The Red Acorn

John McElroy

Contents

THE RED ACORN

BY

John McElroy

Preface

The name given this story is that made glorious by the valor and achievements of the splendid First Division of the Fourteenth Army Corps, the cognizance of which was a crimson acorn, worn on the breasts of its gallant soldiers, and borne upon their battle flags. There are few gatherings of men into which one can go to-day without finding some one wearing, as his most cherished ornament, a red acorn, frequently wrought in gold and studded with precious stones, and which tells that its wearer is a veteran of Mill Springs, Perryville, Shiloh, Corinth, Stone River, Chickamauga, Mission Ridge, Atlanta, Jonesville, March to the Sea, and Bentonville.

The Fourteenth Corps was the heart of the grand old Army of the Cumberland--an army that never new defeat. Its nucleus was a few scattered regiments in Eastern Kentucky, in 1861, which had the good fortune to be commanded by Gen. George H. Thomas. With them he won the first real victory that blessed our arms. It grew as he grew, and under his superb leadership it was shaped and welded and tempered into one of the mightiest military weapons the world ever saw. With it Thomas wrung victory from defeat on the bloody fields of Stone River and Chickamauga; with it he dealt the final crushing blow of the Atlanta campaign, and with it defeat was again turned to victory at Bentonville.

The characters introduced into the story all belonged to or co-operated with the First Division of the Fourteenth Corps. The Corps' badge was the Acorn. As was the custom in the army, the divisions in each Corps were distinguished by the color of the badges--the First's being red, the Second's white, and the Third's blue. There was a time when this explanation was hardly necessary, but now eighteen years have elapsed since the Acorn flags fluttered victoriously over the last field of battle, and a generation has grown up to which they are but a tradition. J. M.

Chapter I. A Declaration.

O, what is so rare as a day in June?
Then, if ever, come perfect days;
Then Heaven tries the Earth if it be in tune,
And over it softly her warm ear lays."
--Lowell.

O f all human teachers they were the grandest who gave us the New Testament, and made it a textbook for Man in every age. Transcendent benefactors of the race, they opened in it a never-failing well-spring of the sweet waters of Consolation and Hope, which have flowed over, fertilized, and made blossom as a rose the twenty-century wide desert of the ills of human existence.

But they were not poets, as most of the authors of the Old Testament were.

They were too much in earnest in their great work of carrying the glad evangel of Redemption to all the earth--they so burned with eagerness to pour their joyful tidings into every ear, that they recked little of the FORM in which the saving intelligence was conveyed.

Had they been poets would they have conceived Heaven as a place with foundations of jasper, sapphires and emeralds, gates of pearl, and streets of burnished gold that shone like glass? Never.

That showed them to be practical men, of a Semitic cast of mind, who addressed hearers that agreed with them in regarding gold and precious stones as the finest things of which the heart could dream.

Had they been such lovers of God's handiwork in Nature as the Greek religious teachers--who were also poets--they would have painted us a Heaven vaulted by the breath of opening flowers, and made musical by the sweet songs of birds in the first rapture of finding their young mates.

In other words they would have given us a picture of earth on a perfect June day.

On the afternoon of such a day as this Rachel Bond sat beneath an apple-tree at the crest of a moderate hill, and looked dreamily away to where, beyond the village of Sardis at the foot of the hill, the Miami River marked the beautiful valley like a silver ribbon carelessly flung upon a web of green velvet. Rather she seemed to be looking there, for the light that usually shown outward in those luminous eyes was turned inward. The little volume of poems had dropped unheeded from the white hand. It had done its office: the passion of its lines had keyed her thoughts to a harmony that suffused her whole being, until all seemed as naturally a part of the glorious day as the fleecy clouds in the sapphire sky, the cheerful hum of the bees, and the apple-blossoms' luxurious scent.

Her love--and, quite as much, her girlish ambition--had been crowned with violets and bays some weeks before, when the fever-heat of patriotism seemed to bring another passion in Harry Glen's bosom to the eruptive point, and there came the long-waited-for avowal of his love, which was made on the evening before his company departed to respond to the call for troops which followed the fall of Fort Sumter.

Does it seem harsh to say that she had sought to bring about this DENOUE-MENT? Rather, it seems that her efforts were commendable. She was a young woman of marriageable age. She believed her her mission in life was marriage to some man who would make her a good husband, and whom she would in turn love, honor, and strive to make happy. Harry Glen's family was the equal of her's in social station, and a little above it in wealth. to this he added educational and personal advantages that made him the most desirable match in Sardis. Starting with the premises given above, her first conclusion was the natural one that she should marry the best man available, and the next that that man was Harry Glen.

Her efforts had been bounded by the strictest code of maidenly ethics, and so artistically developed that the only persons who penetrated their skillful veiling, and detected her as a "designing creature," were two or three maiden friends, whose maneuvers toward the same objective were brought to naught by her success.

It must be admitted that refining causists may find room for censure in this making Ambition the advance guard to spy out the ground that Love is to occupy. But, after all, is there not a great deal of mistake about the way that true love begins? If we had the data before us we should be pained by the enlightenment that, in the vast majority of cases the regard of young people for each other is fixed in the first instance by motives that will bear quite as little scrutiny as Miss Rachel Bond's.

We can afford to be careless how the germ of love is planted. The main thing is how it is watered and tended, and brought to a lasting and beautiful growth. Rachel's ambition gratified, there had been a steady rise toward flood in the tide of her affections. She was not long in growing to love Harry with all the intensity of a really ardent nature.

After the meeting at which Harry had signed the recruiting roll, he had taken her home up the long, sloping hill, through moonlight as soft, as inspiring, as glorifying as that which had melted even the frosty Goddess of Maidenhood, so that she stooped from her heavenly unapproachableness, and kissed the handsome Endymion as he slept.

Though little and that commonplace was said as they walked, subtle womanly instinct prepared Rachel's mind for what was coming, and her grasp upon Harry's arm assumed a new feeling that hurried him on to the crisis.

They stopped beneath the old apple-tree, at the crest of the hill, and in front of the house. Its gnarled and twisted limbs had been but freshly clothed in a suit of fragrant green leaves.

The ruddy bonfires, lighted for the war-meeting, still burned in the village below. The hum of supplementary speeches to the excited crowds that still lingered about came to their ears, mingled with cheers from throat rapidly growing hoarse, and the throb and wail of fife and drum. Then, uplifted on the voices of hundreds who sang it as only men, and men swayed by powerful emotions can, rose the ever-glorious "Star-Spangled Banner," loftiest and most inspiring of national hymns. Through its long, forceful measures, which have the sweep and ring of marching battalions, swung the singers, with a passionate earnestness that made every note and word glow with meaning. The swelling paean told of the heroism and sacrifice with which the foundations of the Nation were laid, of the glory to which the land had risen, and then its mood changing to one of direness and wrath, it foretold the just punishment of those who broke the peace of a happy land.

The mood of the Sardis people was that patriotic exaltation which reigned in every city and village of the North on that memorable night of April, 1861.

But Rachel and Harry had left far behind them this passion of the multitude, which had set their own to throbbing, even as the roar of a cannon will waken the vibrations of harp-strings. Around where they stood was the peace of the night and sleep. The perfume of violets and hyacinths, and of myriads of opening buds seemed shed by the moon with her silvery rays through the soft, dewy air; a few nocturnal insects droned hither and thither, and "drowsy tinklings lulled the distant folds."

As their steps were arrested Rachel released her grasp from Harry's arm, but he caught her hand before it fell to her side, and held it fast. She turned her face frankly toward him, and he looked down with anxious eyes upon the broad white forehead, framed in silken black hair, upon great eyes, flaming with a meaning that he feared to interpret, upon the eloquent lines about the mobile, sensitive mouth, all now lifted into almost supernatural beauty by the moonlight's spiritualizing magic.

What he said he could never afterward recall. His first memory was that of a pause in his speech, when he saw the ripe, red lips turned toward him with a gesture of the proud head that was both an assent and invitation. The kiss that he pressed there thrilled him with the intoxication of unexpectedly rewarded love, and Rachel with the gladness of triumph.

What they afterward said was as incoherent as the conversations of those rapturous moments ever are.

"You know we leave in the morning?" he said, when at last it became necessary for him to go.

"Yes," she answered calmly. "And perhaps it is better that it should be so--that we be apart for a little while to consider this new-found happiness and understand it. I shall be sustained with the thought that in giving you to the country I have given more than any one else. I know that you will do something that will make me still prouder of you, and my presentiments, which never fail me, assure me that you will return to me safely."

His face showed a little disappointment with the answer.

She reached above her head, and breaking off a bud handed it to him, saying in the words of Juliet:

"Sweet, good-night: This bud of love, by Summer's ripening breath, May prove a beauteous flower, when next we meet."

He kissed the bud, and put it in his bosom; kissed her again passionately, and descended the hill to prepare for his departure in the morning.

She was with the rest of the village at the depot to bid the company good-bye, and was amazed to find how far the process of developing the bud into the flower had gone in her heart since parting with her lover. Her previous partiality and admiration for him appeared now very tame and colorless, beside the emotions that stirred her at the sight of him marching with erect grace at the head of his company. But while all about her were tears and sobs, and modest girls revealing unsuspecting attachments in the agitation of parting, her eyes were undimmed. She was proud and serene, a heightening of the color in her cheeks being the only sign of unusual feeling. Harry came to her for a moment, held her hand tightly in his, took the bud from his bosom, touched it significantly with his lips, and sprang upon the train which was beginning to move away.

The days that followed were halcyon for her. While the other women of Sardis, whose loved ones were gone, were bewailing the dangers they would encounter, her proud spirit only contemplated the chances that Harry would have for winning fame. Battles meant bright laurels for him in which she would have a rightful share.

Her mental food became the poetry of love, chivalry and glorious war. The lyric had a vivid personal interest. Tales of romantic daring and achievement were suggestions of possibilities in Harry's career. Her waking hours were mainly spent, book in hand, under the old apple-tree that daily grew dearer to her.

The exalted mood in which we found her was broken in upon by the sound of some one shutting the gate below very emphatically. Looking down she saw her father approaching with such visible signs in face and demeanor of strong excitement that she arose and went to him.

"Why, father, what can be the matter?" she said, stopping in front of him, with the open book pressed to her breast.

"Matter enough, I'm afraid, Rachel. There's been a battle near a place called Rich Mountain, in Western Virginia, and Harry Glen's---"

"O, father," she said, growing very white, "Harry's killed."

"No; not killed." The old man's lip curled with scorn. "It's worse. He seems to've suddenly discovered he wasn't prepared to die; he didn't want to rush all at once into the presence of his Maker. Mebbe he didn't think it'd be good manners. You know he was always stronger on etikwet than anything else. In short, he's showed the white feather. A dozen or more letters have come from the boys telling all about it, and the town's talking of nothing else. There's one of the letters. It's from Jake Alspaugh, who quite working for me to enlist. Read it yourself."

The old gentleman threw the letter upon the grass, and strode on angrily into the house. Rachel smoothed out the crumpled sheet, and read with a growing sickness at heart:

Mr. Bond--Deer Sur:

i taik my pen in hand to lett you no that with the exception of an occashunal tuch of roomaticks, an boonions all over my fete from hard marchin, ime all rite, an i hope you ar injoin the saim blessin. Weve jest had an awful big fite, and the way we warmed it to the secshers jest beat the jews. i doant expect theyve stopt runnin yit. All the Sardis boys done bully except Lieutenant Harry Glen. The smell of burnt powder seamed to onsettle his narves. He tuk powerful sick all at wunst, jest as the trail was gittin rather fresh, and he lay groanin wen the rest of the company marched off into the fite. He doant find the klime-it here as healthy as it is in Sardis. i 'stinguished myself and have bin promoted, and ive got a Rebel gun for you with a bore big enuff to put a walnut in, and it'll jest nock your hole darned shoulder off every time you shoot it. No more yours til deth send me some finecut tobacker for heavens sake.

Jacob Alspaugh.

Rachel tore the letter into a thousand fragments, and flung the volume of poems into the ditch below. She hastened to her room, and no one saw her again until the next morning, when she came down dressed in somber black, her face pale, and her colorless lips tightly compressed.

Chapter II. First Shots.

"Cowards fear to die; but courage stout, Rather than live in snuff, will be put out."
--Sir Walter Raleigh, on "The Snuff of a Candle."

All military courage of any value is the offspring of pride and will. The existence of what is called "natural courage" may well be doubted. What is frequently mistaken for it is either perfect self-command, or a stolid indifference, arising from dull-brained inability to comprehend what really is danger.

The first instincts of man teach him to shun all sources of harm, and if his senses are sufficiently acute to perceive danger, his natural disposition is to avoid encountering it. This disposition can only be overcome by the exercise of the power of pride and will--pride to aspire to the accomplishment of certain things, even though risk attend, and will to carry out those aspirations.

Harry Glen was apparently not deficient in either pride or will. The close observer, however, seemed to see as his mastering sentiment a certain starile selfishness, not uncommon among the youths of his training and position in the slow-living, hum-drum country towns of Ohio. The only son of a weakly-fondling mother and a father too earnestly treading the narrow path of early diligences and small savings by which a man becomes the richest in his village, to pay any attention to him, Harry grew up a self-indulgent, self-sufficient boy. His course at the seminary and college naturally developed this into a snobbish assumption that he was of finer clay than the commonality, and in some way selected by fortune for her finer displays and luxurious purposes. I have termed this a "sterile selfishness," to distinguish it from that grand egoism which in large minds is fruitful of high accomplishments and great deeds, and to denote a force which, in the sons of the average "rich" men of the county seats, is apt to expend itself in satisfaction at having finer clothes and faster horses and pleasanter homes, than the average--in a pride of white hands and a scorn of drudgery.

When Harry signed his name upon the recruiting roll--largely impelled thereto by the delicately-flattering suggestion that he should lead off for the youth of Sardis--he had not the slightest misgiving that by so doing he would subject himself to any of the ills and discomforts incidental to carrying out the enterprise upon which they were embarking. He, like every one else, had no very clear idea of what the company would be called upon to do or undergo; but no doubt obtruded itself into his mind that whatever might be disagreeable in it would fall to some one else's lot, and he continue to have the same pleasant exemption that had been his good fortune so far through life.

And though the company was unexpectedly ordered to the field in the rugged mountains of Western Virginia, instead of to pleasant quarters about Washington, there was nothing to shake this comfortable belief. The slack discipline of the first three months' service, and the confusion of ideas that prevailed in the beginning of the war as to military duties and responsibilities, enabled him to spend all the time he chose away from his company and with congenial spirits, about headquarters, and to make of the expedition, so far as he was concerned, a pleasant picnic. Occasionally little shadows were thrown by the sight of corpses brought in, with ugly-looking bullet holes in head or breast, but these were always of the class he looked down upon, and he connected their bad luck in some way with their condition in life. Doubtless some one had to go where there was danger of being shot, as some one had to dig ditches and help to pry wagons out of the mud, but there was something rather preposterous in the thought that anything of this kind was incumbent upon him.

The mutterings of the men against an officer, who would not share their hardships and duties, did not reach his ears, nor yet the gibes of the more earnest of the officers at the "young headquarter swells," whose interest and zeal were nothing to what they would have taken in a fishing excursion.

It came about very naturally and very soon that this continual avoidance of duty in directions where danger might be encountered was stigmatized by the harsher name of cowardice. Neither did this come to his knowledge, and he was consequently ignorant that he had delivered a fatal stab to his reputation one fine morning when, the regiment being ordered out with three days' rations and forty rounds of cartridges, the sergeant who was sent in search of him returned and reported that he was sick in his tent. Jacob Alspaugh expressed the conclusion instantly arrived at by every one in the regiment:

"It's all you could expect of one of them kid-glove fellers, to weaken when it came to serious business."

Harry's self-sufficiency had left so little room for anything that did not directly concern his own comfort, that he could not understand the deadly earnestness of the men he saw file out of camp, or that there was any urgent call for him to join them in their undertaking.

"Bob Bennett's always going where there's no need of it," he said to a companion, as he saw the last of the regiment disappear into the woods on the mountain side. "He could have staid back here with us just as well as not, instead of trudging off through the heat over these devilish roads, and probably get into a scrape for which no one will thank him."

"Yes," said Ned Burnleigh, with his affected drawl, "what the devil's the use, I'd like to know, for a fellah's putting himself out to do things, when there's any quantity of other fellahs, that can't be better employed, ready and even anxious to do them."

"That's so. But it's getting awful hot here. Let's go over to the shade, where we were yesterday, and have Dick bring us a bucket of cold spring water and the bottles and things."

"Abe!" said Jake Alspaugh to his file-leader--a red-headed, pock-marked man, whose normal condition was that of outspoken disgust at every thing--"this means a fight."

"Your news would've been fresh and interesting last night," growled Abe Bolton. "I suppose that's what we brought our guns along for."

"Yes; but somebody's likely to get killed."

"Well, you nor me don't have to pay their life insurance, as I know on."

"But it may be you or me,"

"The devil'd be might anxious for green wood before he'd call you in."

"Come, now, don't talk that way. This is a mighty serious time."

"I'll make it a durned sight seriouser for you if you don't keep them splay feet o'your'n offen my heels when we're marching."

"Don't you think we'd better pay, or--something?"

"You might try taking up a collection."

"Try starting a hymn, Jake," said a slender young man at his right elbow, whose face showed a color more intimately connected with the contents of his canteen than the heat of the day. "Line it out, and we'll all join in. Something like this, for example:

'Hark, from the tombs a doleful sound   Mine ears attend the cry. Ye living men, come view the ground   Where you must shortly lie.'"

Alspaugh shuddered visibly.

"Come, spunk up, Jake," continued the slender young man. "Think how proud all your relations will be of you, if you die for your country."

"I'm mad at all of my relations, and I don't want to do nothing to please 'em," sighed Jake.

"But I hope you're not so greedy as to want to live always?" said the slender young man, who answered roll-call to Kent Edwards.

"No, but I don't want to be knocked off like a green apple, before I'm ripe and ready."

"Better be knocked off green and unripe," said Kent, his railing mood changing to one of sad introspection, "than to prematurely fall, from a worm gnawing at your heart."

Jake's fright was not so great as to make him forego the opportunity for a brutal retort:

"You mean the 'worm of the still,' I s'pose. Well, it don't gnaw at my heart so much as at some other folkses' that I know'd."

Kent's face crimsoned still deeper, and he half raised his musket, as if to strike him, but at that moment came the order to march, and the regiment moved forward.

The enemy was by this time known to be near, and the men marched in that silence that comes from tense expectation.

The day was intensely hot, and the stagnant, sultry air was perfumed with the thousand sweet odors that rise in the West Virginia forests in the first flush of Summer.

The road wound around the steep mountain side, through great thickets of glossy-leaved laurel, by banks of fragrant honeysuckle, by beds of millions of sweet-breathing, velvety pansies, nestling under huge shadowy rocks, by acres of white puccoon flowers, each as lovely as the lily that grows by cool Siloam's shady rill--all scattered there with Nature's reckless profusion, where no eye saw them from year to year save those of the infrequent hunter, those of the thousands of gaily-plumaged birds that sang and screamed through the branches of the trees above, and those of the hideous rattlesnakes that crawled and hissed in the crevices of the shelving rocks.

At last the regiment halted under the grateful shadows of the broad-topped oaks and chestnuts. A patriarchal pheasant, drumming on a log near by some uxorious communication to his brooding mate, distended his round eyes in amazement at the strange irruption of men and horses, and then whirred away in a transport of fear. A crimson crested woodpecker ceased his ominous tapping, and flew boldly to a neighboring branch, where he could inspect the new arrival to good advantage and determine his character.

The men threw themselves down for a moment's rest, on the springing moss that covered the whole mountain side. A hum of comment and conversation arose. Jake Alspaugh began to think that there was not likely to be any fight after all, and his spirits rose proportionately. Abe Bolton growled that the cowardly officers had no doubt deliberately misled the regiment, that a fight might be avoided. Kent Edwards saw a nodding May-apple flower--as fair as a calla and as odorous as a pink--at a little distance, and hastened to pick it. He came back with it in the muzzle of his gun, and his hands full of violets.

A thick-bodied rattlesnake crawled slowly and clumsily out from the shelter of a little ledge, his fearful eyes gleaming with deadly intentions against a ground-squirrel frisking upon the end of a mossy log, near where Captain Bob Bennett was seated, poring over a troublesome detail in the "Tactics." The snake saw the man, and his awkward movement changed at once into one of electric alertness. He sounded his terrible rattle, and his dull diamonds and stripes lighted up with the glare that shines through an enraged man's face. The thick body seemed to lengthen out and gain a world of sinuous suppleness. With the quickness of a flash he was coiled, with head erect, forked tongue protruding, and eyes flaming like satanic jewels.

A shout appraised Captain Bennett of his danger. He dropped the book, sprang to his feet with a quickness that matched the snake's, and instinctively drew his sword. Stepping a little to one side as the reptile launched itself at him, he dexterously cut it in two with a sweeping stroke. A shout of applause rose from the excited boys, who gathered around to inspect the slain serpent and congratulate the Captain upon his skillful disposition of his assailant.

"O, that's only my old bat-stroke that used to worry the boys in town-hall so much," said the Captain carelessly. "It's queer what things turn out useful to a man, and when he least expects them."

A long, ringing yell from a thousand throats cleft the air, and with its last notes came the rattle of musketry from the brow of the hill across the little ravine. The bullets sang viciously overhead. They cut the leaves and branches with sharp little crashes, and struck men's bodies with a peculiar slap. A score of men in the disordered group fell back dead or dying upon the green moss.

"Of course, we might've knowed them muddle-headed officers 'd run us right slap into a hornets' nest of Rebels before they knowed a thing about it," grumbled Abe Bolton, hastily tearing a cartridge with his teeth, and forcing it into his gun.

"Hold on, my weak-kneed patriot," said Kent Edwards, catching Jake Alspaugh by the collar, and turning him around so that he faced the enemy again. "It's awful bad manners to rush out of a matinee just as the performance begins. You disturb the people who've come to enjoy the show. Keep you seat till the curatin goes down. You'll find enough to interest you."

The same sudden inspiration of common-sense that had flashed upon Captain Bennett, in encountering the snake now raised him to the level of this emergency. He comprehended that the volley they had received had emptied every Rebel gun. The distance was so short that the enemy could be reached before they had time to re-load. But no time must be lost in attempting to form, or in having the order regularly given by the Colonel. He sprang toward the enemy, waving his sword, and shouted in tones that echoed back from the cliffs:

"Attention, BATTALION! Charge bayonets! FORWARD, DOUBLE-QUICK,

MARCH!"

A swelling cheer answered him. His own company ran forward to follow his impetuous lead. The others joined in rapidly. Away they dashed down the side of the declivity, and in an instant more were swarming up the opposite side toward the astonished Rebels. Among these divided councils reigned. Some were excited snapping unloaded guns at the oncoming foe; others were fixing bayonets, and sturdily urging their comrades to do likewise, and meet the rushing wave of cold steel with a counter wave. The weaker-hearted ones were already clambering up the mountain-side out of reach of harm.

There was no time for debate. The blue line led by Bennett flung itself upon the dark-brown mass of Rebels like an angry wave dashing over a flimsy bank of sand, and in an instant there was nothing to be done but pursue the disrupted and flying fragments. It was all over.

Chapter III. A Race.

"Some have greatness thrust upon them." -- Twelfth Night.

The unexpected volley probably disturbed private Jacob Alspaugh's mind more than that of any other man in the regiment. It produced there an effect akin to the sensation of nauseous emetic in his stomach.

He had long enjoyed the enviable distinction of being the "best man" among combative youths of Sardis, and his zeal and invariable success in the fistic tournaments which form so large a part of the interest in life of a certain class of young men in villages, had led his townsmen to entertain extravagant hopes as to his achievements in the field.

But, like most of his class, his courage was purely physical, and a low order of that type. He was bold in those encounters where he knew that his superior strength and agility rendered small the chances of his receiving any serious bodily harm, but of that high pride and mounting spirit which lead to soldierly deeds he had none.

The sight of the dying men on each side shriveled his heart with a deadly panic.

"O, Kent," he groaned, "Lemme go, and let's git out o' here. This's just awful, and it'll be ten times wuss in another minnit. Let's git behind that big rock there, as quick as the Lord'll let us."

He turned to pull away from Kent's detaining hand, when he heard Captain Bennett's order to the regiment to charge, and the hand relaxed its hold. Jake faced to the front again and saw Kent and Abe Bolton, and the rest of the boys rush forward, leaving him and a score of other weak-kneed irresolutes standing alone behind.

Again he thought he would seek the refuge of the rock, but at that moment the Union line swept up to the Rebels, scattering them as a wave does dry sand.

Jake's mental motions were reasonably rapid. Now he was not long in realizing that all the danger was past, and that he had an opportunity of gaining credit cheaply. He acted promptly. Fixing his bayonet, he gave a fearful yell and started forward on a run for the position which the regiment had gained.

He was soon in the lead of the pursuers, and appeared, by his later zeal, to be making amends for his earlier tardiness. As he ran ahead he shouted savagely:

"Run down the hellions! Shoot 'em! Stab 'em! Bay'net 'em! Don't let one of 'em git away."

There is an excitement in a man-chase that is not even approached by any other kind of hunting, and Jake soon became fairly intoxicated with it.

He quickly overtook one or two of the slower-paced Rebels, who surrendered quietly, and were handed by him over to the other boys as they came up, and conducted by them to the rear.

Becoming more excited he sped on, entirely unmindful of how far he was outstripping his comrades.

A hundred yards ahead of him was a tall, gaunt Virginian, clad in butternut-colored jeans of queer cut and pattern, and a great bell-crowned hat of rough, gray beaver. Though his gait was shambling and his huge splay feet rose and fell in the most awkward way, he went over the ground with a swiftness that made it rather doubtful whether Jake was gaining on him at all. But the latter was encouraged by the sings of his chase's distress. First the bell-crowned hat flew off and rolled behind, and Jake could not resist the temptation to give it a kick which sent it spinning into a clump of honeysuckles. Then the Rebel flung off a haversack, whose flapping interfered with his speed, and this was followed by a clumsily-constructed cedar canteen. The thought flashed into Jake's mind that this was probably filled with the much-vaunted peach-brandy of that section; and as ardent sprits were one of his weaknesses, the temptation to stop and pick up the canteen was very strong, but he conquered it and hurried on after his prey. Next followed the fugitive's belt, loaded down with an antique cartridge-box, a savage knife made from a rasp and handled with buckhorn, and a fierce-looking horse-pistol with a flint-lock.

"I seemed to be bustin' up a moosyum o' revolutionary relics," said Jake afterward, in describing the incident. "The feller dropped keepsakes from his forefathers like a bird moltin' its feathers on a windy day. I begun to think that if I kep up the chase purty soon he'd begin to shed Continental money and knee-britches."

The fugitive turned off to the right into a narrow path that wound through the laurel thickets. Jake followed with all the energy that remained in him, confident that a short distance more would bring him so close to his game that he could force his surrender by a threat of bayoneting. He caught up to within a rod of the Rebel, and was already foreshortening his gun for a lunge in case of refusal to surrender on demand, when he was amazed to see the Rebel whirl around, level his gun at him, and order HIS surrender. Jake was so astonished that he stumbled, fell forward and dropped his gun. As he raised his eyes he saw three or four other Rebels step out from behind a rock, and level their guns upon him with an expression of blood-thirstiness that seemed simply fiendish.

Then it flashed upon him how far away he was from all his comrades, and that the labyrinth of laurel made them even more remote. With this realization came the involuntary groan:

"O, Lordy! it's all up with me. I'm a goner, sure!"

His courage did not ooze out of his fingers, like the historic Bob Acres's; it vanished like gas from a rent balloon. He clasped his hands and tried to think of some prayer.

"Now I lay me," he murmured.

"Shan't we shoot the varmint?" said one of the Rebels, with a motion of his gun in harmony with that idea.

"O, mister--mister--GOOD mister, DON'T! PLEASE don't! I swear I didn't mean to do no harm to you."

"Wall, ye acted monty quare fur a man that didn't mean no harm," said the pursued man, regaining his breath with some difficulty. "A-chasin' me down with thet ar prod on yer gun, an' a-threatenin' to stick hit inter me at every jump. Only wanted ter see me run, did yer?"

"O, mister, I only done it because I wuz ordered to. I couldn't help myself; I swear I couldn't."

"Whar's the ossifers thet wuz a-orderin' ye? Whar's the captins that wuz puttin' ye up ter hit? Thar wan't no one in a mile of ye. Guess we'd better shoot ye."

Again Jake raised his voice in abject appeal for mercy. There was nothing he was not willing to promise if only his life were only spared.

"Wouldn't hit be better ter bay'net him?" suggested one of the Rebels, entirely unmoved, as his comrades were, by Jake's piteous pleadings. "Ef we go ter shootin' 'round yere hit'll liekly bring the Yankees right onter us."

"I 'spect hit would be better ter take him back a little ways, any way," said the man whom Jake had pursued. "Pick up his gun thar, Eph. Come along, you, an' be monty peart about hit, fur we're in a powerful bad frame o' mind ter be fooled with. I wouldn't gin a fi'-penny-bit fur all yer blue-bellied life's worth. The boys ar jest pizen mad from seein' so many o' thar kin and folks killed by yer crowd o' thievin' Hessians."

Grateful for even a momentary respite, Jake rose from his knees with alacrity and humbly followed one of the Rebels along the path. The others strode behind, and occasionally spurred him into a more rapid pace with a prick from their bayonets.

"O,---ough, mister, don't do that! Don't, PLEASE! You don't know how it hurts. I ain't got no rhinoceros skin to stand such jabs as that. That came purty nigh goin' clean through to my heart."

"Skeet ahead faster, then, or the next punch'll go righ smack through ye, fur sartin. Ef yer skin's so tender what are ye doin' in the army?"

They climbed the mountain laboriously, and started down on the other side. About midway in the descent they came upon a deserted cabin standing near the side of the road.

"By the Lord Harry," said one of the Rebels, "I'm a'most done clean gin out, so I am. I'm tireder nor a claybank hoss arter a hard day's plowin', an' I'm ez dry ez a lime-kiln. I motion that we stop yere an' take a rest. We kin put our Yank in the house thar, an' keep him. I wonder whar the spring is that the folks thet lived yere got thar water from?"

"Ef I don't disremember," said another, "this is the house where little Pete Higgenbottom lived afore the country got ruther onhelthy fur him on account of his partiality for other people's hosses. I made a little trip up yere the time I loss thet little white-faced bay mar of pap's, an I'm purty sure the spring's over thar in the holler."

"Lordy, how they must 've hankered arter the fun o' totin' water to 've lugged hit clar from over tha. I'd've moved the house nigher the spring afore I'd've stood thet ere a month, so I would."

"The distance to the water ortent to bother a feller thet gets along with usin' ez little ez you do," growled the first speaker.

"A man whose nose looks like a red-pepper pod in August, and his shirt like a section o' rich bottom land, hain't no great reason ter make remarks on other folks's use o' water."

Jake plucked up some courage from the relaxation in the savage grimness of his captors, which seemed implied by this rough pleasantry, and with him such recuperation of spirits naturally took the form of brassy self-assertion.

"Don't you fellers know," he began with a manner and tone intended to be placating, but instead was rasping and irritating, "don't you fellers know that the best thing you can do with me is to take me back to our people, and trade me off for one of your fellers that they've ketched?"

"An' don't ye know thet the best thing ye kin do is to keep thet gapin' mouth o' your'n shet, so thet the flies won't git no chance to blow yer throat?" said the man whose nose had been aptly likened to a ripe red-pepper pod, "an' the next best thing's fur ye to git inter that cabin thar quicker'n blazes 'll scorch a feather, an' stay thar without makin' a motion toward gittin' away. Git!" and he made a bayonet thrust at Jake that tore open his blouse and shirt, and laid a great gaping wound along his breast. Jake leaped into the cabin and threw himself down upon the puncheon floor.

"Thar war none of our crowd taken," said another of the squad, who had looked on approvingly. "They wuz all killed, an' the only way to git even is ter send ye whar they are."

Jake made another earnest effort to recall one of the prayers he had derided in his bad boyhood.

Leaving the red-nosed man to guard the prisoner, the rest of the Rebels started for the hollow, in search of water to cool their burning thirst.

They had gained such a distance from the scene of the fight, and were in such an out-of-the-way place, that the thought of being overtaken did not obtrude itself for an instant, either upon their minds or Jake's.

But as they came back up the hill, with a gourd full of spring water for their companion, they were amazed to see a party of blue-coats appear around the bend of the road at a little distance. They dropped the gourd of water, and yelled to the man on guard:

"Kill the Yank, an' run for yer life!" and disappeared themselves, in the direction of the spring.

The guard comprehended the situation and the order. He fired his gun at Jake, but with such nervous haste as to destroy the aim, and send the charge into the puncheon a foot beyond his intended victim, and then ran off with all speed to join his companions. the Union boys sent a few dropping shots after him, all of which missed their mark.

Jake managed to recover his nerves and wits sufficiently to stagger to the door as his comrades came up, and grasp one of the guns the Rebels had left.

Questions and congratulations were showered upon him, but he replied incoherently, and gasped a request for water, as if he were perishing from thirst. While some hunted for this, others sought for traces of the Rebels; so he gained time to fix up a fairly presentable story of a desperate and long-continued bayonet struggle in which he was behaving with the greatest gallantry, although nearly hopeless of success, when the arrival of help changed the aspect of matters. He had so many gaping wounds to confirm the truth of this story, that it was implicitly believed, and he was taken back to camp as on e of the foremost heroes of that eventful day. The Colonel made him a Sergeant as soon as he heard the tale, and regretted much that he could not imitate the example of the great Napoleon, and raise him to a commission, on the scene of his valiant exploits. His cot at the hospital was daily visited by numbers of admiring comrades, to whom he repeated his glowing account of the fight, with marked improvements in manner and detail accompanying every repetition.

He had no desire to leave the hospital during his term of service, but his hurts were all superficial and healed rapidly, so that in a fortnight's time the Surgeon pronounced him fit to return to duty. He cursed inwardly tha officer's zeal in keeping the ranks as full as possible, and went back to his company to find it preparing to go into another fight.

"Hello, Jake," said his comrades, "awful glad to see you back. Now you'll have a chance to get your revenge on those fellows. There'll be enough of us with you to see that you get a fair fight."

"To the devil with their revenge and a fair fight," said Jake to himself. That evening he strolled around to the headquarters tent, and said to the commander of the regiment:

"Colonel, the doctor seems to think that I'm fit to return to duty, but I don't feel all right yet. I've a numbness in my legs, so that I kin hardly walk sometims. It's my old rheumatics, stirred up by sleeping out in the night air. I hear that the man who's been drivin' the headquarters wagin has had to go to the hospital. I want to be at something, even if I can't do duty in the ranks, and I'd like to take his place till him and me gets well."

"All right, Sergeant. You can have the place as long as you wish, or any other that I can give you. I can't do too much for so brave a man."

So it happened that in the next fight the regiment was not gratified by any thrilling episodes of sanguinary, single-handed combats, between the indomitable Jake and bloodthirsty Rebels.

He had deferred his "revenge" indefinitely.

Chapter IV. Disgrace.

For of fortune's sharp adversitie
The worst kind of infortune is this:
A man that hath been in prosperitie,
And it remember when it passed is.
                                   -- Chaucer.

Harry Glen's perfect self-complacency did not molt a feather when the victors returned to camp flushed with their triumph, which, in the eyes of those inexperienced three-months men, had the dimensions of Waterloo. He did not know that in proportion as they magnified their exploit, so was the depth of their contempt felt for those of their comrades who had declined to share the perils and the honors of the expedition with them. He was too thoroughly satisfied with himself and his motives to even imagine that any one could have just cause for complaint at anything he chose to do.

This kept him from understanding or appreciating the force of the biting innuendoes and sarcasms which were made to his very face; and he had stood so aloof from all, that there was nobody who cared to take the friendly trouble of telling him how free the camp conversation was making with his reputation.

He could not help, however, understanding that in some way he had lost caste with the regiment: but he serenely attributed this to mean-spirited jealousy of the superior advantages he was enjoying, and it only made him more anxious for the coming of the time when he could "cut the whole mob of beggars," as Ned Burnleigh phrased it."

A few days more would end the regiment's term of service, and he readily obtained permission to return him in advance.

The first real blow his confidence received was when he walked down the one principal street of Sardis, and was forced to a perception of the fact that there was an absence of that effusive warmth with which the Sardis people had ever before welcomed back their young townsman, of whose good looks and gentlemanliness they had always been proud. Now people looked at him in a curious way. They turned to whisper to each other, with sarcastic smiles and knowing winks, as he came into view, and they did not come forward to offer him their hands as of old. It astonished him that nobody alluded to the company or to anything that had happened to it.

Turning at length from the main street, he entered the lateral one leading to his home. As he did so, he heard one boy call out to another in that piercing treble which boys employ in making their confidential communications to one another, across a street,

"S-a-y-, did you know that Hank Glen 'd got back? and they say he looks pale yet?"

"Has he?" the reply came in high falsetto, palpably tinged with that fine scorn of a healthy boy, for anything which does not exactly square with his young highness's ideas. "Come back to mammy, eh? Well, it's a pity she ever let him go away from her. Hope she'll keep him with her now. He don't seem to do well out of reach of her apron strings."

The whole truth flashed upon him: Envious ones had slandered him at home, as a coward.

He walked onward in a flurry of rage. The thought that he had done anything to deserve criticism could not obtrude itself between the joints of his triple-plated armor of self-esteem.

A swelling contempt for his village critics flushed his heart.

"Spiteful, little-minded country boobies," he said to himself with an impatient shake of his head, as if to adjust his hair, which was his usual sign of excitement, "they've always hated me because I was above them. They take advantage of the least opportunity to show their mean jealousy."

After a moment's pause: "But I don't care. I'd a little rather have their dislike than their good-will. It'll save me a world of trouble in being polite to a lot of curs that I despise. I'm going to leave this dull little burg anyhow, as soon as I can get away. I'm going to Cincinnati, and be with Ned Burnleigh. There is more life there in a day than here in a year. After all, there's nobody here that I care anything for, except father and mother--and--Rachel."

A new train of thought introduced itself at this tardy remembrance of his betrothed. His heat abated. He stopped, and leaning against a shady silver maple began anew a meditation that had occupied his mind very frequently since that memorable night under the old apple tree on the hill-top.

There had been for him but little of that spiritual exaltation which made that night the one supreme one in Rachel's existence; when the rapture of gratified pride and love blended with the radiant moonlight and the subtle fragrance of the flowers into a sweet symphony that would well chord with the song the stars sang together in the morning.

He was denied the pleasure that comes from success, after harrowing doubts and fears. His unfailing consciousness of his own worth had left him little doubt that a favorable answer would promptly follow when he chose to propose to Rachel Bond, or to any other girl, and when this came with the anticipated readiness, he could not help in the midst of his gratification at her assent the intrusion of the disagreeable suspicion that, peradventure, he had not done the best with his personal wares that he might. Possibly there would appear in time some other girl, whom he might prefer to Rachel, and at all events there was no necessity for his committing himself when he did, for Rachel "would have kept," as Ned Burnleigh coarsely put it, when made the recipient of Harry's confidence.

Three months of companionship with Ned Burnleigh, and daily imbibation of that young man's stories of his wonderful conquests among young women of peerless beauty and exalted social station confirmed this feeling, and led him to wish for at least such slackening of the betrothal tether as would permit excursions into a charmed realm like that where Ned reigned supreme.

For the thousandth time--and in each recurrence becoming a little clearer defined and more urgent--came the question:

"Shall I break with Rachel? How can I? And what possible excuse can I assign for it?"

There came no answer to this save the spurs with which base self-love was pricking the sides of his intent, and he recoiled from it--ashamed of himself, it is true, but less ashamed at each renewed consideration of the query.

He hastened home that he might receive a greeting that would efface the memory of the reception he had met with in the street. There, at least, he would be regarded as a hero, returning laurel-crowned from the conflict.

As he entered the door his father, tall, spare and iron-gray, laid down the paper he was reading, and with a noticeable lowering of the temperature of his wonted calm but earnest cordiality, said simply:

"How do you do? When did you get in?"

"Very well, and on the 10:30 train."

"Did all your company come?"

Harry winced, for there was something in his father's manner, more than his words, expressive of strong disapproval. He answered:

"No; I was unwell. The water and the exposure disagreed with me, and I was allowed to come on in advance."

Mr. Glen, the elder, carefully folded the paper he was reading and laid it on the stand, as if its presence would embarrass him in what he was about to say. He took off his eye-glasses, wiped them deliberately, closed them up and hesitated for a moment, holding them between the thumb and fore finger of one hand, before placing them in their case, which he had taken from his pocket with the other.

These were all gestures with which experience had made Harry painfully familiar. He used to describe them to his boy intimates as "the Governor clearing for action." There was something very disagreeable coming, and he awaited it apprehensively.

"Were you"--the father's cold, searching eyes rested for an instant on the glasses in his hand, and then were fixed on his son's face--"were you too ill the day of the fight to accompany your command?"

Harry's glance quailed under the penetrating scrutiny, as was his custom when his father subjected him to a relentless catechism; then he summoned assurance and assumed anger.

"Father," he said, "I certainly did not expect that you would join these mean-spirited curs in their abuse of me, but now I see that---"

"Henry, you evade the question." The calm eyes took on a steely hardness. "You certainly know by this time that I always require direct answers to my questions. Now the point is this: You entered this company to be its leader, and to share all its duties with it. It went into a fight while you remained back in camp. Why was this so? Were you too sick to accompany it?"

"I certainly was not feeling well."

"Were you too ill to go along with your company?"

and--there--was--some--work--in--camp   that--needed--to--be--done--and there was enough without me, and--I--I--"

"That is sufficient," said the elder man with a look of scorn that presently changed into one of deeply wounded pride. "Henry, I know too well your disposition to shirk the unpleasant duties of life, to be much surprised that, when tried by this test, you were found wanting. But this wounds me deeply. People in Sardis think my disposition hard and exacting; they think I care for little except to get all that is due me. But no man here can say that in all his long life Robert Glen shirked or evaded a single duty that he owed to the community or his fellow-men, no matter how dangerous or disagreeable that duty might be. To have you fail in this respect and to take and maintain your place in the front rank with other men is a terrible blow to my pride."

"O, Harry, is that you?" said his mother, coming into the room at that moment and throwing herself into her son's arms. "I was lying down when I heard your voice, and I dressed and hurried down as quickly as possible. I am so glad that you have come home all safe and well. I know that you'll contradict, for your poor mother's sake, all these horrible stories that are worrying her almost to death."

"Unfortunately he has just admitted that those stories are substantially true," said the father curtly.

"I won't believe it," sobbed his mother, "until he tells me so himself. You didn't, did you, back out of a fight, and let that Bob Bennett, whose mother used to be my sewing girl, and whom I supported for months after he was born, and his father died with the cholera and left her nothing, by giving her work and paying her cash, and who is now putting on all sorts of airs because everybody's congratulating her on having such a wonderful son, and nobody's congratulating me at all, and sometimes I almost which I was dead.

Clearness of statement was never one of Mrs. Glen's salient characteristics. Nor did deep emotion help her in this regard. Still it was only too evident that the fountains of her being were moved by having another woman's son exalted over her own. Her maternal pride and social prestige were both quivering under the blow.

Harry met this with a flank movement.

"You both seem decidedly disappointed that I did not get myself wounded or killed," he said.

"That's an unmanly whimper," said his father contemptuously.

"Why, Harry, Bob Bennett didn't get either killed or wounded," said his mother with that defective ratiocination which it is a pretty woman's privilege to indulge in at her own sweet will.

Harry withdrew from the mortifying conference under the plea of the necessity of going to his room to remove the grime of travel.

He was smarting with rage and humiliation. His panoply of conceit was pierced for the first time since the completion of his collegiate course sent him forth into the world a being superior, in his own esteem, to the accidents and conditions that the mass of inferior mortals are subject to. Yet he found reasons to account for his parent's defection to the ranks of his enemies.

"It's no new thing," he said, while carefully dressing for a call upon Rachel in the evening, "for father to be harsh and unjust to me, and mother has one of her nervous spells, when everything goes wrong with her."

"Anyhow," he continued, "there's Ned Burnleigh, who understands me and will do me justice, and he amounts to more than all of Sardis--except Rachel, who loves me and will always believe that what I do is right."

He sat down at his desk and wrote a long letter to Ned, inveighing bitterly against the stupidity and malice of people living in small villages, and informing him of his intention to remove to Cincinnati as soon as an opening could be found for him there, which he begged Ned to busy himself in discovering.

Attired in his most becoming garb, and neglecting nothing that could enhance his personal appearance, he walked slowly up the hill in the evening to Rachel Bond's house. The shrinkage which his self-sufficiency had suffered had left room for a wonderful expansion of his affection for Rachel, whose love and loyalty were now essential to him, to compensate for the falling away of others. The question of whether he should break with her was now one the answering of which could be postponed indefinitely. There was no reason why he should not enjoy the sweet privileges of an affianced lover during his stay in Sardis. What would happen afterward would depend upon the shape that things took in his new home.

He found Rachel sitting on the piazza. Though dressed in the deepest and plainest black she had never looked so surpassingly beautiful. As is usually the case with young women of her type of beauty, grief had toned down the rich coloring that had at times seemed almost too exuberant into that delicate shell-like tint which is the perfection of nature's painting. Her round white arms shone like Juno's, as the outlines were revealed by the graceful motions which threw back the wide sleeves. Her wealth of silken black hair was drawn smoothly back from her white forehead, over her shapely head, and gathered into a simple knot behind. Save a black brooch at her throat, she wore no ornaments--not even a plain ring.

She rose as Harry came upon the piazza, and for a moment her face was rigid with intensity of feeling. This evidence of emotion went as quickly as it came, however, and she extended her hand with calm dignity, saying simply:

"You have returned, Mr. Glen."

In his anxiety to so play the impassioned lover as to conceal the recreancy he had fostered in his own heart, Harry did not notice the coolness of this greeting. Then, too, his self-satisfaction had always done him the invaluable service of preventing a ready perception of the repellant attitudes of others.

He came forward eagerly to press a kiss upon her lips, but she checked him with uplifted hand.

"O, the family's in there, are they?" said he, looking toward the open windows of the parlor. "Well, what matter? Isn't it expected that a fellow will kiss his affianced wife on his return, and not care who knows it?"

He pointed to the old apple-tree where they had plighted their troth that happy night, with a gesture and a look that was a reminder of their former meeting and an invitation to go thither again. She comprehended, but refused with a shudder, and, turning, motioned him to the farther end of the piazza, to which she led the way, moving with a sweeping gracefulness of carriage that Harry thought had wonderfully ripened and perfected in the three months that had elapsed since their parting.

"'Fore gad," he said to himself. (This was a new addition to his expletory vocabulary, which had accrued from Ned Burnleigh's companionship.) "I'd like to put her alongside of one of the girls that Ned's always talking about. I don't believe she's got her equal anywhere."

Arriving at the end of the piazza he impetuously renewed his attempt at an embrace, but her repulse was now unmistakable.

"Sit down," she said, pointing to a chair; "I have something to say to you."

Harry's first thought was a rush of jealously. "Some rascal has supplanted me," he said bitterly, but under his breath.

She took a chair near by, put away the arm he would have placed about her waist, drew from her pocket a dainty handkerchief bordered with black, and opened it deliberately. It shed a delicate odor of violets.

Harry waited anxiously for her to speak.

"This mourning which I wear," she began gently, "I put on when I received the news of your downfall."

"My downfall?" broke in Harry hotly. "Great heavens, you don't say that you, too, have been carried away by this wretched village slander?"

"I put it on," she continued, unmindful of the interruption, "because I suffered a loss which was greater than any merely physical death could have occasioned."

"I don't understand you."

"My faith in you as a man superior to your fellows died then. This was a much more cruel blow than your bodily death would have been."

"'Fore gad, you take a pleasant view of my decease--a much cooler one, I must confess, than I am able to take of that interesting event in my history."

Her great eyes blazed, and she seemed about to reply hotly, but she restrained herself and went on with measured calmness:

"The reason I selected you from among all other men, and loved you, and joyfully accepted as my lot in life to be your devoted wife and helpmate, was that I believed you superior in all manly things to other men. Without such a belief I could love no man."

She paused for an instant, and Harry managed to stammer:

"But what have I done to deserve being thrown over in this unexpected way?"

"You have not done anything. That is the trouble. You have failed to do that which was rightfully expected of you. You have allowed others, who had no better opportunities, to surpass you in doing your manly duty. Whatever else my husband may not be he must not fail in this."

"Rachel, you are hard and cruel."

"No, I am only kind to you and to myself. I know myself too well to make a mistake in this respect. I have seen too many women who have been compelled to defend, apologize, or blush for their husband's acts, and have felt too keenly the abject misery of their lives to take the least chance of adding myself to their sorrowful number. If I were married to you I could endure to be beaten by you and perhaps love you still, but the moment I was compelled to confess your inferiority to some other woman's husband I should hate you, and in the end drag both of us down to miserable graves."

"But let me explain this."

"It would be a waste of time," she answered coldly. "It is sufficient for me to know that you are convicted by general opinion of having failed where a number of commonplace fellows succeeded. You, yourself, admit the justice of this verdict by tame submission to it, making no effort to retrieve your reputation. I can not understand how this could be so if you had any of the qualities that I fondly imagined you possessed in a high degree. But this interview is being protracted to a painful extent. Let us say good night and part."

"Forever?" he stammered.

"Yes."

She held out her hand for farewell. Harry caught it and would have carried it to his lips, but she drew it away.

"No; all that must be ended now," she said, with the first touch of gentleness that had shaded her sad, serious eyes.

"Will you give me no hope?" said Harry, pleadingly.

"When you can make people forget the past--if ever--" she said, "then I will change this dress and you can come back to me."

She bowed and entered the house.

Chapter V. The Lint-scraping and Bandage-making Union.

At length I have acted my severest part: I feel the woman breaking in upon me, And melt about my heart: My tears will flow.
                                        -- Addison.

Rachel Bond's will had carried her triumphantly through a terrible ordeal--how terrible no one could guess, unless he followed her to her room after the interview and saw her alone with her agony. She did not weep. Tears did not lie near the surface with her. The lachrymal glands had none of that ready sensitiveness which gives many superficial women the credit of deep feeling. But when she did weep it was not an April shower, but a midsummer tempest.

Now it was as if her intense grief were a powerful cautery which seared and sealed every duct of the fountain of tears and left her eyes hot and dry as her heart was ashes.

With pallid face and lips set until the blood was forced from them, and they made a thin purplish line in the pale flesh, she walked the floor back and forth, ever back and forth, until a half-stumble, as she was turning in a dreary round, revealed to her that she was almost dropping from exhaustion.

She had thought her love for Harry had received its death-blow when her pride in him had been so rudely shattered. But this meeting, in which she played the part set for herself with a brave perfection that she had hardly deemed possible, had resurrected every dear memory, and her passion sprung into life again to mock and jeer at her efforts to throttle it out of existence. With him toppling from the pedestal on which her husband must stand, she had told herself that there was naught left

but to roll a great stone against the sepulcher in which her love must henceforth lie
buried, hopeless of the coming of any bright angle to unseal the gloomy vault. Yet,
despite the entire approval given this by her judgment, her woman's heart cried bitterly for a return of the joys out of which the beauty had fled forever.

Hours passed in this wrestle with pain. How many she did not know, but when
she came forth it was with the composure of one who had fought the fight and won
the victory, but at a cost that forbade exultation.

There was one ordeal that thus far she had not been called upon to endure.
From the day on which she had donned her sable robes to that of Harry's return no
one had ventured to speak his name in her presence. Even her father and mother,
after the first burst of indignation, had kept silence in pity for her suffering, and
there was that in her bearing that forbade others touching upon a subject in her
hearing that elsewhere was discussed with the hungry avidity of village gossips
masticating a fresh scandal.

But she could not be always spared thus. She had not been so careful of the
feelings of less favored women and girls, inferior to her in brightness, as to gain any
claim for clement treatment now, when the displacement of a portion of her armor of superiority gave those who envied or disliked her an unprotected spot upon
which to launch their irritating little darts.

All the sewing, dorcas and mite societies of the several churches in Sardis had
been merged into one consolidated Lint-Scraping and Bandage-Making Union, in
whose enlarged confines the waves of gossip flowed with as much more force and
volume as other waves gain when the floods unite a number of small pools into one
great lake.

In other days a sensational ripple starting, say in the Episcopalian "Dorcas," was
stilled into calmness ere it passed the calm and stately church boundaries. It would
not do to let its existence be even suspected by the keen eyes of the freely-censori-
ous Presbyterian dames, or the sharp-witted, agile-tongued Methodist ladies.

And, much as these latter were disposed to talk over the weaknesses and foibles
of their absent sisters in the confidential environments of the Mite Society or the
Sewing Circle, they were as reluctant to expose these to the invidious criticisms of
the women of the other churches as if the discussed ones had been their sisters in
fact, and not simply through sectarian affiliation. Church pride, if nothing else,

contributed to the bridling of their tongues, and checking the free circulation of gossip.

"Them stuck-up Presbyterian and Episcopalian women think little enough on us now, the land knows," Mrs. Deborah Pancake explained to a newly-received sister, whom she was instructing in elementary duties. "There's no use giving 'em more reason for looking down upon us. We may talk over each other's short-comings among ourselves, private like, because the Bible tells us to admonish and watch over each other. But it don't say that we're to give outsiders any chance to speak ill of our sisters-in-Christ."

And Mrs. Euphrosyne Pursifer remarked to the latest agreeable accession to the parish of St. Marks, with that graceful indirection that gave her the reputation in Sardis of being a feminine Talleyrand:

"Undoubtedly the ladies in these outside denominations are very worthy women, dear, but a certain circumspection seems advisable in conversing with them on subjects that we may speak of rather freely among ourselves."

The rising fervor of the war spirit melted away most of these barriers to a free interchange of gossip. With the first thrill of pleasure at finding that patriotism had drawn together those whom the churches had long held aloof came to all the gushing impulse to cement the newly-formed relationship by confiding to each other secrets heretofore jealously guarded. Nor should be forgotten the "narrative stimulus" every one feels on gaining new listeners to old stories.

It was so graciously condescending in Mrs. Euphrosyne Pursifer to communicate to Mrs. Elizabeth Baker some few particulars in which her aristocratic associates of St. Marks had grieved her by not rising to her standard of womanly dignity and Christian duty, that Mrs. Baker in turn was only too happy to reciprocate with a similar confidence in regard to her intimate friends of Wesley Chapel.

It was this sudden lapsing of all restraint that made the waves of gossip surge like sweeping billows.

And the flotsam that appeared most frequently of late on their crests, and that was tossed most relentlessly hither and thither, was Rachel Bond's and Harry Glen's conduct and relations to each other.

The Consolidated Lint-scraping and Bandage-making Union was holding a regular session, and gossip was at spring-tide.

"It is certainly queer," said Mrs. Tufis, one of her regulation smiles illuminating her very artificial countenance; "it is singular to the last degree that we don't have Miss Rachel Bond among us. She is such a LOVELY girl. I am very, very fond of her, and her heart is thoroughly in unison with our objects. It would seem impossible for her to keep away."

All this with the acrid sub-flavor of irony and insincerity with which an insincere woman can not help tainting even her most sincere words.

"Yes," said Mrs. Tabitha Grimes, with a premeditated acerbity apparent even in the threading of her needle, into the eye of which she thrust the thread as if piercing the flesh of an enemy with a barb; "yes;" she pulled the thread through with a motion as if she enjoyed its rasping against the steel. "Rachel Bond started into this work quite as brash as Harry Glen started into the war. Her enthusiasm died out about as quickly as his courage, when it came to the actual business, and she found there was nobody to admire her industry, or the way she got herself up, except a parcel of married women."

The milk of human kindness had begun to curdle in Mrs. Grimes's bosom, at an early and now rather remote age. Years of unavailing struggle to convince Mr. Jason Grimes that more of his valuable time should be devoted to providing for the wants of his family, and less to leading the discussion on the condition of the country in the free parliament that met around the stove in the corner grocery, had carried forward this lacteal fermentation until it had converted the milky fluid into a vinegarish whey.

"Well, why not?" asked Elmira Spelter, the main grief of whose life was time's cruel inflexibility in scoring upon her face unconcealable tallies of every one of his yearly flights over her head, "why shouldn't she enjoy these golden days? Youth is passing, to her and to all of us, like an arrow from the bow. It'd be absurd for her to waste her time in this stuffy old place, when there are so many more attractive ones. It ought to be enough that those of us who have only a few remnants of beauty left, should devote them to this work."

"Well," snapped Mrs. Grimes, "your donation of good looks to the cause--even if you give all you got--will be quite modest, something on the widow's mite order. You might easily obey the scriptural injunction, and give them with your right hand without your left knowing what was being done."

Elmira winced under this spiteful bludgeoning, but she rallied and came back at her antagonist.

"Well, my dear," she said quietly, "the thought often occurs to me, that one great reason why we both have been able to keep in the straight and narrow path, is the entire lack of that beauty which so often proves a snare to the feet of even the best-intentioned women."

It was Mrs. Grimes's turn to wince.

"A hit! a palpable hit!" laughed pretty Anna Bayne, who studied and quoted Shakespeare.

"The mention of snares reminds me," said Mrs. Grimes, "that I, at least, did not have to spread any to catch a husband."

"No," returned Elmira, with irritating composure, "the poorer kinds of game are caught without taking that trouble."

"Well"--Mrs. Grimes's temper was rising so rapidly that she was losing her usual skill in this verbal fence--"Jason Grimes, no doubt, has his faults, as all men have; but he is certainly better than no husband at all."

"That's the way for you to think," said Elmira, composedly, disregarding the thrust at her own celibacy. "It's very nice in you to take so cheerful a view of it. SOMEBODY had to marry him, doubtless, and it's real gratifying to see one accepting the visitations of Providence in so commendable a spirit."

To use the language of diplomacy, the relations between these ladies had now become so strained that a rupture seemed unavoidable.

"Heavens, will this quarrel ne'er be mended?" quoted Anna Bayne, not all sorry that these veteran word-swordsmen, dreaded by everybody, were for once turning their weapons on each other.

Peace-making was one of the prerogatives assumed by Mrs. Tufis, as belonging to the social leadership to which she had elected herself. She now hastened to check the rapidly-opening breach.

"Ladies," she said blandly, "the discussion has wandered. Our first remarks were, I believe about Miss Bond, and there was a surmise as to her reasons for discontinuing attendance upon our meetings."

The diversion had the anticipated effect. The two disputants gladly quit each other, to turn upon and rend the object flung in between them.

"Why Rachel Bond don't come here any more?" said Mrs. Grimes, with a sniff that was one of the keenest-edged weapons in her controversial armory. "When you know how little likely she is to do anything that's not going to be for her benefit in some way. She's mighty particular in everything, but more particular in that than in anything else."

"I'll admit that there is reason to suspect a strain of selfishness in Rachel's nature," said Anna Bayne; "but it's the only blemish among her many good qualities. Still, I think you do her an injustice in attributing her absence from our meetings to purely selfish motives."

"Of course, we all know what you mean," said Elmira. "She set her cap for Harry Glen, and played her cards so openly and boldly--"

"I should say 'shamelessly,'" interrupted Mrs. Grimes.

"Shamelessly, my dear?" This from Mrs. Tufis, as if in mild expostulation.

"Shamelessly," repeated Mrs. Grimes, firmly.

"Well, so shamelessly, if you choose," continued Elmira, "as to incur the ill-will of all the rest of the girls--"

"Whom she beat at a game in which they all played their best," interrupted Anna.

"That's an unworthy insinuation," said Elmira, getting very red. "At least, no one can say I played any cards for that stake."

"Wasn't it because all your trumps and suit had been played out in previous games?" This from Mrs. Grimes, whose smarting wounds still called for vengeance.

For an instant a resumption of hostilities was threatened. Mrs. Tufis hastened to interpose:

"There's no doubt in my mind that the poor, dear girl really took very deeply to heart the stories that have been circulated about Harry Glen's conduct, though there are people ready to say that she was quite willing to play the role of the stricken one. It really makes her look very interesting. Mourning and the plain style of wearing her hair suit her very, VERY well. I do not think I ever saw her looking so lovely as she has lately, and I have heard quite a number of GENTLEMEN say the same thing.

"If she'd had real spirit," said Mrs. Grimes, "she'd have dropped Harry Glen without all this heroine-of-a-yellow-covered-novel demonstration, and showed her contempt of the fellow by going ahead just as usual, pretending that his conduct was nothing to her; but she's a deep one. I'll venture anything she's got a well-laid scheme, that none of us dream of."

"Mrs. Tufis,"--it was the calm, even tones of Rachel Bond's voice that fell upon the startled ears of the little coterie of gossipers. She had glided in unobserved by them in the earnestness of their debate. "How long has she been here and what has she heard?" was the thrilling question that each addressed to herself. When they summoned courage to look up at her, they saw her standing with perfectly composed mien, her pale face bearing the pensive expression it had worn for weeks. With subdued and kindly manner she returned the affectionate greetings that each bestowed on her, in imitation of Mrs. Tufis, who was the first to recover her wits and then continued:

"Mrs. Tufis, I come to you, as president of this society, to apologize for my absence from so many of your meetings, and to excuse myself on the ground of indisposition." (Mrs. Grimes darted a significant look at Elmira.) "I also want to announce that, as I have determined to join the corps of nurses for the field hospitals, which Miss Dix, of New York, is organizing, and as I will start for the front soon, I shall have to ask you to excuse me from any farther attendance upon your meetings, and drop my name from your roll."

She replied pleasantly to a flood of questions and expostulations, which the crowd that gathered around poured upon her, and turning, walked quietly away to her home.

Chapter VI. The Awakening.

The nobler nature within him stirred To life, at that woman's deed and w
ord.
-- Whittier.

Deeper emotions than he had felt before in all his life of shallow aimlessness stirred Harry Glen's bosom as he turned away from the door which Rachel Bond closed behind her with a decisive promptness that chorded well with her resolute composure during the interview.

This blow fell much more heavily than any that had preceded it, because it descended from the towering height to which he had raised his expectations of an ardent greeting from a loving girl, eagerly watching for his return.

As was to be expected from one of his nature, he forgot entirely his ruminations upon the advisability of discarding her, and the difficulty he experienced in devising a plan whereby this could be done easily and gracefully. He only thought of himself as the blameless victim of a woman's fickleness. The bitter things he had read and heard of the sex's inconstancy rose in his mind, as acrid bile sometimes ascends in one's throat.

"Here," he said to himself, "is an instance of feminine perfidy equal to anything that Byron ever sneered at. This girl, who was so proud to receive my attentions a little while ago, and who so gladly accepted me for her promised husband, now turns away at the slightest cloud of disapproval falling upon me. And to think, too, how I have given her all my heart, and lavished upon her a love as deep and true as ever a man gave a woman."

He was sure that he had been so badly used as to have sufficient grounds for turning misanthrope and woman-hater. Thin natures are like light wines and weak syrups in the readiness with which they sour.

The moon had risen as it did on that eventful betrothal-night. Again the stars had sunk from sight in the sea of silver splendor rolling from the round, full orb. Again the roadway down the hill lay like a web of fine linen, bleaching upon an emerald meadow. Again the clear waters of the Miami rippled in softly merry music over the white limestone of their shallow bed. Again the river, winding through the pleasant valley, framed in gently rising hill-sides, appeared as great silver ribbon, decorating a mass of heavily-embroidered green velvet. Again Sardis lay at the foot of the hills, its coarse and common place outlines softened into glorious symmetry by the moonlight's wondrous witchery.

He stopped for a moment and glanced at the old apple-tree, under which they had stood when

"Their spirits rushed together at the meeting of their lips."

But its raiment of odorous blossoms was gone. Instead, it bore a load of shapeless, sour, unripened fruit. Instead of the freshling springing grass, at its foot was now a coarse stubble. Instead of the delicately sweet breath of violets and fruit blooms scenting the evening air came the heavy, persistent perfume of tuberoses, and the mawkish scent of gaudy poppies.

"Bah, it smells like a funeral," he said, and he turned away and walked slowly down the hill. "And it is one. My heart and all my hopes lie buried at the foot of that old apple-tree."

It had been suggested that much of the sympathy we lavish upon martyrs is wanton waste, because to many minds, if not in fact to all, there is a positive pleasure in considering oneself a martyr. More absolute truth is contained in this than appears at the first blush. There are very few who do not roll under their tongues as a sweet morsel the belief that their superior goodness or generosity has brought them trouble and affliction from envious and wicked inferiors.

So the honey that mingled with the gall and hysop of Harry Glen's humiliation was the martyr feeling that his holiest affections had been ruthlessly trampled upon by a cold-hearted woman. His desultory readings of Byron furnished his imagination with all the woful suits and trappings necessary to trick himself out as a melancholy hero.

On his way home he had to pass the principal hotel in the place, the front of which on Summer evenings was the Sardis forum for the discussion of national

politics and local gossip. As he approached quietly along the grassy walk he overheard his own name used. He stepped back into the shadow of a large maple and
listened:

"Yes, I seen him as he got off the train," said Nels Hathaway, big, fat, lazy, and
the most inveterate male gossip in the village. "And he is looking mighty well--yes,
MIGHTY well. I said to Tom Botkins, here, 'what a wonderful consitution Harry
Glen has, to be sure, to stand the hardships of the field so well.'"

The sarcasm was so evident that Harry's blood seethed. The Tim Botkins alluded to had been dubbed by Basil Wurmset, the cynic and wit of the village, "apt
appreciation's artful aid." Red-haired, soft eyed, moon-faced, round of belly and
lymphatic of temperament, his principal occupation in life was to play fiddle in
the Sardis string-band, and in the intervals of professional engagements at dances
and picnics, to fill one of the large splint-bottomed chairs in front of the hotel with
his pulpy form, and receive the smart or bitter sayings of the loungers there with
a laught that began before any one else's, and lasted after the others had gotten
through. His laugh alone was as good as that of all the rest of the crowd. It was not
a hearty, resonant laugh, like that from the mouth of a strong-lunged, wholesome-
natured man, which has the mellow roundness of a solo on a French horn. It was
a slovenly, greasy, convictionless laugh, with uncertain tones and ill-defined edges.
Its effect was due to its volume, readiness, and long continuance. Swelling up of
the puffy form, and reddening ripples of the broad face heralded it, it began with a
contagious cackle, it deepened into a flabby guffaw, and after all the others round-
about had finished their cachinnatory tribute it wound up with what was between
a roar and the lazy drone of a bagpipe.

It now rewarded Nels Hathaway's irony, and the rest of the loungers joined in.
Encouraged, Nels continued, as its last echoes died away:

"Yes, he's just as spry and pert as anybody. He seems to have recovered entirely
from all his wounds; none of 'em have disfiggered him any, and his nerves have got
over their terrible strain."

Tim ran promptly through all the notes in his diapason, and the rest joined in
on the middle register.

"Well, I'm not at all surprised," said Mr. Oldunker, a bitter States' Rights Dem-
ocrat, and the oracle of his party. "I told you how it'd be from the first. Harry

Glen was one of them Wide-Awakes that marched around on pleasant evenings last Fall with oil-cloth capes and kerosene lamps. I told you that those fellows'd be no where when the war they were trying to bring on came. I'm not at all astonished that he showed himself lily-livered when he found the people that he was willing to rob of their property standing ready to fight for their homes and their slaves."

"Ready to shoot into a crowd of unsuspecting men, you mean," sneered Basil Wurmset, "and then break their own cursed necks when they saw a little cold steel coming their way."

Tim came in promptly with his risible symphony.

"Well, they didn't run away from any cold steel that Harry Glen displayed," sneered Oldunker.

Tim's laugh was allegro and crescendo at the first, and staccato at the close.

"You seem to forget that Capt. Bob Bennett was a Wide-Awake, too," retorted Wurmset, "though you might have remembered it from his having threatened to lick you for encouraging the boys to stone the lamps in the procession."

Tim cackled, gurgled and roared.

Nels Hathaway had kept silent as long as he could. He must put his oar into the conversational tide.

"I'd give six bits," he said, "to know how the meeting between him and Rachel Bond passes off. He's gone up to the house. The boys seen him, all dressed up his best. But his finery and his perfumed hankerchiefs won't count anything with her, I can tell YOU. She comes of fighting stock, if ever a woman did. The Bonds and Harringtons--her mother's people--are game breeds, both of 'em, and stand right on their record, every time. She'll have precious little traffic with a white-feathered fellow. I think she's been preparing for him the coldest shoulder any young feller in Sardis's got for many a long day."

There was nothing very funny in this speech, but a good deal of risible matter had accumulated in Tim's diaphragm during its delivery which he had to get rid of, and he did.

Harry had heard enough. While Tim's laugh yet resounded he walked away unnoticed, and taking a roundabout course gained his room. There he remained a week, hardly coming down to his meals. It was a terrible week for him, for every waking hour of it he walked through the valley of humiliation, and drank the bitter waters of shame. The joints of his hitherto impenetrable armor of self-conceit had been so pierced by the fine rapier thrusts of Rachel's scorn that it fell from him under the coarse pounding of the village loungers and left him naked and defenseless to their blows. Every nerve and sense ached with acute pain. He now felt all of his father's humiliation, all his mother's querulous sorrow, all his betrothed's anguish and abasement.

Thoughts of suicide, and of flying to some part of the country where he was entirely unknown, crowded upon him incessantly. But with that perversity that nature seemingly delights in, there had arisen in his heart since he had lost her, such a love for Rachel Bond as made life without her, or without her esteem even, seem valueless. To go into a strange part of the country and begin life anew would be to give her up forever, and this he could not do. It would be much preferable to die demonstrating that he was in some degree worthy of her. And a latent manly pride awakened and came to his assistance. He could not be the son of his proud, iron-willed father without some transmission of that sire's courageous qualities. He formed his resolution: He would stay in Sardis, and recover his honor where he had lost it.

At the end of the week he heard the drums beat, the cannon fire, and the people cheer. The company had come home, and was marching proudly down the street to a welcome as enthusiastic as if its members were bronzed veterans returning victoriously from a campaign that had lasted for years.

His mother told him the next day that the company had decided to re-enlist for three years or duration of the war, and that a meeting would be held that evening to carry the intention into execution. When the evening came Harry walked into the town hall, dressed as carefully as he had prepared himself for his visit with Rachel. He found the whole company assembled there, the members smoking, chatting with their friends, and recounting to admiring hearers the wonderful experiences they had gone through. The enlistment papers were being prepared, and some of the boys who had not been examined during the day were undergoing the surgeon's inspection in an adjoining room.

Harry was coldly received by everybody, and winced a little under this contrast with the attentions that all the others were given.

At last all the papers and rolls seemed to be signed, and there was a lull in the proceedings. Harry rose from his seat, as if to address the meeting. Instantly all was silence and attention.

"Comrades," he said, in a firm, even voice, "I have come to say to you that I feel that I made a mistake during our term of service, and I want to apologize to you for my conduct then. More than this, I want to redeem myself. I want to go with you again, and have another chance to---"

He was interrupted by an enthusiastic shout from them all.

"Hurrah! Bully for Lieutenant Glen! Of couse we'll give you another show. Come right along in your old place, and welcome."

There was but one dissenting voice. It was that of Jake Alspaugh:

"No, I'll be durned if we want ye along any more. We've no place for sich fellers with us. We only want them as has sand in their craws."

But the protest was overslaughed by the multitude of assents. At the first interval of silence Harry said:

"No, comrades, I'll not accept a commission again until I'm sure I can do it credit. I'll enlist in the company on the same footing as the rest of the boys, and share everything with you. Give the lieutenancy to our gallant comrade Alspaugh, who has richly earned it."

The suggestion was accepted with more enthusiastic cheering, and Harry, going up to the desk, filled out an enlistment blank, signed it and the company roll, and retired with the surgeon for the physical examination. This finished, he slipped out unnoticed and went to his home. On his way thither he saw Rachel as she passed a brilliantly lighted show-window. She was in traveling costume, and seemed to be going to the depot. She turned her head slightly and bowed a formal recognition.

As their eyes met he saw enough to make him believe that what he had done met her approval.

Chapter VII. Pomp and Circumstances of Glorious War.

> But man, proud man,
> Dressed in a little brief authority,
> Most ignorant of what he's most assured,
>   *   *   *   * Plays such fantastic tricks before high
> Heaven As make the angels weep, who, with our spleens, Would all
> themselves laugh mortal.
>   --Measure for Measure

Abe, you remember how that man who made the speech when our colors were presented to us talked of 'the swelling hearts of our volunteers,' don't you?" said Kent Edwards, as he and Abe Bolton lounged near the parade-ground one fine afternoon, shortly after the arrival of the regiment in camp of instruction. "You remember that that was his favorite figure of rhetoric, and he repeated it several times?"

"Don't know anything about figger of retterick," growled Abe, who, his comrades said, had the evenest temper in the regiment, "for he was always mad. But I do remember that he said that over several times, with a lot o' other things without much pint to 'em, until I thought I'd drop, I was so thirsty and tired."

"Yes? Well, now if you want to get a good idea of what that expression meant, look over there. Not only his heart swells, but he swells all over."

"I should think he did," replied Abe, after a moment's inspection. "Unless his hat has an Injy-rubber band, he'll have to git it cut offen his head, which ought to be hooped, for it can't swell no more without busting."

It was Jacob Alspaugh crossing the parade ground in more than Solomonic splendor of uniform. His inflated form bore upon it all the blue and tinsel pre-scribed by the Army Regulations for the raiment and insignia of a First Lieutenant of Infantry, with such additions as had been suggested by his exuberant fancy. His blue broadcloth was the finest and shiniest. Buttons and bugles seemed masses of barbric gold. From broad-brimmed hat floated the longest ostrich feather procur-able in the shops. Shining leather boots, field-marshal pattern, came above his knees. Yellow gauntlets covered his massive hands and reached nearly to his el-bows, and on his broad shoulders were great glittering epaulets--then seldom worn by anyone, and still more rarely by volunteer officers. He evidently disdained to hide the crimson glories of his sash in the customary modest way, by folding it un-der his belt, but had made of it a broad bandage for his abdominal regions, which gae him the appearance of some gigantic crimson-breasted blue-bird. Behind him trailing, clanking on the ground as he walked, not the modest little sword of his rank, but a long cavalry saber, with glittering steel scabbard. But the sheen of gold and steel was dimmed beside the glow of intense satisfaction with hs make-up that shone in his face. There might be alloy in his gleaming buttons and bullion epau-lets; there was none in his happiness.

"I feel sorry for the poor lilies of the field that he comes near," sighed Kent, sympathetically. "He is like them now, in neither toiling nor spinning, and yet how ashamed he must make them of their inferior rainment."

"Faugh! it makes me sick to see a dunghill like that strutting around in feathers that belong to game birds."

"O, no; no game bird ever wore such plumage as that. You must be thinking of a peacock, or a bird-of-paradise."

"Well, then, blast it, I hate to see a peacock hatched all at once out of a slinking, roupy, barnyard rooster."

"O, no; since circuses are out of the question now, we ought to be glad of so good a substitute. It only needs a brass band, with some colored posters, to be a genuine grand entry, with street parade."

Alspaugh's triumphal march had now brought him within a few feet of them, but they continued to lounge indifferently on the musket box upon which they had been sitting, giving a mere nod as recognition of his presence, and showing no intention of rising to salute.

The glow of satisfaction faded from Alspaugh's horizon, and a cloud overcast it.

"Here, you fellers," he said angrily, "why don't ye git up an' saloot? Don't ye know your business yit?"

"What business, Jake?" asked Kent Edwards, absently, paying most attention to a toad which had hopped out form the cover of a budock leaf, in search of insects for his supper.

Alspaugh's face grew blacker. "The business of paying proper respect to your officers."

"It hasn't occured to me that I am neglecting anything in that line," said Kent, languidly, shifting over to recline upon his left elbow, and with his right hand gathering up a little gravel to flip at the toad; "but maybe you are better acquainted with our business than we are."

Abe contributed to the dialogue a scornful laugh, indicative of a most heartless disbelief in his superior officer's superior intellectuality.

The dark cloud burst in storm: "Don't you know," said Alspaugh, angry in every fiber, "that the reggerlations say that 'when an enlisted man sees an officer approach, he will rise and saloot, and remain standin' and gazin' in a respectful manner until the officer passes five paces beyond him?' Say, don't you know that?"

Kent Edwards flipped a bit of gravel with such good aim that it struck the toad fairly on the head, who blinked his bright eyes in surprise, and hopped back to his covert. "I am really glad," said he, "to know that you have learned SOMETHING of the regulations. Now, don't say another word about it until I run down to the company quarters and catch a fellow for a bet, who wants to put up money that you can never learn a single sentence of them. Don't say another word, and you can stand in with me on the bet."

"Had your head measured since you got this idea into it?" asked Abe Bolton, with well-assumed interest.

"If he did, he had to use a surveyor's chain," suggested Kent, flipping another small pebble in the direction of the toad's retreat.

Alspaugh had grown so great upon the liberal feed of the meat of flattery, that he could hardly make himself believe that he had heard aright, and that these men did not care a fig for himself or his authority. Then recovering confidence in the fidelity of their ears, it seemed to him that such conduct was aggravated mutiny, which military discipline demanded should receive condign punishment on the spot. Had he any confidence in his ability to use the doughy weapon at his side, he would not have resisted the strong temptation to draw his sword and make an example then and there of the contemners of his power and magnificence. But the culprits has shown such an aptitude in the use of arms as to inspire his wholesome respect, and he was very far from sure that they might not make a display of his broadsword an occasion for heaping fresh ridicule upon him. An opportune remembrance came to his aid:

"If it wasn't for the strcit orders we officers got yesterday not to allow ourselves to be provoked under any circumstances into striking our men, I'd learn you fellers mighty quick not to insult your superior officers. I'd bring you to time, I can tell you. But I'll settle with you yit. I'll have you in the guard hose on bread and water in short meter, and then I'll learn you to be respectful and obedient."

"He means 'teach,' instead of 'learn,'" said Kent, apologetically, to Abe. "It's just awful to have a man, wearing shoulder-straps, abuse English grammar in that way. What's grammar done to him to deserve such treatment? He hasn't even a speaking acquaintance with it."

"I 'spose it's because grammar can't hit back. That's the kind he always picks on," answered Abe.

"You'll pay for this," shouted Alspaugh, striding off after the Seargent of the Guard.

At that moment a little drummer appeared by the flagstaff, and beat a lively rataplan.

"That's for dress-parade," said Kent Edwards, rising. "We'd better skip right over to quarters and fall in."

"Wish their dress-parades were in the brimstone flames," growled Abe Bolton, as he rose to accompany his comrade. "All they're for is to stand up as a background, to show off a lot of spruce young officers dressed in fancy rigs."

"Well," said Kent, lightly, as they walked along, "I kind of like that; don't you? We make picturesque backgrounds, don't we? you and I, especially you, the soft, tender, lithe and willowy; and I, the frowning, rugged and adamantine, so to speak. I think the background business is our best hold."

He laughed heartily at his own sarcasm, but Abe was not to be moved by such frivolity, and answered glumly:

"O, yes; laugh about it, if you choose. That's your way: giggle over everything. But when I play background, I want it to be with something worth while in the foreground. I don't hanker after making myself a foil to show off such fellers as our officers are, to good advantage."

"That don't bother me any more than it does a mountain to serve as a background for a nanny goat and a pair of sore-eyed mules!"

"Yes, but the mountain sometimes has an opportunity to drop an avalanche on 'em.'"

At this point of the discussion they arrived at the company grounds, and had scarcely time to snatch up their guns and don their belts before the company moved out to take its place in the regimental line.

The occasion of Lieutenant Alspaugh's elaborate personal ornamentation now manifested itself. By reason of Captain Bennett's absence, he was in command of the company, and was about to make his first appearance on parade in that capacity. Two or three young women, of the hollyhock order of beauty, whom he was very anxious to impress, had been brought to camp, to witness his apotheosis into a commanding officer.

The moment, however, that he placed himself at the head of the company and drew sword, the chill breath of distrust sent the mercury of his self-confidence down to zero. It looked so easy to command a company when some one else was doing it; it was hard when he tried it himself. All the imps of confusion held high revel in his mind when he attempted to give the orders which he had conned until he supposed he had them "dead-letter perfect." he felt his usually-unfailing assurance shrivel up under the gaze of hundreds of mercilessly critical eyes. He managed to stammer out:

"ATTENTION, COMPANY! FORWARD, FILE RIGHT, MARCH!"

But as the company began to execute the order, it seemed to be going just the opposite to what he had commanded, and he called out excitedly:

"Not that way! Not that way! I said 'file right,' and you're going left."

"We are filing right," answered some in the company. "You're turned around; that's what's the matter with you."

So it was. He had forgotten that when standing facing the men, he must give them orders in reverse from what the movement appeared to him. This increased his confusion, until all his drill knowledge seemed gone from him. The sight of his young lady friends, clad in masses of primary colors, stimulated him to a strong effort to recover his audacity, and bracing himself up, he began calling out the guide and step, with a noisy confidence that made him heard all over the parade ground:

"Left! left! left! Hep! hep! hep! Cast them head and eyes to the right!"

Trouble loomed up mountainously as he approached the line. Putting a company into its place on parade is one of the crucial tests of tactical proficiency. To march a company to exactly the right spot, with every man keeping his proper distance from his file-leader--"twenty-eight inches from back to breast," clear down the column, so that when the order "front" was given, every one turns, as if on pivot, and touches elbows with those on each side of him, in a straight, firm wall of men, without any shambling "closing up," or "side-stepping" to the right or left,--to do all this at word of command, looks very simple and easy to the non-military spectator, as many other very difficult things look simple and easy to the inexperienced. But really it is only possible to a thoroughly drilled company, held well in hand by a competent commander. It is something that, if done well, is simply done well, but if not done well, is very bad. It is like an egg that is either good or utterly worthless.

Alspaugh seemed fated to exhaust the category of possible mistakes. Coming on the ground late he found that a gap had been left in the line for his company which was only barely sufficient to receive it when it was aligned and compactly "dressed."

In his nervousness he halted the company before it had reached the right of the gap by ten paces, and so left about one-quarter of the company lapping over on the one to his left. Even this was done with an unsightly jumble. His confusion as to the reversal of right and left still abode with him. He commanded "right face" instead of "front," and was amazed to see the whole one hundred well-drilled men whirl their backs around to the regiment and the commanding officer. A laugh rippled down the ranks of the other companies; even the spectators smiled, and something sounded like swearing by the Adjutant and Sergeant-Major.

Alspaugh lifted his plumed hat, and wiped the beaded perspiration from his brow with the back of one of the yellow gauntlets.

"Order an 'about face,'" whispered the Orderly-Sergeant, whose face was burning with shame at the awkward position in which the company found itself.

"ABOUT--FACE!" gasped Alspaugh.

The men turned on their heels.

"Side-step to the right," whispered the Orderly.

"Side-step to the right," repeated Alspaugh, mechanically.

The men took short side-steps, and following the orders which Alspaugh repeated from the whispered suggestions of the Orderly, the company came clumsily forward into its place, "dressed," and "opened ranks to the rear." When at the command of "parade-rest," Alspaugh dropped his saber's point to the ground, he did it with the crushed feeling of a strutting cock which has been flung into the pond and emerges with dripping feathers.

He raised his heart in sincere thanksgiving that he was at last through, for there was nothing more for him to do during the parade, except to stand still, and at its conclusion the Orderly would have to march the company back to its quarters.

But his woes had still another chapter. The Inspector-General had come to camp to inspect the regiment, and he was on the ground.

Forty years of service in the regular army, with promotion averaging one grade every ten years, making him an old man and a grandfather before he was a Lieutenant-Colonel, had so surcharged Col. Murbank's nature with bitterness as to make even the very air in his vicinity seem roughly astringent. The wicked young Lieutenants who served with him on the Plains used to say that his bark was worse than his bite, because no reasonable bite could ever be so bad as his bark. They even suggested calling him "Peruvian Bark," because a visit to his quarters was worse than a strong does of quinia.

"Yeth, that'th good," said the lisping wit of the crowd. "Evely bite ith a bit, ain't it? And the wortht mutht be a bitter, ath he ith."

The Colonel believed tha the whole duty of man consisted in loving the army regulations, and in keeping their commandments. The best part of all virtue was to observe them to the letter; the most abhorrent form of vice, to violate or disregard even their minor precepts.

His feelings were continually lacerated by contact with volunteers, who cared next to nothing for the FORM of war-making, but everything for its spirit, and the martinet heart within him was bruised and sore when he came upon the ground to inspect the regiment.

Alspaugh's blundering in bringing the company into line awakened this ire from a passivity to activity.

"I'll have that dunderhead's shoulder-straps off inside of a fortnight," he muttered between his teeth.

The unhappy Lietenant's inability to even stand properly during the parade, or repeat an order intensified his rage. When the parade was dismissed the officers, as usual, sheathed their swords, and forming a line with the Adjutant in the center, marched forward to teh commanding and inspecting officers, and saluted. Then the wrath of the old Inspector became vocable.

"What in God's name," he roared, fixing his glance upon Alspaugh so unmistakably that enve the latter's rainbow-clad girls, who had crowded up closely, could not make a mistake as to the victim of the expletives. "What in God's name, sir," repeated the old fellow with purpling face, "do you mean by bringing your company on to the ground in that absurd way, sir? Did you think, sir, that it was a hod of brick--with which I have no doubt you are most familiar--that you could dump down any place and any how, sir? Such misconduct is simply disgraceful, sir, I'd have you know. Simply disgraceful, sir."

He paused for breath, but Alspaugh had no word of defense to offer.

"And what do you mean, sir," resumed the Inspector, after inflating his lungs for another gust, "what in the name of all the piebald circus clowns that ever jiggered around on sawdust, do you mean by coming on parade dressed like the ringmaster of a traveling monkey-show, sir? Haven't you any more idea of the honor of wearing a United States sword--the noblest weapon on earth, sir--than to make yourself look like the drum-major of a band of nigger minstrels, sir! A United States officer ought to be ashamed to make a damned harlequin of himself, sir. I'd have you to understand that most distinctly, sir!"

The Inspector's stock of breath, alas, was not so ample as in the far-off days when his sturdy shoulders bore the modest single-bar, instead of the proud spread eagle of the present. Even had it been, the explosive energy of his speech would have speedily exhausted it. Compelled to stop to pump in a fresh supply, the Colonel of the regiment took advantage of the pause to whisper in his ear:

"Don't be too rough on him, please. He's a good man but green. Promoted from the ranks for courage in action. First appearance on parade. He'll do better if given a chance."

The Inspector's anger was mollified. Addressing himself to all the officers, he continued in a milder tone:

"Gentlemen, you seem to be making progress in acquiring a knowledge of your duties, though you have a world of things yet to learn. I shall say so in my report to the General. You can go to your quarters."

The line of officers dissolved, and the spectators began to melt away. Alspaugh's assurance rose buoyantly the moment that the pressure was removed. He raised his eyes from the ground, and looked for the young ladies. They had turned their backs and were leaving the ground. He hastened after them, fabricating as he walked an explanation, based on personal jealousy, of the Inspector's treatment of him. He was within a step of overtaking them when he heard one say, with toss of flaunting ribbons, and hoidenish giggle:

"Did you EVER see ANY-body wilt as Alspaugh did when old Bite-Your-Head-Off-In-a-Minute was jawing him? It was so awfully FUNNY that I just thought I SHOULD DIE."

The sentence ended with the picturesque rapid CRESCENDO employed by maidens of her type in describing a convulsive experience.

"Just didn't he," joined in another. "I never saw ANY-thing so funny in all my BORN DAYS. I was AFRAID to look at either one of YOU; I knew if I DID I would BURST RIGHT OUT laughing. I couldn't've HELPED it--I know I COULDN'T, if I'd'a knowed I'd'a DIED the next MINUTE."

"This would seem to be a pretty good time to drop the fellow," added the third girl, reflectively.

Alspaugh turned and went in another direction. At the 9 o'clock roll-call he informed the company that the Inspector was well pleased with its appearance on parade.

Chapter VIII. The Tedium of Camp.

And you, good yeoman,
Whose limbs were made in England, show us here
The mettle of your pasture; let us swear
That you are worth your breeding.
                              --Henry V.

To really enjoy life in a Camp of Instruction requires a peculiar cast of mind. It requires a genuine liking for a tread-mill round of merely mechanical duties; it requiers a taste for rising in the chill and cheerless dawn, at the unwelcome summons of "reveille," to a long day filled with a tiresome routine of laborious drills alternating with tedious roll-calls, and wearisome parades and inspections; it requires pleased contentment with walks continually cut short by the camp-guard, and with amusements limited to rough horse-play on the parade-ground, and dull games of cards by sputtering candles in the tent.

As these be tastes and preferences notably absent from the mind of the average young man, our volunteers usually regard their experience in Camp of Instruction as among the most unpleasant of their war memories.

These were the trials that tested Harry Glen's resolution sorely. When he enlisted with the intention of redeeming himself, he naturally expected that the opportunity he desired would be given by a prompt march to the field, and a speedy entrance into an engagement. He nerved himself strenuously for the dredful ordeal of battle, but this became a continually receding point. The bitter defeat at Bull Run was bearing fruit in months of painstaking preparation before venturing upon another collision.

Day by day he saw the chance of retrieving his reputation apparently more remote. Meanwhile discouragements and annoyances grew continually more plentiful and irksome. He painfully learned that the most disagreeable part of war is not the trial of battle, but the daily sacrifices of personal liberty, tastes, feelings and conveniences involved in camp-life, and in the reduction of one's cherished individuality to the dead-level of a passive, obedient, will-less private soldier.

"I do wish the regiment would get orders to move!" said almost hourly each one of a half-million impatient youths fretting in Camps of Instruction through the long Summer of 1861.

"I do wish the regiment would get orders to move!" said Harry Glen angrily one evening, on coming into the Surgeon's tent to have his blistered hands dressed. he had been on fatigue duty during the day, and the Fatigue-Squad had had an obstinate struggle with an old oak stump, which disfigured the parade-ground, and resisted removal like an Irish tenant.

"I am willing--yes, I can say I am anxious, even--to go into battle," he continued, while Dr. Paul Denslow laid plasters of simple cerate on the abraded palms, and then swathed them in bandages. "Anything is preferable to this chopping tough stumps with a dull ax, and drilling six hours a day while the thermometer hangs around the nineties."

"I admit that there are things which would seem pleasanter to a young man of your temperament and previous habits," said the Surgeon, kindly. "Shift over into that arm-stool, which you will find easier, and reat a little while. Julius, bring in that box of cigars."

While Julius, who resembled his illustrious namesake as little in celerity of movement as he did in complexion, was coming, the Surgeon prepared a paper, which he presented to Harry, saying:

"There, that'll keep you off duty to-morrow. After that, we'll see what can be done."

Julius arrived with the cigars as tardily as if he had had to cross a Rubicon in the back room. Two were lighted, and the Surgeon settled himself for a chat.

"Have you become tired of soldier-life?" asked he, studying Harry's face for the effect of the question.

"I can not say that I have become tired of it," said Harry, frankly, "because I must admit that I never had the slightest inclination to it. I had less fancy for becoming a soldier than for any other honorable pursuit that you could mention."

"Then you only joined the army--"

"From a sense of duty merely," said Harry, knocking the ashes from his cigar.

"And the physical and other discomforts now begin to weight nearly as much as that sense of duty?"

"Not at all. It only seems to me that there are more of them than are absolutely essential to the performance of that duty. I want to be of service to the country, but I would prefer that that service be not made unnecessarily onerous."

"Quite natural; quite natural."

"For example, how have the fatigues and pains of my afternoon's chopping contributed a particle toward the suppression of the rebellion? What have my blistered hands to do with the hurts of actual conflict?"

"Let us admit that the connection is somewhat obscure," said Doctor Denslow, philosophically.

"It is easier for you, than for me, to view the matter calmly. Your hands are unhurt. I am the galled jade whose withers are wrung."

"Body and spirit both bruised?" said the Surgeon, half reflectively.

Harry colored. "Yes," he said, rather defiantly. "In addition to desiring to serve my country, I want to vindicate my manhood from some aspersions which have been cast upon it."

"Quite a fair showing of motives. Better, perhaps, than usual, when a careful weighing of the relative proportions of self-esteem, self-interest and higher impulses is made."

"I am free to say that the discouragements I have met with are very different, and perhaps much greater than I contemplated. Nor can I bring myself to belived tha they are necessary. I am trying to be entirely willing to peril life and limb on the field of battle, but instead of placing me where I can do this, and allowing me to concentrate all my energies upon that object, I am kept for months chafing under the petty tyrannies of a bullying officer, and deprived of most of the comforts that I have heretofore regarded as necessary to my existence. What good can be accomplished by diverting forces which should be devoted to the main struggle into this ignoble channel? That's what puzzles and irritates me."

"It seems to be one of the inseperable conditions of the higher forms of achievement that they require vastly more preparation for them than the labor of doing them."

"That's no doubt very philosophical, but it's not satisfactory, for all that."

"My dear boy, learn this grand truth now: That philosophy is never satisfactory; it is only mitigatory. It consists mainly in saying with many fine words: 'What can't be cured must be endured.'"

"I presume that is so. I wish, though, that by the mere syaing so, I could make the endurance easier."

"I can make your lot in the service easier."

"Indeed! how so?"

"By having you appointed my Hospital Steward. I have not secured one yet, and the man who is acting as such is so intemperate that I feel a fresh sense of escape with every day that passes without his mistaking the oxalic axid for Epsom salts, to the destruction of some earnest but constipated young patriot's whole digestive viscera.

"If you accept this position," continued the Surgeon, flinging away his refractory cigar in disgust, and rising to get a fresh one, "you will have the best rank and pay of any non-commissioned officer in the regiment; better, ineed, than that of a Second Lieutenant. You will have your quarters here with me, and be compelled to associate with no one but me, thus reducing your disagreeable companions at a single stroke, to one. And you will escape finally from all subserviency to Lieutenant Alspaugh, or indeed to any other officer in the regiment, except your humble servant. As to food, you will mess with me."

"Those are certainly very strong inducements," said Harry, meditating upon the delightfulness of relief from the myriad of rasping little annoyances which rendered every day of camp-life an infliction.

"Yes, and still farther, you will never need to go under fire, or expose yourself to danger of any kind, unless you choose to."

Harry's face crimsoned to the hue of the western sky where the sun was just going down. He started to answer hotly, but an understanding of the Surgeon's evident kindness and sincerity interposed to deter him. He knew there was no shaft of sarcasm hidden below this plain speech, and after a moment's consideration he replied:

"I am very grateful, I assure you, for your kindness in this matter. I am strongly tempted to accept your offer, bu there are still stronger reasons why I should decline it."

"May I ask your reasons?"

"My reasons for not accepting the appointment?"

"Yes, the reasons which impel you to prefer a dinner of bitter herbs, under Mr. Alspaugh's usually soiled thumb, to a stalled ox and my profitable society," said the Surgeon, gayly.

Harry hesitated a moment, and then decided to speak frankly. "Yes," he said, "your kindness gives you the right to know. To not tell you would show a lack of gratitude. I made a painful blunder before in not staying unflinchingly with my company. The more I think of it, the more I regret it, and the more I am decided not to repeat it, but abide with my comrades and share their fate in all things. I feel that I no longer have a choice in the matter; I must do it. But there goes the drum for roll-call. I must go. Good evening, and very many thanks."

"The young fellow's no callow milksop, after all," said the Surgeon Denslow, as his eyes followed Harry's retreating form. "His gristle is hardening into something like his stern old father's backbone."

Chapter IX. On the March.

"He smelleth the battle afar off, the thunder of the Captains and the shouting." -- Job.

The weary weeks in Camp of Instruction ended with the Summer. September had come, and Nature was hanging out crimson battle-flags everywhere--on the swaying poppy and the heavy-odored geranium. The sumach and the sassafras wore crimson signals of defiance, and the maples blazed with the gaudy red, yellow and orange of warlike pomp.

The regiment made its first step on Kentucky soil with a little bit of pardonable ostentation. Every one looked upon it as the real beginning of its military career. When the transport was securely tied up at the wharf, the Colonel mounted his horse, drew his sword, placed himself at the head of the regiment, and gave the command "Forward." Eleven hundred superb young fellows, marching four abrest, with bayonets fixed, and muskets at "right shoulder shift," strode up the bank after him and went into line of battle at the top, where he made a short soldierly speech, the drums rolled, the colors dipped, the men cheered, and the band played "Star-spangled Banner" and "Dixie."

Three years later the two hundred survivors of this number returning from their "Veteran furlough," without a band and with their tattered colors carefully cased, came off a transport at the same place, without uttering a word other than a little grumbling at the trouble of disposing of some baggage, marched swiftly and silently up the bank, and disappeared before any one fairly realized that they were there. So much had Time and War taught them.

"Now our work may be said to be fairly begun." said the Colonel, turning from the contemplation of his regiment, and scanning anxiously the tops of the distant line of encircling hills, as if he expected to see there signs of the Rebels in strong force. All the rest imitated his example, and studied the horizon solicitously. "And I expect we shall have plenty of it!" continued the Colonel.

"No doubt of that," answered the Major. "They say the Rebels are filling Kentucky with troops, and gonig to fight for every foot of the Old Dark and Bloody Ground. I think we will have to earn all we get of it."

"To-day's papers report," joined in Surgeon Denslow, "that General sherman says it will take two hundred thousand troops to redeem Kentucky."

"Yes," broke in the Colonel testily, "and the same papers agree in pronouncing Sherman crazy. But no matter how many or how few it takes, that's none of our affair. We've got eleven hundred good men in ranks, and we're going to do all that eleven hundred good men can do. God Almighty and Abe Lincoln have got to take care of the rest."

It will be seen that the Colonel was a very practical soldier.

"First think we know, the Colonel will be trying to make us 'leven hundred clean out 'leven thousand Rebs," growled Abe Bolton.

"Suppose the Colonel should imagine himself another Leonidas, and us his Spartan band, and want us to die around him, and start another Thermopylae down her in the mountains, some place," suggested Kent Edwards, "you would cheerfully pass in your checks along with the rest, so as to make the thing an entire success, wouldn't you?"

"The day I'm sent below, I'll take a pile of Rebs along to keep me company," answered Abe, surlily.

Glen, standing in the rear of his company in his place as file-closer, listened to these words, and saw in the dim distance and on the darkling heights the throngs of fierce enemies and avalanches of impeding dangers as are likely to oppress the imagination of a young soldier at such unfavorable moments. The conflict and carnage seemed so imminent that he half expected it to begin that very night, and he stiffened his sinews for the shock.

Lieutenant Alspaugh also heard, studied over the unwelcome possibilities shrouded in the gathering gloom of the distance, and regretted that he had not, before crossing the Ohio, called the Surgeon's attention to some premonitory symptoms of rheumatism, which he felt he might desire to develop into an acute attack in the event of danger assuming an unpleasant proximity.

But as no Rebels appeared on the sweeping semi-circle of hills that shut in Convington on the south, he concluded to hold his disability in abeyance, by a strong effort of the will, until the regiment had penetrated farther into the enemy's country.

For days the regiment marched steadily on through the wonderfully lovely Blue Grass Region, toward the interior of the State, without coming into the neighborhood of any organized body of the Rebels.

Glen's first tremors upon crossing the Ohio subsided so as to permit him to thoroughly enjoy the beauties of the scenery, and the pleasures of out-door life in a region so attractive at that season of the year.

The turnpike, hard and smooth as a city pavement, wound over and around romantic hills--hills crowned with cedar and evergreen laurel, and scarred with cliffs and caverns. It passed through forests, aromatic with ripening nuts and changing leaves, and glorious in the colors of early Autumn. Then its course would traverse farms of gracefully undulating acres, bounded by substantial stone-walls, marked by winding streams of pure spring water, centering around great roomy houses, with huge outside chimneys, and broad piazzas, and with a train of humble negro cabins in the rear. The horses were proud stepping thoroughbreds, the women comely and spirited, the men dignified and athletic, and all seemed well-fed and comfortable. The names of the places along the route recalled to Harry's memory all he had ever read of the desperate battles and massacres and single-handed encounters of Daniel Boone and his associates, with the Indians in the early history of the country.

"This certainly seems an ideal pastoral land--a place where one would naturally locate a charming idyl or bucolic love-story!" he said one evening, to Surgeon Paul Denslow, after descanting at length upon the beauties of the country which they were "redeeming" from the hands of the Rebels.

"Yes, answered Dr. Denslow, "and it's as dull and sleepy and non-progressive as all those places are where they locate what you call your idyls and pastorals! These people haven't got an idea belonging to this century, nor do they want one. They know how to raise handsome girls, distil good whisky, and breed fast horses. This they esteem the end of all human knowledge and understanding. Anything moer is to them vanity and useless vexation of spirit."

At last the regiment halted under the grand old beeches and hickories of teh famous Camp Dick Robinson, in the heart of the Blue Grass Region. In this most picturesque part of the lovely Kentucky River Valley they spent the bright days of October very delightfully.

Nature is as kindly and gracious in Central Kentucky as in any part of the globe upon which her sun shines, and she seemed to be on her best behavior, that she might duly impress the Northern visitors.

The orchards were loaded with fruit, and the forest trees showered nuts upon the ground. In every field were groups of persimmon trees, their branches bend-ingunder a burden of luscious fruit, which the frost had coated with sheeny purple outside, and made sweeter than fine wine within. Over all bent softly brilliant skies, and the bland, bracing air was charged with the electricity of life and happi-ness.

It was the very poetry of soldiering, and Harry began to forget the miseries of life in a Camp of Instruction, and to believe that there was much to be enjoyed, even in the life of an enlisted man.

"This here air or the apple-jack seems to have a wonderfully improving effect on Jake Alspaugh's chronic rheumatics," sneered Abe Bolton.

It was a sunny afternoon. Bolton and Kent Edwards were just ouside of the camp lines, in the shade of a grand old black walnut, and had re-seated themselves to finsih devouring a bucketful of lush persimmons, after having reluctantly risen from that delightful occupation to salute Lieutenant Alspaugh, as he passed out-ward in imposing blue and gold stalwarthood.

"I've been remarking that myself," said Kent, taking out a handful of the shin-ing fruit, and deliberately picking the stems and dead leaves from the sticky sides, preparatory to swallowing it. "He hasn't had an attack since we thought those ne-groes and teams on the hills beyond Cynthiana was John Morgan's Rebel cavalry."

"Yes," continued Abe, helping himself also the mellow date-plums, "his legs are so sound now that he is able to go to every frolic in the country for miles around, and dance all night. He's going to the Quartermaster's now, to get a horse to ride to a dance and candy-pulling at that double log-house four miles down the Harrods-burg Pike. I heard him talking to some other fellows about it when I went up with the squad to bring the rations down to the company."

"Seems to em, come to think of it, that I HAVE heard of some rheumatic symptoms recently. Remember that a couple of weeks ago Pete Sanford got a bullet through his blouse, that scraped his ribs, don't you?"

"Yes," said Abe, spitting the seeds out from a mouthful of honeyed pulp.

"Well, the boys say that Jake went to a candy-pulling frolic down in the Cranston settlement, and got into a killing flirtation with the prettiest girl there. She was taken with his brass buttons, and his circus-horse style generally, but she had another fellow that it didn't suit so well. He showed his disapproval in a way that seems to be the fashion down here; that is, he 'laid for' Jake behind a big rock with a six-foot deer rifle, but mistook Pete Sanford for him."

"The dunderhead's as poor a judge of men as he's marksman. He's a disgrace to Kentucky."

"At all events it served as a hint, which Alspaugh did not fail to take. Since that time there has been two or three dances at Cranston's, but every time Jake has had such twinges of his rheumatism that he did not think it best to 'expose himself to the night air,' and go with the boys."

"O!---ouw!---wh-i-s-s-s-sh!" sputtered Abe, spitting the contents of his mouth out explosively, while his face was contorted as if every nerve and muscle was being twisted violently.

"Why, what is the matter, Abe?" asked Kent, in real alarm. "Have you swallowed a centipede or has the cramp-colic griped you?"

"No! I hain't swallowed no centerboard, nor have I the belly-ache--blast your chucklehead," roared Abe, as he sprang to his feet, rushed to the brook, scooped up some water in his hands, and rinsed his mouth out energetically.

"Well, what can it be, then? You surely ain't doing all that for fun."

"No, I ain't doing it for fun," shouted Abe, angrier still; "and nobody but a double-and twisted idiot would ask such a fool question. I was paying so much attention to your dumbed story that I chewed up a green persimmon--one that hadn't been touched by the frost. It's puckered my mouth so that I will never get it straight again. It's worse than a pound of alum and a gallon of tanbark juice mixed together. O, laugh, if you want to--that's just what I'd expect from you. That's about all the sense you've got."

There was enough excitement in camp to prevent any danger of ennui. The probability of battle gave the daily drills an interest that they never could gain in Ohio. The native Rebels were numerous and defiant, and kept up such demonstrations as led to continual apprehensions of an attack. New regiments came in constantly, and were received with enthusiasm. Kentucky and East Tennessee Loyalists, tall, gaunt, long-haired and quaint-spoken, but burning with enthusiasm for the Government of their fathers, flocked to the camp, doffed their butternut garb, assumed the glue, and enrolled themselves to defend the Union.

At length it became evident that the Rebel "Army of Liberation" was really about crossing the Cumberland Mountains to drive out the "Yankees" and recover possession of Kentucky for the Southern Confederacy.

Outposts were thrown out in all directions to gain the earlies possible intelligence of the progress of the movement, and to make such resistance to it as might be possible. One of these outposts was stationed at Wildcat Gap, an inexpressibly wild and desolate region, sixty miles from Camp Dick Robinson, where the road entering Kentucky from Tennessee at Cumberland Gap crosses the Wildcat range of mountains.

One day the startling news reached camp that an overwhelming Rebel force under Gen. Zollicoffer was on the eve of attacking the slender garrison of Wildcat Gap. The "assembly" was sounded, and the regiment, hastily provided with rations and ammunition, was hurried forward to aid in the defense of the threatened outpost.

Nature, as if in sympathy with the gathering storm of war, ceased her smiling. The blue, bending skies were transformed intoa scowling, leaden-visaged canopy, from which fell a chill incessant rain.

When the order to prepare for the march came, Glen, following the example of his comrades, packed three days' cooked rations in his haversack, made his blankets into a roll, tieing their ends together, threw them scarf-fashion over his shoulder, and took his accustomed place as file-closer in the rear of his company. He was conscious all the time, though he suffered no outward sign to betray the fact, that he was closely watched by the boys who had been with him in Western Virginia, and who were eager to see how he would demean himself in this new emergency.

He was shortly ordered to assist in the inspection of cartridge-boxes and the issuing of cartridges, adn the grim nature of the errand they were about to start upon duly impressed itself upon his mind as he walked down the lines in the melancholy rains, examined each box, and gave the owner the quantity of cartridges required to make up the quota of forty rounds per man.

Those who scrutinized his face as he passed slowly by, saw underneath the dripping eaves of his broad-brimmed hat firm-set lines about his mouth, and a little more luminous light in his eyes.

"Harry Glen's screwing his courage to the sticking point. He's bound to go through this time," said Kent Edwards.

"The more fool he," answered Abe Bolton, adjusting his poncho so as to better protect his cartridges and rations from the rain. "If he wanted to play the warrior all so bold why didn't he improve his opportunities in West Virginia, when it was fine weather and he only had three months to do it in? Now that he's in for three years it will be almighty strange if he can't find a pleasanter time to make his little strut on the field of battle than in this infernal soak."

"I have seen better days than this, as the tramp remarked who had once been a bank cashier," murmured kent, tightening the tompion in his musket-muzzle with a piece of paper, the better to exclude the moisture, and wrapping a part of the poncho around the lock for the same purpose. "Where is that canteen?"

"It's where it'll do you no good until you need it much worse'n you do now. O, I know you of old, Mr. Kent Edwards," continued Abe, with that deep sarcasm, which was his nearest approach to humor. "I may say that I've had the advantages of an intimate acquaintance with you for years, and when I trust you with a full canteen of apple-jack at the beginning of such a march as this'll be, I'll be ready to enlist in the permanent garrison of a lunatic asylum, I will. This canteen ony holds three pints; that's great deal less'n you do. It's full now, and you're empty. Fill up some place else, and tomorrow or next day, when you'd give a farm for a nip, this'll come in mighty handy."

The Hospital Steward approached, and said:

"Captain, the Surgeon presents his compliments and requests that you send four men to convey your First Lieutenant Alspaugh to comfortable quarters which have been prepared for him in the hospital barracks. His rheumatic trouble has suddenly assumed an acute form--brought on doubtless by the change in the weather--and he is suffering greatly. Please instruct the men to be very careful carrying him, so as to avoid all unnecessary pain, and also all exposure to the rain. He will have a good room in the hospital, with a fire in it, and every attention, so that you need have no fears concerning him."

"I never had," said Kent, loud enough to be heard all over the right wing of the company.

"I have," said Abe. "There's every danger in the world that he'll get well."

Away the regiment marched, through the dismal rain, giong as fast as the heavily laden men could be spurred onward by the knowledge of their comrades' imminent need.

It was fearful hard work even so long as the pike lasted, and they had a firm, even foundation for their feet to tread upon. But the pike ended at Crab Orchard, and then they plunged into the worst roads that the South at any time offered to resist the progress of the Union armies. Narrow, tortuous, unworked substitutes for highways wound around and over steep, rocky hills, through miry creek bottoms, and over bridgeless streams, now so swollen as to be absolutely unfordable by less determined men, starting on a less urgent errand.

For three weary, discouraging days they pressed onward through the dispiriting rain and over all the exhausting obstacles. On the morning of the fourth they reached the foot of the range in which Wildcat Gap is situated. They were marching slowly up the steep mountain side, their soaked garments clinging about their weary limbs and clogging their footsteps. Suddenly a sullen boom rolled out of the mist that hung over the distant mountain tops.

Every one stopped, held their breaths, and tried to check the beating of their hearts, that they might hear more.

They needed not. There was no difficulty about hearing the succeeding reports, which became every instant more distinct.

"By God, that's cannon!" said the Colonel. "They're attacking our boys. Throw off everything, boys, and hurry forward!"

Overcoats, blankets, haversacks and knapsacks were hastily pied, and the two most exhausted men in each company placed on guard over them.

Kent and Abe did not contribute their canteen to the company pile. But then its weight was much less of an impediment than when they left Camp Dick Robinson.

They employed the very brief halt of the regiment in swabbing out the barrels of their muskets very carefully, and removing the last traces of moisture from the nipples and hammers.

"At last I stand a show of getting some return from this old piece of gas-tube for the trouble it's been to me," said Kent Edwards, as he ran a pin into the nipple to make assurance doubly sure that it was entirely free. "Think of the transportation charges I have against it, for the time I have lugged it around over Ohio and Kentucky, to say nothing of the manual labor and the mental strain of learning and prectising 'present arms,' 'carry arms,' 'support arms,' and such military monkey-shines under the hot sun of last Summer!"

He pulled off the woolen rag he had twisted around the head of the rammer for a swab, wiped the rammer clean and bright and dropped it into the gun. It fell with a clear ring. Another dextrous movement of the gun sent it flying into the air. Kent caught it as it came down and scrutinized its bright head. He found no smirch of dirt or dampness. "Clean and clear as a whistle inside," he said, approvingly. "She'll make music that our Secession friends will pay attention to, though it may not be as sweet to their ears as 'The Bonnie Blue Flag.'"

"More likely kick the whole northwest quarter section of your shoulder off when you try to shoot it," growled Abe, who had been paying similar close attention to his gun. "If we'd had anybody but a lot of mullet-heads for officers we'd a'been sent up here last week, when the weather and the roads were good, and when we could've done something. Now our boys'll be licked before we can get where we can help 'em."

Glen leaned on his musket, and listening to the deepening roar of battle, was shaken by the surge of emotions natural to the occasion. It seemed as if no one could live through the incessant firing the sound of which rolled down to them. To go up into it was to deliberately venture into certain destruction. Memory made a vehement protest. He recalled all the pleasant things that life had in store for him; all that he could enjoy and accomplish; all that he might be to others; all that others might be to him. Every enjoyment of the past, every happy possibility of the future took on a more entrancing roseatenesss.

Could he give all this up, and die there on the mountain top, in this dull, brutal, unheroic fashion, in the filthy mud and dreary rain, with no one to note or care whether he acted courageously or otherwise?

It did not seem that he was expected to fling his life away like a dumb brute entering the reeking shambles. His youth and abilities had been given him for some other purpose. Again palsying fear and ignoble selfishness tugged at his heart-strings, and he felt all his carefully cultivated resolutions weakening.

"A Sergeant must be left in command of the men guarding this property," said the Colonel. The Captain of Company A will detail one for that duty."

Captain Bennett glanced from one to another of his five Sergeants. Harry's heart gave a swift leap, with hope that he might be ORDERED to remain behind. Then the blood crimsoned his cheeks, for the first time since the sound of the firing struck his ears; he felt that every eye in the Company was upon him, and that his ignoble desire had been read by all in his look of expectancy. Shame came to spur up his faltering will. He set his teeth firmly, pulled the tompion out of his gun, and flung it away disdainfully as if he would never need it again, blew into the muzzle to see if the tube was clear, and wiped off the lock with a fine white handkerchief--one of the relics of his by-gone elegance--which he drew from the breast of his blouse.

"Sergeant Glan--Sergeant Glancey will remain," said the Captain peremptorily. Glancey, the Captain knew, was the only son and support of a widowed mother.

"Now, boys," said the Colonel in tones that rang like bugle notes, "the time has come for us to strike a blow for the Union, and for the fame of the dear old Buckeye State. I need not exhort you to do your duty like men; I know you too well to think that any such words of mine are at all necessary. Forward! QUICK TIME! MARCH!"

The mountain sides rang with the answering cheers from a thousand throats.

The noise of the battle on the distant crest was at first in separate bursts of sound, as regiment after regiment came into position and opened fire. The intervals between these bursts had disappeared, and it had now become a steady roar.

A wild mob came rushing backward from the front.

"My God, our men are whipped!" exclaimed the young Adjutant in tones of Anguish.

"No, no," said Captain Bennett, with cheerful confidence. "These are only the camp riff-raff, who run whenever so much as a cap is burst near them."

So it proved to be. There were teamsters upon their wheel-mules, cooks, officers' servants, both black and white, and civilian employees, mingled with many men in uniform, skulking from their companies. Those were mounted who could seize a mule anywhere, and those who could not were endeavoring to keep up on foot with the panic-stricken riders.

All seemed wild with one idea: To get as far as possible from the terrors raging around the mountain top. They rushed through the regiment and disordered its ranks.

"Who are you a-shovin', young fellow--say?" demanded Abe Bolton, roughly collaring a strapping hulk of a youth, who, hatless, and with his fat cheeks white with fear came plunging against him like a frightened steer.

"O boys, let me pass, and don't go up there! Don't! You'll all be killed. I know it, I'm all the one of my company that got away--I am, really. All the rest are killed."

"Heavens! what a wretched remnant, as the dry-goods man said, when the clerk brought him a piece of selvage as all that the burglars had left of his stock of broadcloth," said Kent Edwards. "It's too bad that you were allowed to get away, either. You're not a proper selection for a relic at all, and you give a bad impression of your company. You ought to have thought of this, and staid up there and got killed, and let some better-looking man got away, that would have done the company credit. Why didn't you think of this?"

"Git!" said Abe, sententiously, with a twist in the coward's collar, that, with the help of an opportune kick by Kent, sent him sprawling down the bank.

"Captain Bennett," shouted the Colonel angrily, "Fix bayonets there in front, and drive these hounds off, or we'll never get there."

A show of savage-looking steel sent the skulkers down a side-path through the woods.

The tumult of the battle heightened with every step the regiment advanced. A turn in the winding road brought them to an opening in the woods which extended clear to the summit. Through this the torrent of noise poured as when a powerful band passes the head of a street. Down this avenue came rolling the crash of thousands of muskets fired with the intense energy of men in mortal combat, the deeper pulsations of the artillery, and even the firece yells of the fighters, as charges were made or repulsed.

Glen felt the blood settle around his heart anew.

"Get out of the road and let the artillery pass! Open up for the artillery!" shouted voices from the rear. Everybody sprang to the side of the road.

There came a sound of blows rained upon horses bodies--of shouts and oaths from exited drivers and eager officers--of rushing wheels and of ironed hoofs striking fire from the grindng stones. Six long-bodied, strong-limbed horses, their hides reeking with sweat, and their nostrils distended with intense effort, tore past, snatching after them, as if it were a toy, a gleaming brass cannon, surrounded by galloping cannoneers, who goaded the draft horses on with blows with the flats of their drawn sabers. Another gun, with its straining horses and galloping attendants, and another, and another, until six great, grim pieces, with their scres of desperately eager men and horses, had rushed by toward the front.

It was a sight to stir the coldest blood. The excited infantry boys, wrought up to the last pitch by the spectacle, sprang back into the road, cheered vociferously, and rushed on after the battery.

Hardly had the echoes of their voices died away, when they heard the battery join its thunders to the din of the fight.

Then wounded men, powder-stained, came straggling back--men with shattered arms and gashed faces and garments soaked with blood from bleeding wounds.

"Hurrah, boys!" each shouted with weakened voice, as his eyes lighted up at sight of the regiment, "We're whipping them; but hurry forward! You're needed."

"If you ain't pretty quick," piped one girl-faced boy, with a pensive smile, as he sat weakly down on a stone and pressed a delicate hand over a round red spot that had just appeared on the breast of his blouse, "you'll miss all the fun. We've about licked 'em already. Oh!--"

Abe and Kent sprang forward to catch him, but he was dead almost before they could reach him. They laid him back tenderly on the brown dead leaves, and ran to regain their places in the ranks.

The regiment was now sweeping around the last curve between it and the line of battle. The smell of burning powder that filled the air, the sight of flowing blood, the shouts of teh fighting men, had awakened every bosom that deep-lying KILLING instinct inherited from our savage ancestry, which slumbers--generally wholly unsuspected--in even the gentlest man's bosom, until some accident gives it a terrible arousing.

Now the slaying fever burned in every soul. They were marching with long, quick strides, but well-closed ranks, elbow touching elbow, and every movement made with the even more than the accuracy of a parade. Harry felt himself swept forward by a current as resistless as that which sets over Niagara.

They came around the little hill, and saw a bank of smoke indicating where the line of battle was.

"Let's finish the canteen now," said Kent. "It may get bored by a bullet and all run out, and you know I hate to waste."

"I suppose we might as well drink it," assented Abe--the first time in the history of the regiment, that he agreed with anybody. "We mayn't be able to do it in ten minutes, and it would be too bad to 've lugged that all the way here, just for some one else to drink."

An Aide, powder-grimed, but radiant with joy, dashed up. "Colonel," he said, "you had better go into line over in that vacant space there, and wait for orders; but I don't think you will have anything to do, for the General believes that the victory is on, and the Rebels are in full retreat."

As he spoke, a mighty cheer rolled around the line of battle, and a band stationed upon a rock which formed the highest part of the mountain, burst forth with the grand strains of "Star-spangled Banner."

The artillery continued to hurl screaming shot and shell down into the narrow gorge, through which the defeated Rebels were flying with mad haste.

Chapter X. The Mountaineer's Revenge.

And if we do but watch the hour,
There never yet was human power
Which could evade, if unforgiven,
The patient search and vigil long
Of him who treasures up a wrong.
                    --Byron.

Harry Glen's first feeling when he found the battle was really over, was that of elation that the crisis to which he had looked forward with so much apprehension, had passed without his receiving any bodily harm. This was soon replaced by regret that the long-coveted opportunity had been suffered to pass unimproved, and still another strong sentiment--that keen sense of disappointment which comes when we have braced ourselves up to encounter an emergency, and it vanishes. There is the feeling of waste of valuable accumulated energy, which is as painful as that of energy misapplied.

Still farther, he felt sadly that the day of his vindication had been again postponed over another weary period of probation.

All around was intense enthusiasm, growing stronger every instant. It was the first battle tha the victors had been engaged in, and they felt the tumultuous joy that the first triumph brings to young soldiers. It was the first encounter upon the soil of Kentucky; it was the first victory between the Cumberland Mountains and the Mississippi River, and the loss of the victors was insignificant, compared with that of the vanquished.

The cold drench from the skies, the dreary mud--even the dead and wounded--were forgotten in the jubilation at the sight of the lately insolent foe flying in confusion down the mountain side, recking for nothing so much as for personal safety.

The band continued to play patriotic airs, and the cannon to thunder long after the last Rebel had disappeared in the thick woods at the bottom of the gloomy gorge.

A detail of men and some wagons were sent back after the regiment's baggage, and the rest of the boys, after a few minutes survey of the battle-field, were set to work building fires, cooking rations and preparing from the branches and brush such shelter as could be made to do substitute duty for the tents left behind.

Little as was Harry's normal inclination to manual labor, it was less than ever now, with these emotions struggling in his mind, and leaving his comrades hard at work, he wandered off to where Hoosier Knob, a commanding eminence on the left of the battle-field seemed to offer the best view of the retreat of the forces of Zollicoffer. Arriving there, he pushed on down the slope to where the enemy's line had stood, and where now were groups of men in blue uniforms, searching for trophies of the fight. In one place a musket would be found; in another a cap with a silver star, or a canteen quaintly fashioned from alternate staves of red and white cedar. Each "find" was proclaimed by the discoverer, and he was immediately surrounded by a group to earnestly inspect and discuss it. It was still the first year of the war; the next year "trophies" were left to rot unnoticed on the battle-fields they covered.

Harry took no interest in relic-hunting, but walked onward toward another prominence that gave hopes of a good view of the Rebels. The glimpses he gained from this of the surging mass of fugitives inflamed him with the excitement of the chase--of the most exciting of chases, a man-hunt. He forgot his fears--forgot how far behind he was leaving all the others, and became eager only to see more of this fascinating sight. Before he was aware of it, he was three or four miles from the Gap.

Here a point ran boldly down from the mountain into the valley, and ended in a bare knob that overlooked the narrow creek bottom, along which the beaten host was forging its way. Harry unhesitatingly descended to this, and stood gazing at the swarming horde below. It was a sight to rivet the attention. The narrow level space through which the creek meandered between the two parrallel ranges of heights was crowded as far as he could see with an army which defeat had degraded to a demoralized mob. All semblance of military organization had well-nigh disappeared. Horsemen and footmen, infantry, cavalry and artillery, officers and privates, ambulances creaking under their load of wounded and dying, ponderous artillery forges, wagons loaded with food, wagons loaded with ammunition, and wagons loaded with luxuries for the delectation of the higher officers,--all huddled and crowded together, and struggled forward with feverish haste over the logs, rocks, gullies and the deep waters of the swollen stream, and up its slippery banks, through the quicksands and quagmires which every passing foot and wheel beat into a still more grievous obstacle for those that followed. Hopelessly fagged horses fell for the last time under the merciless blows of their frightened masters, and added their great bulks to the impediments of the road.

The men were sullen and depressed--cast down by the wretchedness of earth and sky, and embittered against their officers and each other for the blood uselessly shed--oppressed with hunger and weariness, and momentarily fearful that new misfortunes were about to descend upon them. In brief, it was one of the saddest spectacles that human history can present: that of a beaten and disorganized army in full retreat, and an army so new to soldiership and discipline as to be able to make nothing but the worst out of so great a calamity--it was a rout after a repulse.

Nearly all of the passing thousands were too much engrossed in the miseries of their toilsome progress to notice the blue-coated figure on the bare knob above the road. But the rear of the fugitives was brought up by a squad of men moving much more leisurely, and with some show of order. They did not plunge into the mass of men and animals and vehicles, and struggle with them in the morass which the road had now become, but deliberately picked their way along the sides of the valley where the walking was easier. They saw Harry, and understood as soon as they saw, who he was. Two or three responded to their first impulse, and raising their guns to their shoulders, fired at him. A bullet slapped against the rock upon which he was partially leaning, and fell at his feet. Another spattered mud in his face, and flew away, singing viciously.

At the reports the fear-harrassed mob shuddered and surged forward through its entire length.

The companions of those who fired seemed to reproach them with angry gestures, pointing to the effect upon the panicky mass. Then the whole squad rushed forward toward the hill.

Deadly fear clutched Harry Glen's heart as the angry notes of the bullets jarred on his senses. Then pride and the animal instinct of fighting for life flamed upward. So swiftly that he was scarcely conscious of what he was doing he snatched a cartridge from the box, tore its end between his teeth, and rammed it home. He replaced the ramrod in its thimbles with one quick thrust, and as he raised his eyes from the nipple upon which he had placed the cap, he saw that the Rebel squad had gained the foot of the knoll and started up its side. He raised teh gun to fire, but as he did so he heard a voice call out from behind him:

"Skeet outen thar! Skeet outen thar! Come up heah, quick!"

Harry looked in the direction of the voice. He saw a tall, slender, black-haired man standing in the woods at the upper edge of the cleared space. He was dressed in butternut jeans, and looked so much like the Rebels in front that Harry thought he was one of them. The stranger noticed his indecision, and called out again still more peremptorily:

"Skeet outen thar, I tell ye! Skeet outen thar! Come up heah. I'm a friend--I'm Union."

His rifle came to his face at the same instant, and Harry saw the flame and white smoke puff from it, and the sickening thought flashed into his mind that the shot was fired at him, and that he would feel the deadly ball pierce his body! Before he could more than formulate this he heard the bullet pass him with a screech, and strike somewhere with a plainly sharp slap. Turning his head he saw the leading Rebel stagger and fall. Harry thre his gun up, with the readiness acquired in old hunting days, and fired at the next of his foes, who also fell! The other Rebels, as they came up, gathered around their fallen comrades.

Harry ran back to where the stranger was, as rapidly as the clinging mud and the steep hillside would permit him.

"Purty fa'r shot that," said the stranger, setting down the heavy rifle he was carefully reloading, and extending his hand cordially as Harry came panting up. "That's what I call mouty neat shooting--knock yer man over at 150 yards, down hill, with that ole smooth-bore, and without no rest. The oldest han' at the business couldn't've done no better."

Harry was too much agitated to heed the compliment to his markmanship. He looked back anxiously and asked:

"Are they coming on yet?"

"Skacely they hain't," said the stranger, with a very obvious sneer. "Skacely they hain't comin' on no more. They've hed enuff, they hev. Two of their best men dropt inter blue blazes on the first jump will take all the aidge off ther appetite for larks. I know 'em."

"But they will come on. They'll pursue us. They'll never let us go now," said Harry, reloading his gun with hands trembling from the exertion and excitement.

He was yet too young a soldier to understand that his enemy's fright might be greater than his own.

"Nary a time they won't," said the stranger, derisively. "Them fellers are jest like Injuns; they're red-hot till one or two gits knocked over, an' then they cool down mouty suddent. Why, me an' two others stopt the whole of Zollicoffer's army for two days by shootin' the officer in command of the advance-guard jest ez they war a-comin' up the hill this side of Barboursville. Fact! They'd a' been at Wildcat last Friday ef we hedn't skeered 'em so. They stopt an' hunted the whole country round for bushwhackers afore they'd move ary other step."

"But who are you?" asked Harry, looking again at his companion's butternut garb.

"I'm called Long Jim Forner, an' I've the name o' bein' the pizenest Union man in the Rockassel Mountains. Thar's a good s'tifkit o' my p'litical principles" (pointing with his thumb to where lay the men who had felln under their bullets). Harry looked again in that direction. Part of the squad were looking apprehensively toward hiim, as if they feared a volley from bushwhackers concealed near him, and others were taking from the bodies of the dead the weapons, belts, and other articles which it was not best to leave for the pursuers, and still others were pointing to the rapidly growing distance between them and main body, apparently adjuring haste in following.

The great mental and bodily strain Harry had undergone since he had first heard the sound of cannon in the morning at the foot of Wildcat should have made him desperately weary. But the sight of the man falling before his gun had fermented in his blood a fierce intoxication, as unknown, as unsuspected before as the passion of love had been before its first keen transports thrilled his heart. Like that ecstacy, this fever now consumed him. All fear of harm to himself vanished in its flame. He had actually slain one enemy. Why not another? He raised his musket. The mountaineer laid his hand upon it.

"No," he said, "that's not the game to hunt. They'll do when thar's nothin' better to be had, but now powder an' lead kin be used to more advantage. Besides they're outen range o' your smooth-bore now. Come."

As Fortner threw his rifle across his shoulder Harry looked at it curiously. It had a long, heavy, six sided barrel, with a large bore, double triggers, and a gaily striped hickory ramrod in its thimbles. The stock, of fine, curly rock-maple, was ornamented with silver stars and crescents, and in the breech were cunning little receptacles for tow and patches, and other rifle necessaries, each closed by a polished silver cover that shut with a snap. It was evidently the triumph of some renowned kentucky gunsmith's skill.

The mountaineer's foot was on the soil he had trodden since childhood, and Harry found it quite difficult to keep pace with his strong, quick stride. His step landed firm and sure on the sloping surfaces, where Harry slipped or shambled. Clinging vines and sharp briers were avoided without an apparent effort, where every one grasped Harry, or tore his face and hands.

The instinct of the wolf or the panther seemed to lead Fortner by the shortest courses through the pathless woods to where he came unperceived close upon the flank of the mass of harassed fugitives. Then creeping behind a convenient tree with the supple lightness of the leopard crouching for a spring, he scanned with eager eyes the mounted officers within range. Selecting his prey he muttered:

"'Tain't HIM, but he'll hev to do, THIS time."

The weapon rang out sharply. The stricken officer threw up his sword arm, his bridle arm clutched his saddle-pommel, as if resisting the attempt of Death to unhorse him. Then the muscles all relaxed, and he fell into he arms of those who had hurried to him.

Harry fired into the mass the next instant; a few random shots replied, and another impetus of fear spurred the mob onward.

Fortner and Harry sped away to another point of interception, where the same scene was repeated, and then to another, and then to a third, Fortner muttering after each shot his disappointment at not finding the one whom he anxiously sought.

When they hurried away the third time they were compelled to make a wide circuit, for the little valley suddenly broadened out into a considerable plain. Upon this the long-drawn-out line of fugitives gathered in a compact, turmoiling mass.

"That's Little Rockassel Ford," said Fortner, pointing with his left hand to the base of the mountain that rose steeply above the farther side of the commotion. "That's Rockassel Mountain runnin' up thar inter the clouds. The Little Rockassel River runs round hits foot. That's what's a-stoppin' 'em. They'll hev a turrible time gittin' acrost hit. Hit's mouty hard crossin' at enny time, but hit's awful now, fur the Rockassel's boomin'. The big rains hev sent her up kitin', an' hit's now breast-deep thar in the Ford. We'll git round whar we kin see hit all."

Another wide detour to keep themselves in the concealment of the woods brough Fortner and Harry out upon an acclivity that almost overhung the ford, and those gathered around it. The two Unionists crawled cautiously through the cedars and laurel to the very edge of the cliff and looked down upon their enemies. They were so near that everything was plainly visible, and the hum of conversation reached their ears. They could even hear the commands of the officers vainly trying to restore order, the curses of the teamsters upon their jaded animals, the ribald songs of the few whose canteens furnished them with forgetfulness of defeat, and contempt for the surrounding misery.

All the flooding showers which had been falling upon hundreds of square miles of precipitous mountin sides were now gorging through the crooked, narrow throat of the Little Rockcastle. The torrent filled the ragged banks to the brim, and in their greedy swirl undermined and tore from there logs, great trees, and even rocks.

This wasthe barrier that stayed the flight of the fugitive throng, and it was this that they strove to put between thm and the presumed revengeful victors.

On the bank, field and line officers labored to calm their men and restore organization. It was in vain that they pointed out that there had been no pursuit thus far, and the unlikelihood of there being one. When did Panic yield to Reason? In those demoralized ears the thunder of the cannon at Wildcat, the crash of the bursting shells, and the deadly whistle of bullets still rang louder than any words officers could speak.

The worst frightened crowded into the stream in a frenzy, and struggled wildly with the current that swept their feet off the slimy limestone bottom, with the logs and trees dashing along like so many catapult-bolts, and with the horses and teams urged on by men more fear-stricken still. On the steep slope on the other side glimmered numbers of little fires where those who were lucky enough to get across were warming and drying themselves.

"Heavens!" said Harry with an anticipatory shudder, "if our men should come up, the first cannon shot would make half these men drown themselves in trying to get away."

Fortner heeded him not. The mountaineer's eyes were fixed upon a tall, imperious looking man, whose collar bore the silver stars of a Colonel.

"He has found his man at last," said Harry, noticing his companion's attitude, and picking up his own gun in readiness for what might come.

Fortner half-cocked his rifle, took from its nipple the cap that had been tehre an hour and flung it away. He picked the powder out if the tube, replaced it with fresh from his horn, selected another cap carefully, fitted it on the nipple, and let the hammer down with the faintest snap to force it to its place.

His eyes had the look of a rattlesnake's when it coils for a spring, and his breast swelled out as if he was summoning all his strength. He stepped forward to a tree so lightly that there came no rustle from the dead leaves he trod upon. Harry took his place on the other side of the tree, and cocked his musket.

So close were they to hundreds of Rebels with arms in their hands, that it seemed simply an invitation to death to call their attention.

Fortner turned and waved Harry back as he heard him approach, but Glen had apparently exhausted all his capacity for fearing, in the march upon Wildcat, and he was now calmly desperate.

The Colonel rode out from the throng toward the level spot at the base of the ledge upon which the two were concealed. The horse he bestrode was a magnificent thoroughbred, whose fine action could not be concealed, even by his great fatigue.

"Go and find Mars," said the Colonel to an orderly, "and tell him to build a fire against that rock there, and make us some coffee. We will not be able to get across the ford before midnight." The orderly rode off, and the Colonel dismounted and walked forward with the cramped gait of a man who had been long in the saddle.

Still louder yells arose from the ford. A powerful horse, ridden by an officer who was trying to force his way across, had slipped on the river's glassy bedstones, in the midst of a compact throng, and carried many with it down into the deep water below the crossing.

The Colonel's lip curled with contempt as he continued his walk.

A sharp little click sounded from Fortner's rifle. He had set the hair trigger.

He stepped out clear of the tree, and gave a peculiar whistle. The Colonel started as he heard the sound, looked up, saw who uttered it, and instinctly reached his hand back to the holster for a revolver.

Down would scarcely have been ruffled by Fortner's light touch upon the trigger.

Fire flamed from the rifle's muzzle.

The Colonel's haughty eyes became sterner than ever. The holster was torn as he wrenched the revolver out. A clutch at the mane, and he fell forward on the wet brown leaves--dead!

Dumb amazement fille dthe horse's great eyes; he stretched out his neck and smelled his lifeless master inquiringly.

A shot from Harry's musket, fifty from the astounded Rebels, and the two Unionists sped away unhurt into the cover of the dark cedars.

Chapter XI. Through the Mountains and the Night.

God sits upon the Throne of Kings,
And Judges unto judgement brings:
   Why then so long
   Maintain your wrong,
And favor lawlesss things?

Defend the poor, the fatherless;
Their crying injuries redress:
   And vindicate
   The desolate,
Whom wicked men oppress.
  --George Sandy's Paraphrase of Psalm XXXII.

Fortner and Glen were soon so far away from the Ford that the only reminder of its neighborhood were occasional glimpses, caught through rifts in he forest, of the lofty slope of Rockcastle Mountain, now outlined in the gathering darkness by twinkling fires, which increased in number, and climbed higher towards the clouds as fast as the fugitives succeeded in struggling across the river.

"That's a wonderful sight," said Harry, as they paused on a summit to rest and catch breath. "It reminds me of some of the war scenes in Scott, or the Illiad."

"Hit looks ter me like a gineral coon-hunt," said Fortner, "on'y over thar hit's the coons, an' not the hunters, that hev the torches. I wish I could put a bum-shell inter every fire."

"You are merciless."

"No more'n they are. They've ez little marcy ez a pack o' wolves in a sheep-pen."

"Well," continued Fortner, meditatively, "Ole Rockassel's gittin' a glut to-night. She'd orten't ter need no more now fur a hundred yeahs."

"I don't understand you," said Harry.

"Why, they say thet the Rockassel hez ter hev a man every Spring an' Fall. The Injuns believed hit, an' hit's bin so ever sence the white folks come inter the country. Last Spring hit war the turn o' the Fortner kin to gi'n her a man, an' she levied on a fust cousin o' mine--a son o' Aunt Debby Brill. But less jog on; we've got a good piece fur ter go."

It was now night--black and starless, and the dense woods through which they were traveling made the darkness thick and impenetrable. But no check in Fortner's speed hinted at any ignorance of the course or encountering of obstacles. He continued to stride forward with the same swift, certain step as in the day time. But for Harry, who could see nothing but his leader's head and shoulders, and, whose every effort was required to keep these in sight, the journey was full of painful toil. The relaxation from the intense strain manifested itself in proportion as they seemed to recede from the presence of the enemy, and his spirits flagged continually.

In the daylight the brush and briers had been annoying and hurtful, and the roughness of the way very trying. Now the one was wounding and cruel; the other made every step with his jaded limbs a torture. With the low spirits engendered by the great fatigue, came a return of the old fears and tremors. The continual wails of the wildcats roundabout filled him with gloomy forebodings. Every hair of his head stood stiffly up in mortal terror when a huge catamount, screaming like a fiend, leaped down from a tree, and confronted them for an instant with hideously-gleaming yellow eyes.

"Cuss-an'-burn the nasty varmint!" said Fortner angrily, snatching up a pine knot from his feet and flinging it at the beast, which vanished into the darkness with another curdling scream.

"Don't that man know what fear is?" wondered Harry, ignorant that the true mountaineer feels toward these vociferous felidae about the same contempt with which a plainsman regards a coyote.

At length Fortner slackened his pace, and began to move with caution.

"Are we coming upon the enemy again?" asked Harry, in a loud whisper, which had yet a perceptible quaver in it.

"No," answered Fortner, "but we're a-comin' ter what is every bit an' grain ez dangersome. Heah's whar the path winds round Blacksnake Clift, an' ye'll hev ter be ez keeful o' your footin' ez ef ye war treadin' the slippery ways o' sin. The path's no wider 'n a hoss's back, an' no better ter walk on. On the right hand side hit's several rods down ter whar the creek's tearin' 'long like a mad dog. Heah hit now, can't ye?"

For some time the roar of the torrent sweeping the gorge had filled Harry's ears.

"Ye want ter walk slow," continued Fortner, "an' feel keefully with yer foot every time afore ye sot hit squar'ly down. Keep yer left hand a-feelin' the rocks above yer, so's ter make shore all the time thet ye're close ter 'em. 'Bout half way, thar's a big break in the path. Hit's jess a long step across hit. Take one step arter I say thet I'm acrost; the feel keerfully with yer left foot fur the aidge o' the break, an' then step out ez long ez ye kin with yer right. That'll bring ye over. Be shore o' yer feet, an ye'll be all right."

Harry trembled more than at any time before. They were already on the path around the steep cliff. The darkness was inky. The roar of the waters below rose loudly--angrily. The wails of the wildcats behind, overhead and in front of them, made it seem as if the sighing pines and cedars were inhabited with lost spirits shrieking warnings of impending disaster.

Harry's foot came down upon a boulder which turned under his weight. He regained his balance with a start, but the stone toppled over. He listened. There were scores of heart-beats before it splashed in the water below.

"Not so much as a twig between here and eternity," he said to himself, with a shudder. Then aloud: "Can't we stay here, some place, and not go along there to-night?"

The roar of the water drowned his voice before it reached Fortner's ears, and Harry, obeying the instinct to accept leadership, followed the mountaineer trem-blingly.

In a little while he felt--more than saw--Fortner stop, adjust his feet, and make a long stride forward with one of them. Glen collected himself for the same effort.

He had need of all of his resolution, for the many narrow escapes which he had made from slipping into the hungry torrent, had shaken every nerve.

"I'm over," called out Fortner. "Ye try hit now."

Harry balanced his gun so as to embarrass him the least, and carefully felt with his left foot for the edge of the chasm. The catamount announced his renewed presence by a vindictive scream. The clouds parted just enough to let through a rift of gray light, but it fell not upon the brink of the black gap in the path. It showed for an instant the whirlpool, with fragments of tree trunks, of ghastly likeness to drowned human bodies, eddying dizzily around.

"Come on," called out Fortner, impatiently.

Harry stepped out desperately. For a mental eternity he hung in air. His hands relaxed and his gun dropped with a crash and a splash. Then his foot touched the other side with nervous doubtfulness. It slipped, and he felt himself falling--falling into all that he feared. Fortner grasped his collar with a strong hand, and dragged him up against the rocky wall of the path.

"Thar, yer all right," he said, panting with the exertion, "but hit wuz a mouty loud call for ye. Gabriel's ho'n couldn't've made a much mo' powerful one."

"I've lost my gun," said Harry, regretfully, as soon as he could compose himself.

"Cuss-an'-burn the blasted ole smooth-bore," said Fortner, contemptuously. "Don't waste no tear on that ole kick-out-behind. We'll go 'long 'tween Wildcat an' the Ford, an' pick up a wagon-load uv ez good shooters ez thet clumsy chunk o' pot-metal wuz. Shake yourself together. We've on'y got a mile or so ter go now."

In Harry's condition, the "mile or so" seemed to be stretching out a long ways around the globe, and he began to ask himself how near he was to the much-referred-to "heart of the Southern Confederacy."

At length a little fading toward gray of the thick blackness, to that they had emerged from the heavy woods into more open country. Harry thought they were come to fields, but he could see nothing, and without remark plodded painfully after his leader.

Suddenly a large pack of dogs immediately in front of them broke the stillness with a startling diapason, ranging from the deep bass of the mastiff to the ringing bark of the fox-hounds. Mingled with this was the sound of the whole pack rushing fiercely forward. Fortner stopped in his tracks so abruptly that Glen stumbled against him. The mountaineer gave the peculiar whistle he had uttered at the Ford. The rush ceased instantly. The deep growls of the mastiffs and bull-dogs stopped likewise; only the hounds and the shrill-voiced young dogs continued barking.

The darkness was rent by a long narrow lane of light. A door had been opened in a tightly-closed house, just beyond the dogs.

"Down, Tige! Git out, Beauty!" said Forstner, imperiously. "Lay down, Watch! Quiet Bruno!"

The clamors of the gang changed to little yelps of welcome.

"Is that you, Jim?" inquired a high-pitched but not unpleasant voice, from the door.

"Yes, Aunt Debby," answered Fortner, "an' I hev some one with me."

As the two approached, surrounded by the fawning dogs, a slender, erect woman appeared in the doorway, holding above her head, by its nail and chain, one of the rude iron lamps common in the houses of the South.

"Everything all right, Aunt Debby?" asked Fortner, as, after entering, he turned from firmly securing the door, by placing across it a strong wooden bar that rested in the timbers on either side.

"Yes, thank God!" she said with quiet fervor. She stepped with graceful freedom over the floor, and hung the lamp up by thrusting the nail into a crack in one of the logs forming the walls of the room. "An' how is hit with ye?" she asked, facing Fortner, with her large gray eyes eloquent with solicitude.

"O, ez fur me, I'm jes ez sound ez when I left heah last week, 'cept thet I'm tireder 'n a plow mule at night, an' hongrier nor a b'ar thet's lived all Winter by suckin' hits paws."

"I s'pose y' air tired an' hongry; ye look hit," said the woman, with a compassionate glance at Harry, who had sunk limpy into a chair before the glowing wood-fire that filled up a large part of the end of the room.

"Set down by the fire," she continued, "an' I'll git ye some pone an' milk. Thar's nothin' better ter start in on when yer rale empty." She went to a rude cupboard in the farther part of the room, whence the note of colliding crockery soon gave information that she was busy.

Fortner took a bunch of tow from his pouch, and with it wiped off every particle of dampness from the outside of his rifle, after which he laid the gun on two wooden hooks above the fireplace, and hung the accouterments on deer horns at its breech.

"Pull off yer shoes an' toast yer feet," he said to Harry. "The fire'll draw the tiredness right out."

Harry's relaxed fingers fumbled vainly with the wet and obstinate shoe-strings. Aunt Debby came up with a large bowl of milk in each hand, and a great circular loaf of corn-bread under her arm. She placed her burden upon the floor, and with quick, deft fingers loosened the stubborn knots without an apparent effort, drew off the muddy shoes and set them in a dark corner near the fireplace before Harry fairly realized that he had let a woman do this humble office for him. The sight and smell of food aroused him from the torpor of intense fatigue, and he devoured the homely fare set before him with a relish that he had never before felt for victuals. As he ate his senses awakened so that he studied his hostess with interest. Hair which the advancing years, while bleaching to a snowy white had still been unable to rob of the curling waves of girlhood, rippled over a broad white brow, sober but scarcely wrinkled; large, serious but gentle gray eyes, and a small, firm mouth, filled with even white teeth were the salient features of a face at once resolute, refined and womanly. Long, slender hands, small feet, covered with coarse but well-fitting shoes, a slight, erect figure, suggestive of nervous strength, and clad in a shapely homespun gown stamped her as a superior specimen of the class of mountaineer woman to which she belonged.

"Heah's 'nuther pone, honey," she said to Fortner, as she handed both of them segments of another disk of corn-bread, to replace that which they had ravenously devoured. "An' le' me fill yer bowls agin. Hit takes a powerful sight o' bread an' milk ter do when one's rale hongry. But 'tain't like meat vittels. Ye can't eat 'nuff ter do ye harm."

She took from its place behind the rough stones that formed the jam of the fireplace a rude broom, made by shaving down to near its end long slender strips from a stick of pliant green hickory, then turning these over the end and confining them by a band into an exaggerated mop or brush. With this she swept back from the hearth of uneven stones the live coals flung out by the fire.

"Thar's some walnut sticks amongst thet wood," she said as she replaced the hearth-broom, "an' they pops awful."

From a pouch-like basket, made of skilfully interwoven hickory strips, and hanging against the wall, she took a half-finished stocking and a ball of yarn. Drawing a low rocking-chair up into the light, she seated herself and began knitting.

As he neared the last of his second bowl of milk Fortner bethought himself, and glanced at Aunt Debby. Her work had fallen from her nervous hands and lay idly in her lap, while her great eyes were fixed hungrily upon him.

"They've bin fouten over ter Wildcat to-day," he said, answering their inquiry, without waiting to empty his mouth.

"Yes, I heard the cannons," she said with such gentle voice as made her dialect seem quaint and sweet. "I clim up on Bald Rock at the top o' the mounting an' lissened. I could see the smoke raisin', but I couldn't tell nothin'. Much uv a fout?"

"Awful big'un. Biggest 'un sence Buner Vister. Ole Zollicoffer pitched his whole army onter Kunnel Gerrard's rijimint. Some other rijiments cum up ter help Kunnel Garrard, an' both sides fit like devis fur three or fur hours, an' the dead jess lay in winrows, an'---"

The demands of Fortner's unappeased appetite here rose superior to his desire to impart information. He stopped to munch the last bit of corn-bread and drain his bowl to the bottom.

"Yes," said Aunt Debby, inhospitably disregarding the exhaustion of the provender, and speaking a little more quickly than her wont, "but which side whipt?"

"Our'n, in course," said Fortner, with nettled surprise at the question. "Our'n, in course. Old Zollicoffer got ez bad a licken ez ever Gineral Zach Taylor gi'n the Mexicans."

"Rayally?" she said. Gratification showed itself in little lines that coursed about her mouth, and her eyes illumined as when a light shines through a window.

"Yes," answered Fortner. "Like hounds, and run clean ter the Ford, whar they're now a-fouten an' strugglin to git acrost, and drowndin' like so many stampeded cattle."

"Glory! Thank God!" said Aunt Debby. Her earnestness expressed itself more by the intensity of the tone than its rise.

"Evidently a tolerable regular attendant at Methodist camp-meetings," thought Harry, rousing a little from the torpor into which he was falling.

Her faded check flushed with a little confusion at having suffered this outburst, and picking up her knitting she nervously resumed work.

Fortner looked wistfully at the bottom of his emptied bowl. Aunt Debby took it away and speedily returned with it filled. She came back with an air of eager expectancy that Fortner would continue his narrative. But unsatisfied hunger still dominated him, and he had thoughts and mouth only for food. She sad down and resumed her knitting with an apparent effort at composing herself.

For a full minute the needles clicked industriously. Then they stopped; the long, slender fingers clenched themselves about the ball of yarn; she faced Fortner, her eyes shining with a less brilliant but intenser light.

"Jim Fortner," she said with low, measured distinctness, "why don't ye go on? Is thar somethin' that ye'r afeered ter tell me? What hez hapened ter our folks? Don't flinch from tellin' me the wust. I'm allers willin' ter bow ter the will o' the Lord without a murmur. On'y let me know what hit is."

"Why, Aunt Debby, thar hain't been nothin' happened ter 'em," said Fortner, deeply surprised. "Thar ain't nothin' ter tell ye 'bout 'em. They're all safe. They're in Kunnel Garrard's rijimint, ez ye know, an' hit fit behind breastworks, and didn't lose nobody, scacely--leastwise none uv our kin."

She rose quickly from her chair. The ball of yarn fell from her lap and rolled unheeded toward the glowing coals under the forelog. With arm outstretched, hands clasped, and eyes directed upward in fervent appeal, there was much to recall that Deborah from whom she took her name--that prophetess and priestess who, standing under the waving palm trees of Ball-Tamar, inspired her countrymen to go forth and overthrow and destroy their Canaanitish oppressors.

"O, God!" she said in low, thrilling tones, "Thou's aforetimes gi'n me much ter be thankful fur, as well ez much ter dumbly ba'r when Thy rod smote me fur reasons thet I couldn't understand. Thou knows how gladly I'd've gi'n not on'y my pore, nigh-spent life, but also those o' my kinsmen, which I prize much higher, fur sech a vict'ry ez this over the inimies of Thee an' Thy people. But Thou'st gi'n hit free ez Thy marcy, without axin' blood sacrifice from any on us. I kin on'y praise Thee an' Thy goodness all my days."

Fortner rose and listend with bowed head while she spoke. When she finished he snatched up the ball of shriveling yarn and quenched its smoking with his hand.

Looking fixedly at this he said softly: "Aunt Debby, honey, I hain't tole ye all yit."

"No, Jim?"

"No," said he, slowly winding up the yarn, "Arter the fouten wuz thru with at the Gap I slipt down the mounting, an' come in on the r'ar uv those fellers, an' me an' this ere man drapt two on 'em."

"I kinder 'spected ye would do something uv thet sort."

"Then we tuk a short cut an' overtuk 'em agin, an' we drapt another."

Aunt Debby's eyes expressed surprise at this continued good fortune.

"An' then we tuk 'nuther short cut, an' saved 'nuther one."

Aunt Debby waited for him to continue.

"At last--jess ez they come ter the Ford--I seed OUR man."

"Seed Kunnel Bill Pennington?" The great gray eyes were blazing now.

"Yes." Fortner's speech was the spiritless drawl of the mountains, and it had now become so languid that it seemed doubtful if after the enunciation of each word whether vitality enough remained to evolve a successor. "Yes," he repeated with a yawn, as he stuck the ball of yarn upon the needles and gave the whole a toss which landed it in the wall-basket, "an' I GOT him, tew."

"O, just God! Air ye shore?"

"Jess ez shore ez in the last great day thar'll be some 'un settin' in judgement atween him an' me. I wanted him ter be jess ez shore about me. I came out in plain sight, and drawed his attention. He knowed me at fust glimpse, an' pulled his revolver. I kivered his heart with the sights an' tetcht the trigger. I'm sorry now thet I didn't shoot him thru the belly, so thet he'd been a week a-dyin' an' every minnit he'd remembered what he wuz killed fur. But I wuz so afeered that I would not kill him ef I hit him some place else'n the heart--thet's a wayall pizen varmints hev--thet I didn't da'r resk hit. I wuz detarmined ter git him, too, ef I had ter foller him clean ter Cumberland Gap."

"Ye done God's vengence," said Aunt Debby sternly. "An' yit hit wuz very soon ter expect hit." She clasped her hands upon her forehead and rocked back and forth, gazing fixedly into the mass of incandescent coals.

"Hit's gwine to cla'r up ter-morrow," said Fortner, returning from an inspection of the sky at the door. "Le's potter off ter bed," he continued rousing up Harry. They removed their outer garments and crawled into one of the comfortable beds in the room.

Later in the night a sharp pain in one of Harry's over-strained legs awoke him out of his deep slumber, for a few minutes. Aunt Debby was still seated before the fire in her chair, rocking back and forth, and singing softly:

"Thy saints in all this glorious war,   Shall conquer ere they die. They see the triumph from afar--   By faith they bring hit nigh. Sure I must suffer ef I would reign;   Increase my courage, Lord. I'll bear the toil, endure the pain."

He went to sleep again with the sweet strains ringing in his ears, as if in some way a part of the marvelous happenings of that most eventful day.

Chapter XII. Aunt Debby Brill.

Beneath the dark waves where the dead go down,
   There are gulfs of night more deep;
But little they care, whom the waves once drown,
   How far from the litght they sleep.

And dark though Sorrow's fearful billows be,
   They have caverns darker still.
O God! that Sorrow's waves were like the sea,
   Whose topmost waters kill.
                    -Anonymous.

It was nearly noon when Harry awoke. The awakening came slowly and with pain. In all his previous experiences he had had no hint even of such mental and bodily exhaustion as now oppressed him. Every muscle and tendon was aching a bitter complaint against the strain it had been subjected to the day before. Dull, pulseless pain smoldered in some; in others it was the keen throb of the toothache. Continued lying in one position was unendurable; changing it, a thrill of anguish; and the new posture as intolerable as the first. His brain galled and twinged as did his body. To think was as acute pain as to use his sinews. Yet he could not help thinking any more than he could help turning in the bed, though to turn was torture.

Every organ of thought was bruised and sore. The fearful events of the day before would continue to thrust themselves upon his mind. To put them out required painful effort; to recall and comprehend them was even worse. Reflecting upon them now, with unstrung nerves, made them seem a hundred-fold more terrible than when they were the spontaneous offspring of hot blood. With the reflection came the thoguhts that this was but a prelude--an introduction--to an infinitely horrible saturnalia of violence and blood, through which he was to be hurried until released by his own destruction. This became a nightmare that threatened to stagnate the blood in his veins. He gasped, turned his back to the wall with an effort that thrilled him with pain, and opened his eyes.

Naught that he saw reminded him of the preceding day. Sunny peace and contentment reigned. The door stood wide open, and as it faced the south, the noonday sun pushed in--clear to the opposite wall--a broad band of mellow light, vividly telling of the glory he was shedding where roof nor shade checked his genial glow. On the smooth, hard, ashen floor, in the center of this bright zone, sat a matronly cat, giving with tongue and paw dainty finishing touches to her morning toilet, and watching with maternal pride a kittenish game of hide-and-seek on the front step. Through the open doorway came the self-complacent cackling of hens, celebrating their latest additions to their nests, and the exultant call of a cock to his feathered harem to come, admire and partake of some especially fat worm, which he had just unearthed. Farther away speckled Guinea chickens were clamoring their satisfaction at the improvement in the weather. Still farther, gentle tinklings hinted of peacfully-browsing sheep.

Inside the house, bunches of sweet-smelling medicinal herbs, hanging agains the walls to dry, made the air heavy with their odors. Aunt Debby was at work near the bright zone of sun-rays, spinning yarn with a "big wheel." She held in one hand a long slender roll of carded wool, and in the other a short stick, with which she turned the wheel. Setting it to whirling with a long sweep of the stick against a spoke, she would walk backward while the roll was twisted out into a long, thin thread, and then walk forward as they yarn was wound upon the spindle. When she walked backward, the spindle hummed sharply; when she came forward it droned. There was a stately rhythm in both, to which her footsteps and graceful sway of body kept time, and all blended harmoniously with the camp-meeting melody she was softly singing:

"Jesus, I my cross have taken,
   All to leave and follow Thee;

Naked, poor, despised, forsaken,
   Thou from hence my all shalt be.
Perish every fond ambition--
   All I've sought, or hoped, or known;
Yet how rich is my condition--
   God and Heaven still my own."

A world of memories of a joyous past, unflecked by a single one of the miseries of the present, crowded in upon Harry on the wings of this well-remembered tune. It was a favorite hymn at the Methodist church in Sardis, and the last time he had heard it was when he had accompanied Rachel to the church to attend services conducted by a noted evangelist.

Ah, Rachel!--what of her?

He had not thought of her since a swift recollection of her words at the parting scene on the piazza had come to spur up his faltering resolution, as the regiment advanced up the side of Wildcat. Now one bitter thought of how useless all that he had gone through with the day before was to rehabilitate himself in her good opinion was speedily chased from his mind by the still bitterer one of the contempt she must feel for him, did she but know of his present abject prostration.

After all, might not the occurrences of yesterday be but the memories of a nightmare? They seemed too unreal for probability. Perhaps he was just recovering consciousness after the delirium of a fever.

The walnut sticks in the fireplace popped as sharply as pistols, and he trembled from head to foot.

"Heavens, I'm a bigger coward than ever," he said bitterly, and turning himself painfully in bed, he fixed his eyes upon the wall. "I was led to believe," he continued, "that after I had once been under fire, I would cease to dread it. Now, it seems to me more dreadful than I ever imagined it to be."

Aunt Debby's wheel hummed and droned still louder, but her pleasant tones rode on the cadences like an Aeolian harp in a rising wind:

"Man may trouble and distress me,   'T will but drive me to Thy breast; Life with trials hard may press me;   Heaven will bring me sweeter rest. O, 'tis not in grief to harm me,   While Thy love is left to me. O, 'twere not in joy to charm me,

Were that joy unmixed with Thee."

He wondered weakly why ther were no monasteries in this land and age, to serve as harbors or refuge for those who shrank from the fearfulness of war.

He turned over again wearily, and Aunt Debby, looking toward him, encountered his wide-open eyes.

"Yer awake, air ye?" she said kindly. "Hope I didn't disturb you. I wuz tryin' ter make ez little noise ez possible."

"No, you didn't rouse me. It's hard for me to sleep in daylight, even when fatigued, as I am."

"Ef ye want ter git up now," she said, stopping the whell by pressing the stick against a spoke, and laying the "roll" in her hand upon the wheel-head, "I'll hev some breakfast fur ye in a jiffy. Ye kin rise an' dress while I run down ter the spring arter a fresh bucket o' water."

She covered her head with a "slat sun-bonnet," which she took from a peg in the wall, lifted a cedar waterpail from a shelf supported by other long pegs, poured its contents into a large cast-iron teakettle swinging over the fire, and whisked out of the door. Presently the notes of her hymn mingled in plaintive harmony with the sparkling but no sweeter song of a robin redbreast, twittering his delight in the warm sunshine amid the crimson apples of the tree that overhung the spring.

"Will ye hev a fresh drink?" she asked Harry, on her return.

He took the gourdful of clear, cool water, which she offered him, and drank heartily.

"Thet hez the name o' bein' the best spring in these parts," she said, pleased with his appreciation.

"An' hit's a never-failin' spring, too. We've plenty o' water the dryest times, when everybody else's goes dry."

"That IS delicious water," said Harry.

"An' now I'll git ye yor breakfast in a minnit. The teakittle's a-bilin', the coffee's ground, the pone's done, an' when I fry a little ham, everything will be ready."

As her culinary methods and utensils differed wholly from anything Harry had ever seen, he studied them with great interest sharpened not a little by a growing appetite for breakfast.

The clumsy iron teakettle swung on a hook at the end of a chain fastened somewhere in the throat of the chimney. On the rough stones forming the hearth were a half-dozen "ovens" and "skillets"--circular, cast-iron vessels standing on legs, high enough to allow a layer of live coals to be placed beneath them. They were covered by a lid with a ledge around it, to retain the mass of coals heaped on top. The cook's scepter was a wooden hook, with which she moved the kettles and ovens and lifted lids, while the restless fire scorched her amrs and face ruddier than cherry.

It was a primitive way, and so wasteful of wood that it required a tree to furnish fuel enough to prepare breakfast; but under the hands of a skillful woman those ovens and skillets turned out viands with a flavor that no modern appliance can equal.

The joists of the house were thickly hung with the small delicious hams of the country--hams made from young and tender hogs, which had lived and fattened upon the acorns, fragrant hickory-nuts and dainty beechnuts of the abundant "mast" of the forest, until the were saturated with their delicate, nutty flavor. This was farther enriched by a piquancy gained from the smoke of the burning hickory and oak, with which they were cured, and the absorption of odors from the scented herbs in the rooms where they were drying. Many have sung the praises of Kentucky's horses, whisy and women, but no poet has tuned his lyre to the more fruitful theme of Kentucky's mast-fed, smoke-cured, herb-scented hams. For such a man waits a crown of enduring bays.

Slices of this savory ham, fried in a skillet--the truth of history forces the reluctant confession that the march of progress had not yet brought the grid-iron and its virtues to the mountains--a hot pone of golden-yellow meal, whose steaming sweetness had not been allowed to distill off, but had been forced back into the loaf by the hot oven-lid; coffee as black and strong as the virile infusions which cheer the hearts of the true believers in the tents of the Turk, and cream from cows that cropped the odorous and juicy grasses of mountain meadows, made a breakfast that could not have been more appetizing if composed by a French CHEF, and garnished by a polyglot bill-of-fare.

Moved thereto by the hospitable urgings of Aunt Debby, and his own appetite, Harry ate heartily. Under the influence of the comfortable meal, the cheerful sunshine, and the rousing of the energies that follow a change from a recumbent to an erect posture, his spirits rose to a manlier pitch. As he could not walk without pain he took his seat in a slat-bottomed chair by the side of the hearth, and Aunt Debby, knitting in hand, occupied a low rocker nearly opposite.

"Where's Mr. Fortner?" asked Harry.

"Jim got up, arly, an' arter eatin' a snac said he'd go out an' take a look around--mebbe he mout go ez fur ez the Ford."

As if to accompany Harry's instinctie tremor over the possibilities attending the resumption of Fortner's prowling around the flanks of Zollicoffer's army, the fire shot off a whole volley of sharp little explosions.

Harry sprang two or three inches above his chair, then reddened violently, and essayed to conceal his confusion by assiduous attention with the poker to the wants of the fire.

Aunt Debby regarded him with gentle compassion.

"Yer all shuck up by the happenin's yesterday," she said with such tactful sympathy that his sensitive mettle was not offended. "'Tis nateral ye should be. Hit's allers so. Folks kin say what they please, but fouten's terrible tryin' to the narves, no matter who does hit. My husband wuz in the Mexican War, an' he's offen tole me thet fur weeks arter the battle o' Buner Visty he couldn't heah a twig snap withouten his heart poppin' right up inter his mouth, an' hit wuz so with everybody else, much ez they tried ter play off unconsarned like."

"Ah, really?" said Henry, deeply interested in all the concerned this woman, whose remarkable qualities were impressing themselves upon his recognition. "What part of the army did your husband belong to?"

"He wuz in the Kentucky rigimint commanded by Kunnel Henry Clay, son o' the great Henry Clay, who wuz killed thar. My husband was promoted to a Leftenant fur his brav'ry in the battle."

"Then this is not your first experience with war?"

"No, indeed," said she, with just a trace of pride swelling in the temple's delicate network of blue veins. "The Fortners an' the Brills air soljer families, an' ther young men hev shouldered ther guns whenever the country needed fouten-men. Great gran'fathers Brill an' Fortner come inter the State along with Dan'l boone nigh onter a hundred years ago, and sence then them an' ther descendents hev fit Injuns, Brittishers an' Mexikins evr'y time an inimy raised a sword agin the country."

"Many of them lose their lives?"

"Yes, ev'ry war hez cost the families some member. Gran'fathes Brill an' Fort-ner war both on 'em killed at the Injun ambush at Blue Licks. I wuz on'y a baby when my father wuz killed at the massacre of Winchester's men at the River Raisin. My brother---"

"father of the man I was with yesterday?"

"No; HIS father wuz my oldest brother. My youngest brother--the 'baby' o' the family--wuz mortally wounded by a copper ball in the charge on the Bishop's Palace at the takin' o' Monterey."

"And your husband--he went through the war safely, did he?"

The pleasant, mobile lines upon the woman's face congealed into stony hardness. At the moment of Harry's question she was beginning to count the stitches in her work for some feminine mystery of "narrowing" or "turning." She stopped, and hands and knittng dropped into her lap.

"My husband," she said slowly and bitterly, "wuz spared by the Mexikins thet he fit, but not by his own countrymen an' neighbors, amongst whom he wuz brung up. His blood wuz not poured out on the soil he invaded, but wuz drunk by the land his forefathers an' kinsmen hed died fur. The godless Greasers on the River Grande war kinder ter him nor the CHRISTIAN gentlemen on the Rockassel."

The intensity and bitterness of the utterance revealed a long conning of the expression of bitter truths.

"He lost his life, then," said Harry, partially comprehending, "in some of the troubles around here?"

"He wuz killed, bekase he wouldn't help brek down what hit hed cost so much ter build up. He wuz killed, bekase he thot a pore man's life wuth mo'en a rich man's nigger. He wuz killed, bekase he b'lieved this whole country belonged ter the men who'd fit fur hit an' made hit what hit is, an' thet hit wuzn't a plantation fur a passel o' slave-drivers ter boss an' divide up jess ez hit suited 'em."

"Why, I thought all you Kentuckians were strongly in favor of keeping the negores in slavery," said Harry in amazement.

"Keepin the niggers ez slaves ain't the question at all. We folks air ez fur from bein' Abolitionists ez ennybody. Hit's a battle now with a lot uv 'ristocrats who'd take our rights away."

"I don't quite understand your position," said Harry.

"Hit's bekase ye don't understand the country. The people down heah air divided into three classes. Fust thar's the few very rich fam'lies that hev big farms over in the Blue Grass with lots o' niggers ter work 'em. Then thar's the middle class--like the Fortners an' the Brills--thet hev small farms in the creek vallies, an' wherever thar's good land on the mounting sides; who hev no niggers, an' who try ter lead God-fearin', hard-workin' lives, an' support ther fam'lies decently. Lastly thar's the pore white trash, thet lives 'way up in the hollers an' on the wuthless lands about the headwaters. They've little patches o' corn ter make ther breadstuff, an' depend on huntin', fishin', an' stealin' fur the rest o' their vittles. They've half-a-dozen guns in every cabin, but nary a hoe; they've more yaller dogs then the rest o' us hev sheep, an they find hit a good deal handier ter kill other folks's hogs than ter raise ther own pork."

"Hardly desirable neighbors, I should think," ventured Harry.

"Hit's war all the time between our kind o' people, and them other kinds. Both on 'em hates us like pizen, an' on our side--well, we air Christians, but we recken thet when Christ tole us ter love our inimies, an' do good ter them ez despitefully used us, he couldn't hev hed no idee how mean people would git ter be long arter he left the airth."

Harry could not help smiling at this new adaptation of Scriptural mandate.

"The low-down white hates us bekase we ain't mean an' ornery ez they air, an' hold ourselves above 'em. The big-bugs hates us bekase we won't knuckle down ter 'em, ez ther niggers an' the pore whites do. So hit's cat-an'-dog all the time. We don't belong ter the same parties, we don't jine the same churches, an' thar's more or less trouble a-gwine on batween us an' them continnerly."

"Then when the war broke out you took different sides as usual?"

"Of course! of course! The big nigger-owners an' the ornery whites who air just ez much ther slaves ez ef they'd been bot an' paid fur with ther own money, became red-hot Secessioners, while our people stuck ter the Union. The very old Satan hisself seemed ter take possession ov 'em, and stir 'em up ter do all manner o' cruelty ter conquer us inter jinin' in with 'em. The Brills an' Fortners hed allers been leaders agin the other people,an' now the Rebels hissed their white slaves onter our men, ez one sets dogs onter steers in the corn. The chief man among 'em wuz Kunnel Bill Pennington."

Harry looked up with a start.

"Yes, the same one who got his reward yesterd," she continued, interpreting the expression of his eyes. "The Penningtons air the richest family this side o' Danville. They an' the Brills an' Fortners hev allers been mortal enemies. Thar's bin blood shed in ev'ry gineration. Kunnel Bill's father limpt ter his grae on 'count of a bullet in his hip, which wuz lodged thar soon arter I'd flung on the floor a ten dollar gold piece he'd crowded inter my hand at a dance, where he'd come 'ithout ary invite. The bullet wuz from teh rifle ov a young man named David Brill, thet I married the next day, jest ez he wuz startin' fur Mexico. He volunteered a little airlier then he'd intended, fur his father's wheat wuz not nearly all harvested, but hit wuz thot best ter git himself out o' the way o' the Penningtons, who wuz a mouty revengeful family, an' besides they then hed the law on ther side. Ez soon ez he come back from teh war Ole Kunnel Bill, an' Young Kunnel Bill, an' all the rest o' the Pennington clan an' connection begun watchin' fur a chance ter git even with him. The Ole Kunnel used ter vow an' swar thet he'd never leave the airth ontil Dave Brill wuz under the clods o' the valley. But he hed ter go last year, spite o' hisself, an' leave David Brill 'live an' well an' becomin' more an' more lookt up ter ev'ry day by the people, while the Penningtons war gittin' wuss and wuss hated. We hed a son, too, the very apple of our eyes, who wuz growin' up jest like his father---"

The quaver of an ill-repressed sob blurred her tones. She closed her eyes firmly, as if to choke back the brimming tears, and then rising from her seat, busied herself brushing the coals and ashes back into the fire.

"Thet walnut pops so awfully," she said, "thet a body hez to sweep nearly ev'ry minnit ter keep the harth at all clean."

"The death of his father made no change in the younger Col. Pennington? He kept up the quarrel the same as ever, did he?" asked Harry, deeply interested in teh narrative.

"Wussen ever! Wussen ever! He got bitterer ev'ry day. He laid his defeat when he wuz runnin' fur the Legislatur at our door. He hired bullies ter git inter a quarrel with David, at public getherin's, an' kill him in sech a way ez ter have a plea o' self-defense ter cla'r themselves on, but David tuck too good keer o' hisself ter git ketched that a-way, an' he hurt one o' the bullies so bad thet he niver quite got over hit. He an' Kunnel Pennington leveled ther weepons on each other at a barbecue near London last Fall, but the bystanders interfered, an' prevented bloodshed fur a time."

"When the war broke out, we never believed hit would reach us. Thar mout be trouble in Louisville and Cincinnati--some even thought hit likely that thar would be fouten' in Lexington--but way up in the mountings we'd be peaceable an' safe allers. Our young men formed theirselves inter a company o' Home Gyards, an' elected my husband their Capting. Kunnel Pennington gathered together 'bout a hundred o' the poorest, orneriest shakes on the headwaters, an' tuck them off ter jine Sidney Johnson, an' drive the Yankees 'way from Louisville. Everybody said hit wuz the best riddance o' bad rubbish the country 'd ever knowed, and when they wuz gone our chances fur peace seemed better'n ever.

"All the flurry made by ther gwine 'way hed died down, an' ez we heered nothin' from 'em, or the war, people's minds got quiet ag'in, an' they sot 'bout hur-ryin' up their Spring work.

"One bright, sweet mornin' in May, I wuz at my work in the yard with Fort-ner--thet wuz my son's name--fixin' up the kittles ter dye some yarn fur a coat fur him. Husband 'd went ter the other side o' the hill, whar the new terbacker ground wuz, ter cut out some trees that shaded the plants. The skies wuz ez bright an' fa'r ez the good Lord ever made 'em. I could heah the ringin' o' David's ax, ez he chopped away, an'h hit seemed ter be sayin' ter me cheefully all the time: 'Heah I am--hard at work.' The smoke from some brush-piles that he'd sot afire riz up slowly an' gently, fur thar wuz no wind a-stirring. The birds sung gayly 'bout their work o' nest-buildin', an' I couldn't help singin' about mine. I left the kittles fur a minnit ter run down the gyardin walk, ter see how my bed o' pinks wuz comin' out, an' I sung ez I run.

"Jest then a passel o' men come stringin' up the road ter the bars. They looked like some o' them that Kunnel Pennington tuck 'way with him, but they rid better critters then any o' them ever hed, an' they were dressed in a sorter soljer-cloze, an' all o' 'em toted guns.

"Something sent a chill ter my very heart the moment I laid eyes on 'em. Hit a'most stopped beatin' when I see Kunnel Bill Pennington a little ways behind 'em, with a feather in his hat, an' sword an' pistols in his belt. When they waited at the bars fur him ter come up, I knowed instantly what they were arter.

"'Fortner,' I said ter my son, tryin' ter speak ez low ez possible; 'Fortner, honey, slip back through the bushes ez quick ez the Lord'll let ye, an tell yer daddy that Bill Pennington an' his gang air heah arter him. Sneak away, but when ye air out o' sight, run fur yer life, honey.'

"He turned ter go, but tat that minnit Bill Pennington shouted out:

"'Stop thar! Don't ye send thet boy away! Ef he moves a step, I'll put a bullet through his brain!' Fortner would've run in spite o' him, but I wuz so skeered for him thet I jumped ter his side an' ketched his arm.

"'Keep quiet, honey,' I said. 'Likely they won't find yer daddy at all.'

"Vain hope! Ez I spoke, the sound o' David's ax rung out clearly and steadily. The cannons at Wildcat, yesterday, didn't sound no louder ter me. I could even tell that he wuz choppin' a beech tree. The licks was ex a-sharp an' ringin' ez ef the ax struck iron.

"Bill Pennington lit offen his beast, an' walked toward me, with his sword a-clatterin' an' his spurs a-jinglin'.

"'Whar's that Yankeefied scalawag of a husband o' your'n? Whar's Dave Brill?' he said savagely.

"Hit seemed ter me that every stroke from over the hill said ez plainly ez tongue could utter words: 'Heah I am. Come over heah!' I tried ter gain time ter think o' something.

"'He started this mornin' on Roan Molly fer Mt. Vernon, to 'tend court,' I said, knowin' thet I didn't dare hesitate ter make up a story.

"'Kunnel, thet air's a lie,' said Jake Johnson, who knowed us. 'Thar's Dave Brill's Roan Molly over thar, in the pasture.'

"'An' this hain't court-day in Mt. Vernon, neither,' said another.

"'I know your husband's on the place, I wuz tole so this mornin',' said Kunnel Bill. 'Hit'll be much better fur ye, ef ye tell me whar he is. Hit'll at least save yer house from bein' sot afire.'

"Ring! ring! went David's ax, ez ef hit war a trumpet, shoutin' ter the whole world: 'Heah I am. Come over heah!'

"'Ye kin burn our house ef yer that big a villain,' I said; 'but I can't tell ye no different.'

"'Kunnel, thet's him a-choppin' over thar,' said Jake Johnson. 'I know he's cl'ared some new ground fur terbacker on thet air hill-side.'

"'I believe hit is,' said Kunnel Bill, listenin' a minnit. 'Parker, ye an' Haygood go over thar an' git him, while some o' the rest o' ye look 'bout the stable an' fodder-stack thar. Mind my orders, an' see thet they are carried out.'

"His manner made me fear everything. A thought flashed inter my mind. Thar wuz thet horn thar."--Harry followed her eyes with his, and saw hanging on hooks against the wall one of the long tin horns, used in the South to call the men-folks of the farms to their meals. It was crushed and battered to uselessness.--"I thought I'd blow hit an' attract his attention. He mout then see them a-comin' an' git away. I ran inter the house an' snatched the horn down, but afore I could put hit ter my lips, Bill Pennington jerked hit 'way from me, an' stamped on hit.

"'Deb Brill,' said he, with a mortally hateful look, 'yer peart an' sassy an' bold, an' hev allers been so, an' so 's yer Yankeefied husband. Ye've hed yer own way offen--too offen. Now I'll heve mine, an' wipe out some long-standin' scores. Dave Brill hez capped a lifetime o' plague an' disturbance ter his betters, by becomin' a trator to his country, an' inducin' others ter be traitors. He must be quieted. come out an' listen.'

"He pulled me out inter the yard. Dave wuz still choppin' away. Fur nearly every day fur night thirty years, the sound o' his ax hed been music in my ears. I had larned to know hit, even afore we wuz lovers, fur his father's land jined my father's, an' hit seems ter me that I could tell he note o' his ax from thet o' everybody else, a'most ez airly ez I could tell a robin's song from a blackbird's. Girl, woman, wife an' mother, I hed listened to hit while I knit, wove, or spun, every stroke minglin' with the sounds o' my wheel or loom an' the song o' the birds, an' tellin' me whar he wuz, an' thet he wuz toilin' cheefully fur me an' mine.

"Now, fur the fust time in all these years, hits steady strong beat brought mis'ry ter my ears. Hit wuz ez the tollin' of bell fur some one not yit dead. My heart o'ny beat ez fast ez he chopped. Hit would give a great jump when the sound o' the blow reached me, an' then stand still until the next one came.

"At last came a long--O, so long pause.

"'They've got thar,' said Bill Pennington, cranin' forward his head ter ketch the fust sound. 'He's seed 'em, an' is tryin' ter git 'way. But he kin never do hit. I know the men I sent ter do the job.'

"Two rifle shots sounded a'most together, an' then immediately arter wuz a couple o' boastful Injun-like yells.

"'Thar, Deb, heah thet? Ye'r a widder now. Be thankful thet I let ye off so easy. I ought by rights ter burn yer house, an' put thet boy o' your'n whar he'll do no harm. but this'll do fur an example ter these mounting traitors. They've lost their leader, an' ther hain't no one ter take his place. They'll know now thet we're in dead airnest. Boys, go inter the house an' git all the guns thar is thar, an' what vittles an' blankets ye want; but make haste, fur we must git away from heah in a hurry.'

"I run ez fast ez my feet'd carry me to whar David lay stone dead. Fortner saddled his colt an' galloped off ter his cousin Jim Fortner's, ter rouse the Home Gyard. The colt reached Jim's house, bekase hits mammy wuz thar; but my son never did. In takin' the shortest road, he hed ter cross the dangerousest ford on the Rockassel. The young beast wuz skeered nigh ter death, an' hits rider wuz drowned."

Chapter XIII. "An Apple Jack Raid."

This kind o' sojerin' ain't a mite like our October trainin', A chap could clear right out from there, ef it only looked like rainin'; And the Cunnels, too, could kiver up their shappoes with bandanners, An' send the Insines skootin' to the bar-room, with their banners, (Fear o' gittin' on 'em spotted,) an' a feller could cry quarter Ef he fired away his ramrod arter tu much rum an' water.
--James Russel Lowell.

The morning after the battle, Kent Edwards was strolling around the camp at Wildcat. "Shades of my hot-throated ancestors who swallowed several fine farms by the tumblerful, how thirsty I am!" he said at length. "It's no wonder these Kentuckians are such hard drinkers. There's something in the atmosphere that makes me drier the farther we advance into the State. Maybe the pursuit of glory has something desiccating in it. At least, all the warriors I ever heard of seemed composed of clay that required as much moistening as unslaked lime. I will hie me to teh hill of frankincense and the mountain of myrrh; in other words, I'll go back where Abe is, and get what's left in the canteen."

He found his saturine comrade sitting on a log by a comfortable fire, restoring buttons which, like soldiers, had become "missing by reason of exigencies of the campaign."

The temptation to believe that inanimate matter can be actuated by obstinate malice is almost irresistible when one has to do with the long skeins of black thread which the soldiers use for their sewing. These skeins resolve themselves, upon the pulling of the first thread, into bunches of entanglement more hopelessly perverse than the Gordian knot, or the snarls in a child's hair. To the inexperienced victim, desirous of securing the wherewithal to sew a button on, nothing seems easier than to pull a thread out of the bunch of loose filament that lies before him. Rash man! That simple mesh hat a baffling power like unto the Labyrinth of Arsino, and long labor of fingers and teeth aided by heated and improper language, frequently fails to extract so much as a half foot of thread.

Abe had stuck his needle down into the log beside him. Near, were the buttons he had fished out of his pocket, and he was laboring with clumsy fingers and rising temper at an obdurate bunch of thread.

"I've been round looking over the field," said Kent, as he came up.

A contemptuous snort answered him.

"You ought to've been along. I saw a great many interesting things."

"O, yes, I s'pose. Awful interesting. Lot o' dead men laying around in the mud. 'Bout as interesting, I should say, as a spell o' setting on a Coroner's jury. The things you find interesting would bore anybody else to death."

Abe gave the obstinate clump a savage twist which only made its knots more rebellious, and he looked as if strongly tempted to throw it into the fire.

"Don't do it, Abe," said Kent, with a laugh that irritated Abe worse still. "Thread's thread, out here, a hundred miles from nowhere. You don't know where you'll get any more. Save it--my dear fellow--save it. Perchance you may yet sweetly beguile many an hour of your elegant leisure in unraveling its fantastic convolutions with your taper fingers, and---"

"Lord! Lord!" said Abe with an expression of deep weariness, but without looking in Kent's direction, "Who's pulled the string o' that clack-mill and set it going? When it gets started once it rolls out big words like punkins dropping out o' the tail of a wagon going up hill. And there's no way o' stopping it, either. You've just got to wiat till it runs down."

"The Proverbs say so fittingly that 'A fool delighteth not in wise instruction,'" said Kent, as he stepped around to the other side of the fire. His foot fell upon a projecting twig, the other end of which flew up and landed a very hot coal on the back of Abe's hand. Abe's action followed that of the twig, in teh suddenness of his upspringing. He hurled an oath and a firebrand at his comrade.

"This is really becoming domestic," said Kent as he laughingly dodged. "The gentle amenities could not cluster more thickly around our fireside, even if we were married."

When Abe resumed his seat he did not come down exactly upon the spot from which he had arisen. It was a little farther to the right, where he had stuck the needle. He had forgotten about it, but he rose with a howl when it keenly reminded him that like the star-spangled banner, it "was still there."

"Don't rise on my account, I beg," said Kent with a deprecatory wave of the hand, as he hurried off to wher he could laugh with safety. A saucy drummer-boy, who neglected this precaution, received a cuff from Abe's heavy hand that thrilled the rest of the drum-corps with delight.

When Abe's wrath subsided from this ebullient stage back to its customary one of simmer, Kent ventured to return.

"Say," said he, pulling over the coats and blankets near the fire, "where's the canteen?"

"There it is by the cups. Can't you see it? If it was a snake it'd bite you."

"It's done that already, several times, or rather its contents have. You know what the Bible says, 'Biteth liek a serpent and stingeth like an adder?' Ah, here it is. But gloomy forebodings seize me: it is suspiciously light. Paradoxically, its lightness induces gravity in me. But that pun is entirely too fine-drawn for camp atmosphere."

He shook the canteen near his ear. "Alas! no gurgle responds to my fond caresses--

Canteen, Mavourneen, O, why art thou silent,
Thou voice of my heart?
It is--woe is me--it is empty."

"Of course it is--you were the last one at it."

"I hurl that foul imputation back into thy teeth base knave. Thou thyself art a very daughter of a horse-leech with a canteen of whisky."

Abe looked at him inquiringly. "You must've found some, some place," he said, "or you wouldn't be so awful glib. It's taken 'bout half-a-pint to loosen your tongue so that it'd run this way. I know you."

"No, I've not found a spoonful. The eloquence of thirst is the only inspiration I have at present. I fain would stay its cravings by quaffing a beaker of mountain-distilled hair-curler. Mayhap this humble receptacle contains yet a few drops which escaped thy ravenous thirst."

Kent turned the canteen upside down and placed its mouth upon his tongue. "No," he said, with deep dejection, "all that delicious fluid of yesterday is now like the Father of his Country."

"Eh?" asked Abe, puzzled.

"Because it is no more--it is no more. It belongs to the unreturning past."

"I say," he continued after a moment's pause, "let's go out and hunt for some. there must be plenty in this neighborhood. Nature never makes a want without providing something to supply it. Therefore, judging from my thirst, this country ought to be full of distilleries."

They buckled on their belts, picked up their guns and started out, directing their steps to the front.

In spite of the sunshine the walk through the battle-field was depressing. A chafing wind fretted through the naked limbs of the oaks and chestnuts, and drew moans from the pines and the hemlocks. The brown, dead leaves rustled into little tawny hillocks, behind protecting logs and rocks. Frequently those took on the shape of long, narrow mounds as if they covered the graves of some ill-fated being, who like themselves, had fallen to the earth to rot in dull obscurity. The clear little streams that in Summer-time murmured musically down the slopes, under canopies of nodding roses and fragrant sweet-brier, were now turbid torrents, brawling like churls drunken with much wine, and tearing out with savage wantonness their banks, matted with the roots of the blue violets, and the white-flowered puccoon.

Scattered over the mountain-side were fatigue-parties engaged in hunting up the dead, and burying them in shallow graves, hastily dug in clay so red that it seemed as if saturated with the blood shed the day before. The buriers thrust their hands into the pockets of the dead with the flinching, nauseated air of men touching filth, and took from the garments seeping with water and blood, watches, letters, ambrotypes, money and trinkets, some of which they studied to gain a clue to the dead man's identity, some retained as souvenirs, but threw the most back into the grave with an air of loathing. The faces of the dead with their staring eyes and open mouths and long, lank hair, cloyed with the sand and mud thrown up by the beating rain, looked indescribably repulsive.

The buriers found it better to begin their work by covering the features with a cap or a broad-brimmed hat. It was difficult for the coarsest of them to fling a spadeful of dank clay directly upon the wide-open eyes and seemingly-speaking mouth.

"Those fellows' souls," said Kent, regarding the corpses, "seem to have left their earthly houses in such haste that they forgot to close the doors and windows after them. Somewhere I ahve read of a superstition that bodily tenements left in this way were liable to be entered and occupied by evil spirits, and from this rose the custom of piously closing the eyes and mouths of deceased friends."

"No worse spirit's likely to get into them than was shot out of 'em," growled Abe. "A Rebel with a gun is as bad an evil spirit as I ever expect to meet. But let's go on. It's another kind of an evil spirit that we are interested in just now--one that'll enter into and occupy our empty canteen."

"You're right. It's the enemy that my friend Shakspere says we 'put into our mouths to steal away our brains.' By the way, what a weary hunt he must have in your cranium for a load worth stealing."

"Thee goes that clack-mill again. Great Caesar! if the boys only had legs as active as your tongue what a racer the regiment would be! Cavalry'd be nowhere."

Toward the foot of the mountain their path led them across a noisy, swollen little creek, whose overflowing waters were dyed deeply red and yellow by the load of hill caly they were carrying away in their headlong haste. A little to the left lay a corpse of more striking appearance than any they had yet seen. It was that of a tall, slender, gracefully formed young man, clad in an officer's uniform of rich gray cloth, lavishly ornamented with gilt buttons and gold lace. The features were strong, but delicately cut, and the dark skin smooth and fine-textured. One shapely hand still clasped the hilt of a richly ornamented sword, with which he had evidently been directing his men, and his staring gray eyes seemed yet filled with the anger of battle. A bullet had reached him as he stood upon a little knoll, striving to stay the headlong flight. Falling backward his head touched the edge of the swift running water, which was now filling his long, black locks with slimy sediment.

"The ounce o' lead that done that piece o' work," said Abe, "was better'n a horseload o' gold. A few more used with as good judgement would bring the rebellion to an end in short meter."

"Yes," answered Kent, "he's one of the Chivalry; one of the main props; one of the fellows who are trying to bring about Secession in the hopes of being Dukes, or

Marquises, or Earls--High Keepers of His Majesty Jeff. Davis's China Spittoons, or Grand Custodians of the Prince of South Carolina's Plug Tobacco, when the Southern Confederacy gains its independence."

"Well," said Abe, raising the Rebel's hat on the point of his bayonet, and laying it across the corpse's face, "he's changed bosses much sooner than he expected. Jeff. Davis's blood-relation, who presides over the Sulphur Confederacy, will put on his shoulder-straps with a branding-iron, and serve up his rations for him red-hot. I only wish he had more going along with him to keep him company."

"Save your feelings against the Secessionists for expression with your gun in the next fight, and come along. I'm getting thirstier every minute."

They walked on rapidly for a couple or three hours, without finding much encouragement in their search. The rugged mountain sides were but thinly peopled, and the few poor cabins they saw in the distance they decided were not promising enough of results to justify clambering up to where they were perched. At last, almost wearied out, they halted for a little while to rest and scan the interminable waves of summits that stretched out before them.

"Ah," said Kent, rising suddenly, "let's go on. Hope dawns at last. I smell apples. That's a perfume my nose never mistakes. We're near an orchard. Where there's an orchard there's likely to be a pretty good style of house, and where in Kentucky there's a good style of house there's a likelihood of being plenty of good whisky. Now there's a train of brilliant inductive reasoning that shows that nature intended me to be a great natural philosopher. Come on, Abe."

The smell of apples certainly did grow more palpable as they proceeded, and Abe muttered that even if they did not get any thing to drink they would probably get enough of the fruit to make an agreeable change in their diet.

They emerged from the woods into a cleared space where a number of roads and paths focused. To the right was a little opening in the mountain-side, hardly large enough to be called a valley, but designated in the language of the region as a "hollow." At its mouth stood a couple of diminutive log-cabins, of the rudest possible construction, and roofed with "clapboards" held in place by stones and poles. A long string of wooden troughs, supported upon props, conducted the water from an elevated spring to the roof of one of the cabins, and the water could be seen issuing again from underneath the logs at one side of the cabin. A very primitive cider mill--two wooden rollers fastened in a frame, and moved by a long sapling sweep attached to one of them--stood near. The ground was covered with rotting apple pomace, from which arose the odor that had reached Kent's nose.

"Hello!" said the latter, "here's luck; here's richness! We've succeeded beyond our most sanguine expectations, as the boy said, who ran away from school to catch minnows, and caught a ducking, a bad cold and a licking. We've struck an apple-jack distillery, and as they've been at work lately, they've probably left enough somewhere to give us all that we can drink."

Abe's sigh was eloquent of a disbelief that such a consummation was possible, short of the blissful hereafter.

Inside of one of the cabins they found a still about the size of a tub, with a worm of similar small proportions, kept cook by the flow from the spring. Some tubs and barrels, in which the lees of cider were rapidly turning to vinegar, gave off a fuity, spirituous odor, but for awhile their eager search did not discover a bit of the distilled product. At last, Kent, with a cry of triumph, dragged from a place of cunning concealment a small jug, stopped with a corncob. He smelled it hungrily.

"Yes, here is some. It's apple-jack, not a week old, and as rank as a Major General. Phew! I can smell every stick they burned to distil it. Abe, watch me closely while I drink. I magnanimously take the lead, out of consideration for you. If I ain't dead in five minutes, you try it."

"O, stop monkeying, and drink," was the impatient answer.

Kent put the jug to his mouth and took a long draught. "Shade of old Father Noah, the first drunkard," he said as he wiped the tears from his eyes, "another swig like that would pull out all the rivets in my internal pipings. Heavens! it went down like pulling a cat out of a hole by the tail. I'm afraid to wipe my mouth, lest my breath burn a hole in the sleeve of my blouse."

Three-quarters of an hour later, the spirits in the jug were lowering and those in the men rising with unequal rapidity. Under the influence of the fiery stimulant, Kent's sanguine temperament boiled and bubbled over. Imagination painted the present and future in hues of dazzling radiance. Everything was as delightful as it could be now, and would become more charming as time rolled on. But with Abe Bolton drinking tended to develop moroseness into savagery.

"Ah, comfort me with apple-jack, and stay me with flagons of it," said Kent

Edwards, setting down the jug with the circumspection of a man not yet too drunk to suspect that he is losing exact control of his legs and arms. "That gets better the deeper down you go. First it was like swallowing a chestnut burr; now, old hand-made Bourbon couldn't be smoother."

"A man can get used to a'most anything," said Bolton.

"I get gladder every day, Abe, that I came into the army. I wouldn't have missed all this experience for the finest farm in the Miami Valley.

"'Twere worth ten years of peaceful life, To soldier have a day,'

Sir Walter Scott says--as I improve him."

"'Specially one of them soaking days when we were marching through the mud to Wildcat."

"O, those were just thrown in to make us appreciate good weather when we have it. Otherwise we wouldn't. You know what the song says:

'For Spring would be but gloomy weather, If we had nothing else but Spring.'"

"Well, for my part, one o' them days was enough to p'ison six months o' sun-shine. I declare, I believe I'll feel mildewed for the rest of my life. I know if I pulled off my clothes you could scrape the green mold off my back."

"And I'm sure that if we'd had the whole army to pick from, we couldn't've got in with a better lot of boys and officers. Every one of them's true blue, and a MAN all the way through. It's the best regiment in the army, and our company's the best company in the regiment, and I flatter myself the company hasn't got two other as good men as we are."

"Your modesty'll ruin you yet, Kent," said Abe, sardonically. "It's very painful to see a man going 'round unerrating himself as you do. If I could only get you to have a proper opinion of yourself--that is, believe that you are a bigger man than General Scott or George B. McClellan, I'd have some hopes of you."

"We'll have one grand, big battle with the Secessionists now, pretty soon--everything's getting ripe for it--and we'll whip them like Wellington whipped Napoleon at Waterloo. Our regiment will cover itself with glory, in which you and I will have a big share. Then we'll march back to Sardis with flags flying and drums beating, everybody turning out, and the bands playing 'See, the Conquering Hero Comes,' when you and I come down the street, and we'll be heroes for the rest of our natural lives."

"Go ahead, and tell the rest of it to the mash-tubs and the still. I've heard as much as I can stand, an I must have a breath of fresh air. I'm going into the other cabin to see what's there."

Kent followed him to the door, with the jug in his hand.

"Kent, there's a man coming down the path there," said Abe, pulling himself together, after the manner of a half-drunken man whose attention is powerfully distracted.

"Where?" asked Kent, setting the jug down with solicitous gentleness, and reaching back for his musket.

"There, by that big chestnut. Can't you see him? or have you got so much whisky in you, that you can't see anything? He's in Rebel clothes, and he's got a gun. I'm going to shoot him."

"Maybe he's one of these loyal Kentuckians. Hold on a minute, till you are sure," said Kent, half cocking his own gun.

"The last words of General Washington were 'Never trust a nigger with a gun.' A man with that kind o' cloze has no business carrying weapons around in this country. I'm going to shoot."

"If you shoot with your hands wobbling that way, you'll make him aas full of holes as a skimmer. That'd be cruel. Steady yourself up a little, while I talk to him.

"Halt, there!" commanded Kent, with a thick tongue. "Who are you, and how many are with you?"

"I'm a Union man," said Fortner, for it was he, "an' I'm alone."

"Lay down your gun and come up here, if you are a friend," ordered Kent.

The swaggering imperiousness in Edward's tone nettled Fortner as much as the order itself. "I don't make a practice of layin' down my gun for no man," he said proudly. "I'm ez good Union ez ary of you'uns dar be, an' I don't take no orders from ye. I could've killed ye both, ef I'd a wanted ter, afore ye ever seed me."

Bolton's gun cracked, and the bullet buried itself in the thick, soft bark of the chestnut, just above Fortner's head, and threw dust and chips in his eyes. He brushed them away angrily, and instinctively raised his rifle. Kent took this as his cue to fire, but his aim was even worse than Abe's.

"Ruined again by strong drink," he muttered despairingly, as he saw the failure of his shot. "Nothing but new apple jack could make me miss so fair a mark."

"Now, ye fellers, lay down YORE guns!" shouted Fortner, springing forward to where they were, with his rifle cocked. "Lay 'em down! I say. Lay 'em down, or I'll let daylight through ye!"

"He's got us, Abe," said Kent, laying down his musket reluctantly. His example was followed by Abe, who, however, did not place his gun so far that he could not readily pick it up again, if Fortner gave him an instant's opportunity. Fortner noticed this, and pushed the musket farther away with his foot, still covering the two with his rifle.

"Ye see now," he said "thet I hev ye at my marcy, ef I wanted ter kill or capture ye. Efi I gin ye back yer guns, ye'll admit thet I'm yer friend, and not yer inimy, won't ye?"

"It'll certainly look like an overture to a permanent and disinterested friendship," said Kent, brightening up; and Abe, who was gathering himself up for a spring to catch Fortner's rifle, let his muscles relax again.

"Well, ye kin take up yer guns agin and load 'em," said Fortner, letting down the hammer of his rifle. "I'm Jim Fortner, supposed ter be the pizenest Union man on the Rockassel! Come along ter my house, an' I'll gin ye a good meal o' vittels. Hit's on'y a little piece off, an' I've got thar one of yer fellers. His name's Harry Glen.

Chapter XIV. In the Hospital.

As the tall ship whose lofty prore Shall never stem the billows more Deserted by her gallant band, Amid the breakers lies astrand-- Soon his couch lay Rhoderick Dhu, And oft his fevered limbs he threw In toss abrupt, as when her sides Lie rocking in the advancing tides, That shake her frame with ceaseless beat, Yet can not heave her from her seat;-- O, how unlike her course on sea! Or his free step on hill and lea!

--Lady of the Lake.

An Army Hospital is the vestibule of the Cemetery--the ante-room where the recruiting-agents of Death--Wounds and Disease--assemble their conscripts to prepare them for the ranks from which there is neither desertion nor discharge. Therein enter those who are to lay aside "this muddy vesture of decay," for the changeless garb of the Beyond. Thither troop the Wasted and Stricken to rest a little, and prepare for the last great journey, the first milestone of which is placed over their heads.

Humanity and Science have done much for the Army Hospital, but still its swinging doors wave two to the tomb where they return one to health and activity.

It was a broiling hot day when Rachel Bond descended from the ambulance which had brought her from the station to camp.

She shielded her eyes with a plam-leaf fan, and surveyed the surroundings of the post of duty to which she had been assigned. She found herself in a little city of rough plank barracks, arranged in geometrically correct streets and angles about a great plain of a parade ground, from which the heat radiated as from a glowing stove. A flag drooped as if wilted from the top of a tall pole standing on the side of the parade-ground opposite her. Languidly pacing in front of the Colonel's tent was an Orderly, who had been selected in the morning for his spruce neatness, but who now looked like some enormous blue vegetable, rapidly withering under the sun's blistering rays.

Beyond were the barracks, baking and sweltering, cracking their rough, unpainted sides into yawning fissures, and filling the smothering air with resinous odors distilled from the fat knots in the refuse planking of which they were built. Beyond these was the line of camp-guards--bright gun-barrels and bayonets glistening painfully, and those who bore them walking with as weary slowness as was consistent with any motion whatever, along their beats.

On straw in the oven-like barracks, and under the few trees in the campground, lay the flushed and panting soldiers, waiting wearily for that relief which the descending sun would bring.

The hospital to which Rachel had been brought differed from the rest of the sheds in the camp by being whitewashed within and without, which made it radiate a still more unendurable heat than its duller-lustered companions. A powerful odor of chloride of lime and carbolic acid shocked her sensitive nostrils with their tales of all the repulsiveness those disinfectants were intended to destroy or hide.

Several dejected, hollow-eyed convalescents, whose uniforms hung about their wasted bodies as they would about wooden crosses, sat on benches in the scanty shade by one side of the building, and fanned themselves weakly with fans clumsily fashioned from old newspapers. They looked up as the trim, lady-like figure stepped lightly down from the ambulance, and the long-absent luster returned briefly to their sad eyes.

"That looks like home, Jim," said one of the fever-wasted.

"That it does. Lord! she looks as fresh and sweet as the Johnny-jump-ups down by our old spring-house. I expect she's come down here to find somebody that belongs to her that's sick. Don't I wish it was me!"

"I wouldn't mind being a brother, or a cousin, or a sweetheart to her myself. That'd be better luck than to be given a sutler-shop. Just see her move! She's got a purtier gait than our thoroughbred colt."

"IT does one's eyes good to look at her. It makes me feel better than a cart-load of the stuff that old Pillbags forces down our throats."

"You're a-talking. She's a lady--every inch of her--genuine, simon-pure, fast colors, all-wool, a yard wide, as fine as silk, and bright a a May morning."

"And as wholesome as Spring sunshine."

All unconscious that her appearance was to the invalids who looked upon her like a sweet, health-giving breeze bursting through a tainted atmosphere, Rachel passed wearily along the burning walks toward the Surgeon's office, with a growing heart-sickness at the unwelcome appearance of the task she had elected for herself.

The journey had been full of irritating discomforts. Heat, dust, and soiled linen are only annoyances to a man; they are real miseries to a woman. The marvel is not that Joan of Arc dared the perils of battle, but that she endured the continued wretchedness of camp uncleanliness, to the triumphant end.

With her throat parched, garments "sticky," hair, eyes, ears and nostrils filled with irritating dust, and a feeling that collar and cuffs were, as ladies phrase it, "a sight to behold," Rachel's heoric enthusiasm ebbed to the bottom. Ushered into the Surgeon's office she was presented to a red-faced, harsh-eyed man, past the middle age, who neither rose nor apologized to her for being discovered in the undress of a hot day. He montioned her to a seat with the wave of the fan he was vigorously using, and taking her letter of introduction, adjusted eye-glasses upon a ripe-colored nose, and read it with a scowl that rippled his face with furrows.

"So you're the first of the women nurses that's to be assigned to me," he said ungraciously, after finishing the letter, and scanning her severely for a moment over the top of his glasses. "I suppose I have to have 'em."

The manner hurt Rachel even more than the words. Before she could frame a reply he continued:

"I don't take much stock in this idea of women nurses, especially when they're young and pretty." He scowled at Rachel as if she had committed a crime in being young and beautiful. "But the country's full of women with a Quixotic notion of being Florence Nightingales, and they've badgered the Government into accepting their services. I suppose I'll have to take my share of them. Ever nursed?"

"No, sir," responded Rachel, compressing as much ahughtiness as possible into the answer.

"Of course not. Girls at your age are not at all likely to know anything that is useful, and least of all how to nurse a sick man. I hardly know which is the worst, a young one who don't know anything, or a middle-aged one who thinks she knows it all, and continually interferes with the management of a case. I believe though, I'd rather have had the middle-aged one to start with. She'd be more likely to tend to her business, and not have her head turned by the attentions of the good-looking young officers who swarm around her. Mind, I'll not allow any flirting here."

Rachel's face crimsoned. "You forget yourself," she said, cuttingly; "or perhaps you have nothing to forget. At least, man an effort to remember that I'm a lady."

The bristly eyebrows straightened down to a level line over the small blue eyes, and unpleasant furrows drew themselves around the corners of his mouth. "YOU forget," he said, "that if you enter upon these duties you are in the military service and subject to your superior officers. You forget the necessity of the most rigid discipline, and that it is my duty to explain and enforce this."

"I certainly expect to obey orders," said Rachel, a little overawed.

"You may rightly expect to," he answere with a slight sneer; "because it will be a matter of necessity--you will have to. We must have instant and unquestioning obedience to orders here, as well as everywhere else in the Army, or it would be like a rope of sand--of no strength whatever--no strength, whatever."

"I know it," answered Rachel, depressed even more by th apparition of martial law than she had been by the heat.

"And what I have been telling you is only the beginning," continued the Surgeon, noting the effect of his words, and exulting in their humbling power. "The cornerstone of everything military is obedience--prompt, unfailing obedience, by everybody, soldier or officer, to his superiors. Without it---"

"Major Moxon," said an officer, entering and saluting, "the General presents his compliments, and desires to know why his repeated orders in regard to the furloughing of men have been so persistently disregarded."

"Because," said the Surgeon, getting purplish-red about the cheeks and nose, " because the matter's one which I consider outside of his province--beyond his control, sir. I am Chief of the Medical Department, as you are perhaps aware, sir."

"We presumed that you were taking that view of the matter, from your course," answered the Aide calmly. "I am not here to argue the matter with you, but simply to direct you to consider yourself under arrest. Charges are being prepared against you, to which I will add specifications based on this interview. Good afternoon, sir." The Aide saluted stiffly and moved away, leaving the Surgeon in a state of collapse at the prospect of what he had brought upon himself by his injudicious contumacy. Mis Rachel was in that state of wonderment that comes to pupils at seeing their teachers rebel agains their own precepts. The Surgeon was too much engrossed in his own affairs to pay farther heed to her. He tapped a bell.

"Orderly," he said, to the soldier who responded, "conduct this young woman to Dr. Denslow. Inform him that she is to be with us as a nurse, and ask him to be kind enough to assign her suitable quarters. Good afternoon, ma'am."

In another office, much smaller and far less luxuriously furnished, she found Dr. Denslow, a hazel-eyed, brown-bearded man of thirty, whose shoulder-straps bore the modest bars of Captain. The reader has already made his acquaintance. He received her with the pleasant, manly sympathy for her sex, which had already made him one of the most popular of family physicians in the city where he was practicing at the outbreak of the war.

Rachel's depressed spirits rose again at his cordial reception.

"I am so busy," he said, after a brief exchange of commonplaces, "that I'll not have the time to give you much information this afternoon as to your duties, and I know that you are so fatigued with your journey and the heat that you will not care to do anything but rest and refresh yourself. I will therefore show you immediately to your quarters."

"This will be your field of labor," he said, as he led her down the long aisle between rows of cots toward her room. "It's not a cheerful one to contemplate at first. Human suffering is always a depressing spectacle, and you will see here more of it and more varied agony than you can find anywhere outside of an army hospital's walls. But as the deed is so is the duty, and the glory of doing it. To one who wants to serve God and his fellow-creatures--which I take it is the highest form of religion--here is an opportunity that he may bless God for giving him. Here he can earn a brighter crown than is given them who die at the stake for opinion's sake."

So earnest was his enthusiasm that Rachel felt herself lifted up by it, in spite of her discomforts. But then she turned her eyes away from his impassioned face, and looked over the array of white beds, each with its pale and haggard occupant, his eyes blazing with the delirium of fever, or closed in the langor of exhaustion, with limbs tossing as the febrile fire seethed the blood, or quivering with the last agonies.

Groans, prayers, and not a few oaths fell on her ears. The repulsive smell of the disinfectants, the nauseating odor of the sick room where hundreds of invalids were lying, the horrible effluvia of the typhus rose on the hot air, and seemed part of the misery which so strongly assailed her other senses.

She was sick at heart, and with every feeling in active revolt, but without a word she turned and followed Dr. Denslow to a hot, close, little room which had been cut off one end of the hospital, though not so separated from it but that the sounds and odors from the sick wards continually filtered in through the wide cracks in its plank sides. An iron bedstead, of the same pattern as that upon which the sick lay, stood in one corner, and in another was a rudely-fashioned stand, upon which was a tin-basin, a cake of yellow bar-soap, and a bucket of water for washing. This was all the furniture.

As the door closed behind the Doctor, Rachel threw herself upon the cot, in a fit of despair at the wreck of all her fancies, and the repulsiveness of the career upon which she had embarked.

"I can not--I will not--live here a week," she said to herself, over and over again. "I will die for the lack of comforts--of the decencies of life, even--to say nothing of being poisoned by these horrible smells, or driven distracted by the raving sick and that boor of a Surgeon. But I can not draw back; I would rather die than go back to Sardis with a confession of failure at the very outset of my attempt to play the heroine."

Then she remembered her last words to Harry Glen: "I only know that you have failed where a number of commonplace men have succeeded, and that is sufficient."

Would she subject herself to having him throw these words in her teeth? No. Any shape of trial and death, rather.

Chapter XV. Making an Acquaintance with Duty.

And with light in her looks she entered the chamber of sickness. Noiselessly moved about the assiduous, careful attendants, Moistening the feverish lip, and teh aching brow, and in silence Closing the sightless eyes of the dead, and concealing their faces, Where on their pallets they lay like drifts of snow by the roadside. Many a languid head upraised as Evangeline entered, Turned on its pillow of pain to gaze while she passed for her presence Fell on their hearts like a ray of sun on the walls of a prison, And as she looked around she saw how Death the Consoler, Laying his hand on many a heart hade healed it forever.
>   --Evangaline.

Nervously bolting the rude door after Dr. Denslow's departure, Rachel tossed her hat into one corner, and without farther undressing flung herself down upon the coarse blankets of the cot, in utter exhaustion of mind and body. Nature, beneficent ever to Youth and Health, at once drew the kindly curtains of Sleep, and the world and its woes became oblivion.

Early the next morning the shrill REVEILLE called for a resumption of the day's activities. She was awakened by the fifes screaming a strenuously cheeful jig, but lay for some minutes without opening her eyes. She was so perfectly healthful in every way that the tribulations of the previous day had left no other traces than a slight wariness. But every sense began informing her that yesterday's experience was not a nightmare of her sleep, but a waking reality. The morning sun was already pouring hot beams upon the thin roof over her head. Through the wide cracks in the partition came the groans and the nauseating odors which had depressed her so on the day before. Mingled with these was the smell of spoiled coffee and ill-cooked food floating in from the kitchen, where a detail of slovenly and untaught cooks were preparing breakfast.

She shuddered and opened her eyes.

The rude garniture of her room, thickly covered with coarse dust, and destitute of everything to make life comfortable, looked even more repugnant than it had the evening before.

The attack of sickness at heart at the position in which she found herself came on with renewed intensity, for the hatefulness of everything connected with the lot she had chosen seemed to have augmented during the passing hours. She tried to gain a little respite by throwing one white arm over her eyes, so as to shut out all sight, that she might imagine for a moment at least that she was back under the old apple tree at Sardis, before all this sorrow had come into her life.

"It is not possible," she murmured to herself, "that Florence Nightingale, and those who assisted her found their work and its surroundings as unlovely as it is here. I won't believe it. In Europe things are different, and the hospitals are made fitting places for women to visit and dwell in."

It would have helped her much if she could have known that the Crimean hospitals, in which Florence Nightingale won world-wide fame, lacked immeasurably of the conveniences and comforts with which American ingenuity and lavish generosity mitigated somewhat the wretchedness of army hospitals.

Lying still became unendurable, she rose, in hopes that action might bring some sort of relief. Such plain toilet was made as the very limited means at her command permitted. The scant privacy afforded by her room was another torture. Maiden modesty suggested a Peeping Tom at every yawning crack in the planking.

At least, neatly attired in a serviceable gray frock, with a dainty white collar at her throat, and her satiny hair brushed smoothly over her forehead, she opened her door and stepped out into the main ward room.

A murmur of appreciation arose from those who looked upon her, and the sick ceased groaning, to feast their eyes upon the fair, fresh apparition of sweet young womanhood. There was such unmistakable pleasure written on every face that for a moment even she herself became a little conscious that her presence was like a grateful shower upon a parched and weary land. But before she could buoy her spirits up with this knowledge they sank again as she perceived Dr. Moxon stalking down the long aisle, with ill-humor expressed in every motion of his bulky figure.

He was frowning deeply; his great feet fell flatly upon the creaking planks, as if he were crushing something at every step, and he rated the occupants of the cots on either side as he passed along.

"No. 4," he said sharply to a gaunt boy, whose cheeks were burning with rising fever, "you've got a relapse. Serves you right for leaving your bed yesterday. Now don't deny it, for I saw you outside myself. I'll send the Wardmaster to the guard-house for that."

"But, Doctor, it wasn't his fault," gasped the sick man, painfully. "I begged so hard to go out that he couldn't refuse me. It was so hot in here and smelled so badly, that I felt I should die unless I got a breath of fresh air."

"Silence!" thundered the Surgeon; "I'll have no talking back to me. Steward, send that Wardmaster to the guard-house for disobedience of orders. No. 7, you refused to take your medicine yesterday. Steward, double his prescription, and if he shows the least resistance to taking it, have the nurses hold him and force it down his throat. Do you hear? There, why don't you hold still?" (This to a man who was having a large blister applied to his back.)

"It hurts so," answered the sufferer.

"Hurts, eh? Well, I'll show you what hurts some of these days, when I cut your leg off. Well, what do you want, youngster?"

A slender, white-faced boy was standing at the foot of his cot, at "attention," and saluting respectfully.

"If you please," said he, "I'd like to be discharged, and go back to my company. I'm well enough now to do duty, and I'll be entirely well in a short time, if I can get out of doors into the fresh air."

"Indeed," answered Dr. Moxon, with a sneer, "may I inquire when you began to diagnose cases, and offer advice to your superior officers? Why don't you set up in the practice of medicine at once, and apply for a commission as Surgeon in the Army? Step back, an don't ever speak to me again in this manner, or it'll be the worse for you, I can tell you. I know when you are fit to go back to duty, and I won't have patients annoying me with their whims and fancies. Step back, sir."

Thus he passed along, leaving anger and humiliation behind him, as a steamer leaves a wake of waves beaten into a froth.

"Old Sawbones made a mistake with his morning cocktail, and mixed a lot of wormwood with it," said one of the "convalescents," in an undertone to those about him.

"This awful hot weather's spilin' most everything," said another, "and the old man's temper never was any too sweet."

Dr. Moxon came up to Rachel, and regarded her for an instant very unpleasantly. "Young woman," he said in a harsh tone and with a still harsher manner, "the rules of this institution require every attendant to be present at morning roll-call, under pain of punishment. You were not present this morning, but be careful that you are in the future."

Rachel's grief over her own situation had been swallowed up by indignation at the Surgeon's brutality to others. All her higher instincts were on fire at the gratuitous insults to boys, toward whom her womanly sumpathies streamed out. The pugnacious element, large in hers as in all strong natures, asserted itself and invited to the fray. If there was no one else to resist this petty tyrant she would, and mayhap in this she might find such exercise of her heroic qualities that she felt were within her, as would justify herself in her own esteem. She met with a resolute glance his peevish eyes, and said;

"When the rules are communicated to me in a proper manner, I shall take care to obey them, if they are just and proper; but I will not be spoken to in that way by any man."

His eyes fell from the encounter with hers, and the dull mottle in his cheek became crimson with a blush at this assertion of outraged womanly dignity. He turned away, saying gruffly:

"Just as I expected. The moment a woman comes into the hospital, all discipline is at an end."

He moved off angrily. All the inmates saw and overheard. If Rachel's refreshing beauty had captivated them before, her dauntless spirit completed the conquest.

A cheery voice behind her said, "Good morning." There was something so winning in its tones that the set lines in her indignant face relaxed, and she turned softened eyes to meet the frankly genial ones of Dr. Paul Denslow.

"Good morning, Miss---," he repeated, as she hesitated, a little dazed.

"Bond--Rachel Bond's my name. Good morning, sir," she answered, putting out her hand.

As he took it, he said: "I want to make an abject apology. We are ill-prepared to entertain a lady here, and no one knew of your coming. But we certainly intend to mitigate in some degree the desolation of the room to which you were conducted. I left you for the purpose of seeing what the store-room contained that would contribute a trifle toward transforming it into a maiden's bower--"

"Cinderella's fairy godmother couldn't have made the transformation with that room," she said with a little shrug of despair.

"Probably not--probably not--and I lay no claim to even the least of the powers exercised by the old lady with the wand. But I allow no man to surpass me in the matter of good intentions. That is a luxury of which the poorest of us can afford an abundance, and I will not deny myself anything that is so cheap."

Rachel was beguiled into smiling at his merry cynicism.

"Allusions to the pavement in the unmentionable place are barred in this connection," he continued gayly. "On my way to carry out these good intentions--at some one else's expense, remember, all the time--I was called to the bedside of a dying man, and detained there some time. When I at last returned to your room, I judged that you were fast asleep, and I decided not to disturb you."

"I think you would have found it a difficult matter to have roused me. I had sunk on the cot, and was sleeping the sleep of--"

"The just," interposed Dr. Denslow, gallantly.

"No, of the fatigued."

"Well, scientific truth compels me to say that fatigue is a surer and stronger sedative than a clear conscience even. I know, for I have occasionally tried a clear conscience--only by way of experiment, you know," he added, apologetically.

"Well, whatever the case, I was slepping as though on downy beds of ease."

"Then my mind is lightened of a mountain-load of responsibility for having made you pass a miserable night. But let's go in to breakfast. I am opposed to doing anything on an empty stomach--even to holding a pleasant conversation. It invites malaria, and malaria brings a number of disagreeable sensations which people mistake for repentance, remorse, religious awakening, and so on, according to their mental idiosyncrasies, and the state of their digestion."

The breakfast did not help remove the unpleasant impressions already made upon her mind. The cloth that covered the coarse planks of the table was unmistakably a well-worn sheet. Tin cups and platters made humble substitution for china, and were appropriately accompanied by cast-iron knives and two tined forks.

Two Hospital Stewards--denoted by the green bands, embroidered with CADUCEI, around their arms--and the same number of Wardmasters, formed the mess which sat down with Dr. Denslow and Rachel, on benches around the table.

What bouyant cheerfulness could do to raise Rachel's spirits and give an appetizing flavor to the coarse viands, Dr. Denslow did.

"I apprehend," said he, "that you will suspect that in obtaining this steak the indefatigable cook made a mistake, and sliced a piece from a side of sole leather hanging near. This was not the case. It was selected with a deep physiological design. Meat of this character consists almost wholly of fibrine, the least heat-producing constituent of flesh. By excluding all fats and other tender portions, and confining ourselves to fibrine, we are the better able to stand this torrid weather."

One of the Hospital Stewards groaned deeply.

"What is the matter, 'Squills'?" said the Doctor, kindly.

"I was thinking of the monstrous fibber-in here," said "Squills," lugubriously.

"'Squills,' I don't know how I can properly punish the disrespect shown our young lady guest and your superior officer, by that vile pun and the viler implication contained in it."

"This sugar," continued the Doctor, lifting some out of an old tomato can with a large iron spoon, and tendering it to Rachel for her coffee, "has a rich golden color, which is totally absent from the paler varieties to which you are accustomed. Its deeper hue comes from having caught more of the Cuban yellow sun's rays."

"Yes," interjected "Squills," "all the Cuban's yellow sons raise. Their daughters, too, are sometimes almost brown."

Dr. Denslow frowned.

"What a queer odor it has," said Rachel, sniffing it, and staying the spool just over her cup.

"Has it?" said the Doctor, sniffing too. "O, that's nothing. That's only chloroform. The ants were very bad, and we put some in to kill them off."

"I don't believe I'll take any in my coffee, thank you," said Rachel, calmly. "There are times when I don't like it sweetened."

"But you'll certainly take cream, then," he said, breaking off the cover of a can of condensed milk. "Here is some put in the reverse of the homeopathic plan. Instead of being the 30th dilution, it is about the 30th concentration. With this little can, and his pump in good order, a milkman could supply a good big route with 'pure grass-fed milk.' Within these narrow walls are compressed the nutritive juices of an acre of fragrant white clover."

"The Doctor was formerly a lecturer in a medical college," said "Squills" "sotto voce" to Rachel.

Rachel's appetite had seemed sufficient for almost any food, but she confined her breakfast to two or three crackers of hard bread, and a few sups of coffee. The pleasantry had failed of its desired effect. It was like vinegar upon niter, or the singing of songs to an heavy heart.

As they rose from the table the Doctor informed her that he and the Stewards were about to make their morning round of the wards, and that she had better accompany them. She went along without a word.

They walked slowly up and down the long aisles behind the Doctor, who stopped before each cot, and closely examined its occupant's tongue, pulse, and other indicators of his condition, and gave prescriptions, which the Steward wrote down, as to medicine and food. What was better still were his words of sympathy for the very ill and of cheery encouragement for the convalescent, which he bestowed upon every one.

"A visit from Dr. Denslow does a sick man more good," whispered "Squills" to Rachel, as he saw her eyes light up with admiration at the Doctor's tactful kindliness, "than all the drugs in the dispensary. I sometiems believe he's one of them that can cure by a simple laying-on of hands. He's just the opposite of old Moxon, who'd counteract the effect of the best medicine in the world."

"No. 19, Quin. Sulph., grains 16; make four powders, one every three hours," continued "Squills," repeating the directions as he received them, "Spiritus Frumenti, 1 oz., at evening. No. 2 diet. No. 20, Dover's powder 10 grains, at bedtime. No 1 diet. You," addressing himself to Rachel again, "will do even better than Dr. Denslow, soon. Can't you see how the mere sight of you brightens up everybody around here?"

Rachel had no reply ready for so broad a compliment, but its assertion of her high usefulness went far to reconcile her to her position.

She wondered silently if her mission was to be confined to posing as a thing of beauty and a joy forever.

This differed much from her expectations, for she dreaded at each step lest the next bring her fact to face with some horrible task, which she would be expected to undertake. But the Doctor, with his usual tact, was almost imperceptibly inducting her into her duties.

"Would Miss Bond kindly shake this powder into that cup of water and give it to that boy?"

She did so, and was rewarded by the recipient's grateful look, as he said:

"It don't seem at all nasty when YOU give it to me."

"Would she hand tht one this bit of magnesia for his heartburn?"

It was a young Irishman, who received the magnesia with a gallant speech:

"Faith, your white fingers have made it swater than loaf-sugar."

Rachel colored deeply, and those within hearing laughed.

At the next cot a feverish boy tossed wearily. Rachel noticed the uncomfortable arrangement of the folded blanket which did duty as a pillow. She stepped quickly to the head of the cot, took the blanket out, refolded it with a few deft, womanly motinos, and replaced it with a cool surface uppermost.

"O, that is SO good," murmured the boy, half-unclosing his eyes. "It's just as mother would've done."

Dr. Denslow looked earnest approval.

Rachel began to feel an interest kindling in her work. It was not in a womanly nature to resist this cordial appreciation of all she did.

A few cots farther on a boy wanted a letter written home. She was provided with stationary, and taking her place by the side of the cot, received his instructions, and wrote to his anxious parents the first news they had from their only son since they had been informed, two weeks before, that he had been sent to the hospital. When she had finished she rejoined the Doctor, who had by this time nearly completed his round of the ward. As soon as he was through he dismissed Stewards and Wardmasters to their duties, adn returned with her to her room. It was so changed that she thought she ahd made a mistake when she opened the door. The time of her absence had been well employed by a detail of men, whom the Doctor had previously instructed. The floor was as white and clean as strong arms with an abundance of soap and hot water could scrupt it, the walls and ceiling were neatly papered with "Harper's Weeklies," and "Frank Leslies," other papers concealed the roughness of the table and shelves, white sheet and pillow-cases had given the cot an air of inviting neatness, and before it lay a square of rag carpet. The window was shaded with calico curtains, the tin basin and dipper had been scoured to brightness, and beside them stood a cedar water-pail with shining brass hoops.

"Ah," she said, with brightening face, "this is something like living."

"Yes," answered Dr. Denslow, "I imagine it IS some improvement upon the sandy desert in which you spent the night. I hope we will soon be able to make it still more comfortable. We have just started this hospital, and we are sadly destitute of many of the commonest necessaries of such an institution. But everything will get better in a week or so, and while I can not exactly promise you the comforts of a home, I can assure you that life will be made more endurable than it seems to be possible now."

"I do hope none of this has been taken away from any sick man who needs it more than I?" said Rachel, with a remembrance of how much the boys in the ward needed.

"Do not disturb yourself with any such thought. Your comfort has not been bought at the expense of any one else's. I would not give, even to you, anything taht would help restore a sick soldier to his regiment or his home. My first duty, as that of yours and all of us, is to him. He is the man of the occasion. All the rest of us are mere adjuncts to him. We have no reason for being, except to increase his effectiveness."

The earnestness with which he spoke, so different from his light bantering at the breakfast table, made her regard him more attentively.

"I begin to get a glimmering," she said at length, "of the inspiration in this kind of work. Before it has all seemed unutterably repulsive to me. But it has its rewards."

"Yes," said he, lapsing still deeper into a mood which she soon came to recognize in him as a frequent one of spiritual exaltation, "we who toil here, labor amidst the wreck and ruin of war without the benefit of that stirring impulse which fills the souls of those who actually go into battle. The terrors of human suffering which they see but for an instant, as when the lightning in the night shows the ravages of the storm, encompass us about and abide with us continually. We are called upon for another kind of fortitude, and we must look for our reward otherwise than in the victor's laurels. We can only have to animate us our own consciousness of a high duty well done. To one class of minds this is an infinitely rich meed. The old Jewish legend says that Abrahams principal jewel was one worn upon his breast, 'whose light raised those who were bowed down, and healed the sick,' and when he passed from earth it was placed in heaven, where it shown as one of the great stars. Of such kind must be our jewel."

He stopped, and blushing through his beard, as if ashamed of his heroics, said with a light laugh:

"But if there is anything I fear it is self-righteousness which cankereth the soul. Come; I will show you a sight which will repress any tendency you may ever feel to exalt your services to the pinnacle of human merit."

While leading her to a remote part of the hospital he continued: "Of course greater love hath no man than this, that he gave his life for that which he loves. Considered relatively to the person the peasant who falls in the defense of his country gives just as much as the Emperor who may die by his side. In either case the measure of devotion is brim-full. Nothing more can be added to it. But there are accessories and surroundings which apparently make one life of much greater value than another, and make it a vastly richer sacrifice when laid on the altar of patriotism."

"There are certainly degrees of merit, even in yielding up one's life," said Rachel, not altogther unmindful of the sacrifice she herself had made in coming to the front.

"Judged by this standard," the Doctor continued, "the young man whom we are about to see has made a richer offering to his country than it is possible for most men to make. It is almost shames me as to the meagerness of the gift I bring."

"If you be ashamed how must others who give much less feel?"

"He was in the first dawn of manhood," the Doctor went on, without noticing the interruption, "handsome as a heathen god, educated and wealty, and with high aspirations for a distinguished scientific career fermenting in his young blood like new wine. Yet he turned his back upon all this--upon the opening of a happy married life--to carry a private soldier's musket in the ranks, and to die ingloriously by the shot of a skulking bushwhacker. He would not even take a commision, because he wanted that used to encourage some other man, who might need the inducement."

"But why call his death inglorious? If a man braves death why is any one time or place worse than another?"

"Because for a man of his temperament he is dying the cruelest death possible. He had expected, if called upon to yield his life, to purchase with it some great good for his country. But to perish uselessly as he is doing, as if bitten by a snake, is terrible. Here we are. I will tell you before we go in that he has a bullet wound through the body, just grazing an artery and it is only a question of a short time, and the slightest shock, when a fatal hemorrhage will ensue. Be very quiet and careful."

He untied a rope stretched across the entrance to a little wing of the building to keep unnecessary footsteps at a distance.

"How is he this morning?" he asked of a gray-haired nurse seated in front of a door curtained with a blanket.

"Quiet and cheeful as ever," answered the nurse, rising and pulling the blanket aside that they might enter.

The face upon which Rachel's eyes fell when she entered the room impressed her as an unusual combination of refinement and strength. Beyond this she noted little as to the details of the patient's countenance, except that he had hazel eyes, and a clear complexion asserting itself under the deep sun-burning.

When they entered he was languidly fanning himself with a fan which had been ingeniously constructed for him by some inmate, out of a twig of willow bent into a hoop, and covered by pasting paper over it. He gave a faint smile of welcome to the Doctor, but his face lighted up with pleasure when he saw Rachel.

"Good morning, Sanderson," said Dr. Denslow, in a repressed voice. "How do you feel?"

"As usual," whispered Sanderson.

"This is Miss Rachel Bond, who is assigned to our hospital as nurse."

A slight movement of Sanderson's head acknowledged Rachel's bow.

"I am so glad to see you," he whispered, taking hold of her hand. "Sit down there, please."

Rachel took the indicated seat at the head of the cot.

"Doctor," inquired Sanderson, "is it true that McClellan has had to fall back from before Richmond?"

"I have tried hard to keep the news from you," answered Dr. Denslow, reluctantly. "I feat it is too true. Let us hope it is only a temporary reverse, and that it will soon be more than overcome."

"Not in time for me," said Sanderson, in deep dejection. "I have lived several days merely because I wanted to see Richmond taken before I died. I can wait no longer."

The Doctor essayed some confused words of encouragement, but stopped abruptly, and feigning important business in another part of the hospital, hurried out, bidding Rachel await his return.

When he was gone Sanderson lifted Rachel's hand to his lips, and said with deep feeling:

"I am so glad you have come. You remind me of her."

The ebbing life welled up for the last time into such ardent virility that Rachel's first maidenly instinct was to withdraw her hand from his earnest pressure and kiss.

"No, do not take your hand away," he said eagerly. "There need be no shame, for I shall be clay almost before you flush has had time to fade. I infringe on no other's rights, for I see in you only another whom you much resemble."

Rachel suffered her hand to remain within his grasp.

"I would that she knew as you do, that I died thinking of her, next to my country. You will write and tell her so. The Doctor will give you her address, and you can tell her, as only a woman can tell another what the woman-heart hungers for, of my last moments. It is so much better that you should do it than Dr. Denslow, even, grand as he is in every way. You will tell her that there was not a thought of repining--that I felt that giving my life was only partial payment to those who gave theirs to purchase for me every good thing that I have enjoyed. I had twenty-five years of as happy a life as ever a man lived, and she came as its crowning joy. I look forward almost eagerly to what that Power, which has made every succeeding year of my life happier than the previous one, has in store for me in the awakening beyond. Ah, see there! It has come. There goes my life."

She looked in the direction of his gaze, and saw a pool of blood slowly spreading out from under the bed, banking itself against the dust into miniature gulfs and seas. The hand that held hers relaxed, and looking around she saw his eyes closed as if in peaceful sleep.

Dr. Denslow entered while she still gazed on the dead face, and said:

"I am so sorry I left you alone. I did not expect this for some hours."

"How petty and selfish all my life has been," said Rachel, dejectedly, as they left the room.

"Not a particle more than his was, probably," said Dr. Denslow, "until his opportunity came. It is opportunity that makes the hero, as well as the less reputable personage, and I haev no doubt that when yours comes, you will redeem yourself from all blame of selfishness and pettiness."

Chapter XVI. The Ambuscade.

This heavy-headed revel, east and west, Makes us traduced and taxed of other nations; They clepe us drunkards, and with swinish frase Soul our addition: and indeed it takes From our achievements, though performed at hight, The pith and marrow of our attribute.

--Hamlet.

The day spent with Aunt Debby had been of the greatest benefit to Harry Glen. Since his parting with Rachel Bond, there had been going on in his spirit a fermentation like that with which good wine discharges itself of its grossness and impurities, and becomes clear and fine. In this process had vanished the absorbing selfishness of a much-indulged only son, and teh supercilious egotism which came as an almost necessary result of his college curriculum. This spiritual ripening received its perfecting color and bloom from the serene exaltation of Aunt Debby's soul. So filled was she with lofty devotion to the cause, so complete her faith in its holiness, and so unquestioning her belief that it was every one's simple duty to brave all dangers for it, and die if need be without a murmur, that contact with her would have inspired with pure patriotic ardor a nature much less ready for such leavening than Harry's.

As Dr. Denslow had surmised, his faults were mainly superficial, and underneath them was a firm gristle of manhood, which would speedily harden into bone. With the experience he had been having, days would mature this as rapidly as ordinary years. He was himself hardly aware of the transformation, but only felt, as his physical exhaustion disappeared, a new eagerness to participate in the great work of the war. He was gratified to know a little later that this was no transient feeling. In the course of the evening Jim Fortner came back in, with Kent Edwards and Abe Bolton. After they had all satisfied their hunger, Fortner informed Harry and Aunt

Debby that the enemy had fallen back to London, from which point he was sending out wagons into the surrounding country, to gather up food, forage, arms, clothing, ammunition, etc., with the double object of depriving the Union men of them, and adding the same to the Rebel resources. A long train had also been sent out to the Goose Creek Salt Works--twenty-five miles northeast of London--to bring away a lot of salt stored there, of which the Rebels had even more need than of food.

Fortner proposed to go out in the morning, and endeavor to capture some of these wagons. It seemed altogether probably that a few might be caught in such a position that their guards could be killed or driven off.

All readily agreed to this plan, Aunt Debby leading off by volunteering to ride ahead on her mare, as a scout.

Harry suddenly remembered that he was weaponless. "What shall I do for a gun?" he asked, anxiously.

"I declar, I done forgot all 'bout gittin' ye a gun," said Fortner with real concern. "My mind was disturbed by other things," he added with a suspicion of a grin at Edwards and Bolton; but they were leaning back in their chairs fast asleep. Apple jack, fatigue and a hearty supper together made a narcotic too potent to resist.

Fortner rose, spread a few blankets on the floor, added a sack of bran for a pillow, and with some difficulty induced the two sleepers to lie down and take their slumbers in a more natural position.

"I'll find ye a gun," said Aunt Debby, as this operation was finished, and walking to a farther corner of the room, she came back bearing in her hand a rifle very similar to the one Fortner carried.

"Thar," she said, setting the delicately-curved brazen heel down upon the hearth, and holding the muzzle at arm's length while she gazed at the gun with the admiration one can not help feeling for a magnificent weapon, "is ez true a rifle ez ever a man put to his shoulder. Ef I didn't b'lave ye ter be ez true ez steel ye shouldn't tech hit, fur hit b'longed ter the truest man in this livin' world."

"Hit wuz her husband's," explained Fortner, as her lips met firmly, as if choking down bitter memories.

"I'm givin' hit ter ye ter use ez he'd a-used hit ef he war a-livin'," she said, steadying her tones with a perceptible effort. "I'm glad thet my hands can put inter yours the means ter avenge him."

Harry tried in vain to make an appropriate response.

"I'll clean hit up for ye," she said to Harry, as she saw Fortner beginning to furbish up his own rifle for the next day's duties.

That she was no stranger to the work was shown by the skill with which she addressed herself to it. Nothing that a Kentucky mountaineer does has more of the aspect of a labor of love, than his caring for a find rifle, and any of them would have been put to shame by the deftness of Aunt Debby's supple hands. Removing the leathern hood which protected the lock, she carefully rubbed off the hammer and nipple with a wisp of soft fine tow, and picked out the tube with a needle. Wrapping another bit of tow around the end of a wiping-stick, she moistened it slightly in her mouth, and carefully swabbed out of the inside of the barrel every suspicion of dust and dirt. Each of the winding rifles was made clean and free along its whole course. Then the tow swab was lightly touched with sweet, unsalted goose-fat, that it might spread a rust-preventing film over the interior surface. She burnished the silver and brass ornaments, and rubbed the polished stock until it shone. When not a suspicion of soil or dirt remained any where, the delicate double triggers were examined and set so that they would yield at the stroke of a hair, a tuft of lightly-oiled tow was placed over the nipple and another closed the muzzle.

"Thar," said Aunt Deby, setting the gun back against the logs, "is a rifle that'll allers do hits duty, ef the man a-holt of hit does his. Let's see how the ammunition is."

The powder horn was found to be well filled with powder, and the box with caps, but there were only a few bullets.

"I'll run ye some," she said, taking from a shelf a small iron ladle, a few bars of lead, and a pair of bullet molds. "Fur more'n a hunderd years the women uv our fam'ly hev run all the bullets our menfolks shot. They b'lieved hit made 'em lucky. Granfather Fortner killed an Injun chief acrost the Maumee River at the battle of Fallen Timbers with a bullet thet Granmother hed run fur him an' markt with a little cross. Afore the battle begun Franfather tuck the bullet outen his pouch an' put hit inter his mouth, until he could git a chance ter use hit on big game. He brot the chief's scalp hum ter Granmother."

"I believe the bullets you cast for me will do good service," said Harry, with sincerity in his tones.

"I'm sartin of hit," she returned, confidently. "I hev adopted ye in my heart ez a son, an' I feel towards ye ez ef ye were raylly uv my own kin. I know ye'll be a credit to yerself an' me."

While the lead was melting upon the bed of coals she drew out on the hearth, she sat in her low chair with her hands clasped about her knees, and her great gray eyes fixed upon the depths of a mass of glowing embers in the fireplace, as if she saw there vivid pictures of the past or revelations of the future.

"How wonderfully bright an' glowin' hit is in thar," she said musingly; "hit's purer an' brighter then ennything else on arth. 'Purified ez by fire,' the Book says. My God, Thou has sent Thy fires upon me ez a sweepin' flood. Hev they purified me ez Thou wisht? How hit shines an' glows away in thar! Hit seems so deep sometimes thet I kin skeercely see the end. A million times purer an' brighter is the light thet shines from the Throne uv God. THEY'RE lookin' at thet now, while I still tarry heah. Husband an' son, when will I go to ye? When will I finish the work the Lord hez fur me ter do? When will the day uv my freedom come? May-be to-morrer--may-be to-morrer."

She began singing softly:

"An' when a shadder falls acrost the winder
      Of my room,
When I am workin' my app'inted task,
I lift my head to watch the door an' ask
      If he is come;
An' the angel answers sweetly
      In my home:
'Only a few more shadders
      An' He will come.'"

"Aunt Debby, honey," said Fortner, rousing himself from a nap in his chair, "thet thar lead's burnin'. Better run yer bullets."

She started as if waked from a trance, pressed her slender thin hands to her eyes for an instant, and then taking the molds up in herleft hand she raised the ladle with her right, filled them from it, knocked the molded balls out by a tap on the floor, and repeated the process with such dexterous quickness that she had made fifty bullets before harry realized that she was fairly at work.

"Ye men hed better lay down an' git some sleep," she said, as she replaced the molds and ladle on the shelf. "Ye'll need all yer strength to-morrer. I'll neck these bullets, an' git together some vittles fur the trip, an' then I'll lay down a while. We orter start airly--soon arter daybreak."

They did start early the next morning, with Aunt Debby riding upon the roads that wound around the mountain sides, while Fortner led the men through the shorter by-paths.

Noon had passed some hours, and yet they had come across no signs of wagons. Aunt Debby was riding along a road cut out of the rocks about mid-way up the mountain. To her right the descent was almost perpendicular for a hundred feet or more to where a creek ran at the bottom of a cliff. To her left the hill rose up steeply to a great height. Fortner and the others saw Aunt Debby galloping back, waving the red handkerchief which was her signal of the approach of a wagon. After her galloped a Rebel Sergeant, with revolver drawn shouting to her to stop or he would fire. Abe Bolton stepped forward impulsively to shoot the Rebel, missed his footing, and slid down the hill, landing in the orad with such force as to jar into unintelligibiliy a bitter imprecation he had constructed for the emergency. He struck in front of the Sergeant, who instantly fired at Aunt Debby's mare, sending a bullet through the faithful animal, which sank to her knees, and threw her rider to the ground. Without waiting to rise, and he was not certain that he could, Abe fired his musket, but missed both man and horse. He scrambled to his feet, and ran furiously at the Rebel with raised gun. The Sergeant fired wildly at him, when Bolton struck the animal a violent blow across the head. It recoiled, slipped, and in another instant had fallen over the side of the road, and crushed his rider on the rocks below. Five of the wagon-guard who were riding ahead of the wagon galloped forward at the sound of the shots. Fortner, Edwards and Harry Glen fired into these, and three saddles were emptied. The remaining two men whirled their horses around, fired wildly into the air, and dashed back upon the plunging team, with which the driver was vainly struggling. The ground quivered as the frightened animals struck together; they were crushed back upon their haunches, and beat one another cruelly with their mighty hoofs. Wagon, horses and men reeled on the brink an agonizing instant; the white-faced driver dropped the lines and sprang to the secure ground; the riders strained with the energy of deadly fear to tear themselves loose from their steeds, but in vain. Then the frantic mess crashed down the jagged rocks, tearing up the stunted cedars as if they were weeds, and fell with a sounding splash on the limestone bed of the shallow creek.

Fortner, Glen and Edwards came down as quickly as possible, the latter spraining his ankle badly by making a venturesome leap to reach the road first. They found a man that Fortner had shot at stone dead, with a bullet through his temple. The other two had been struck in the body. Their horses stood near, looking wonderingly at their prostrate masters.

Bolton was rubbing his bruises and abrasions, and vituperating everything, from the conduct of the war to the steepness of Kentucky mountains. Aunt Debby had partially recovered from the stunning of her fall, and limped slowly up, with her long riding-skirt raised by one hand. Her lips were compressed, an her great gray eyes blazed with excitement.

They all went to the side of the road, and looked down at the crushed and bleeding mass in the creek.

"My God! that's awful," said Henry, with a rising sickness about his heart, as the excitement began subsiding.

"Plenty good enuf fur scoundrels who rob poor men of all they hev," said Fortner fiercely, as he re-loaded his rifle. "Hit's not bad enuf fur thieves an' robbers."

"Hit's God's judgement on the wicked an' the opporessor," said Aunt Debby, with solemn pitilessness.

"Hadn't we better try to get down there, and help those men out?" suggested Harry. "Perhaps they are not dead yet."

"Aunt Debby, thet thar hoss thet's rain' his head an' whinnyin'," said Fortner, with sudden interest, "is Joel Sprigg's roan geldin', sho's yore bo'n, honey." He pointed to where a shapely head was raised, and almost human agony looked out of great liquid eyes. "Thet wuz the finest hoss in Laurel County, an' they've stole 'im from Joel. Hit'll 'bout break his heart, fur he set a powerful sight o'store on thet there beast. Pore critter! hit makes me sick ter see 'im suffer thet-a-way! I've a mind ter put 'im outen his misery, but I'm afeered I can't shoot 'im, so long ez he looks at me with them big pitiful eyes o' his'n. They go right ter my heart."

"You'd better shoot him," urged Aunt Debby. "Hit's a si ter let an innocent critter suffer thet-a-way."

Fortner raised his rifle, and sent a bullet through the mangled brute's brain.

Aunt Debby's eyes became fixed on a point where, a mile away down the mountain, a bend in the road was visible through an opening in the trees.

"Look out," she said, as the echoes of the shot died away, "thar comes a hull lot on 'em."

They looked and saw plainly a large squad of cavalry, with a wagon behind.

"We must get outen heah, an' thet quick," said Fortner decisively. He caught one of the horses and shortened a stirrup to make the sadle answer for a side-saddle. "Heah, Aunt Debby, let me help ye up, honey. Now Bolton and Edwards, I'll help ye on these ere other critters. Now skeet out ez fast ez the hosse's legs will tote ye. Don't spar 'em a mite. Them fellers'll gin ye to the devil's own chase ez soon ez they get heah, an' see what's bin done. Glen and me'll go acrost the mounting, an' head 'em off on t'other side. Don't come back ef ye heah shootin', but keep straight on, fur we kin take keer o' this crowd without enny help. glen, you sasshay up the mounting thar ez fast ez the Lord'll let ye. I'll be arter ye right spry."

All sped away as directed. Fortner had been loading his gun while speaking. He now rammed the bullet home, and withdrawing his rammer walked over to the cliff beside which the teamster was cowering.

"O, Mister Fortner, don't kill me--please don't!" whined the luckless man, getting awkwardly upon his knees and raising his hands imploringly. "I swar ter God I'll never raise a hand agin a Union man agin ef ye'll only spar my life."

"Kill ye, Pete Hoskins!" said Fortner with unfathomable contempt. "What consete ye hev ter think yer wuth the powder an' lead. I hain't no bullets ter waste on carr'on."

He struck the abject fellow a couple of stinging blows on the face with the ramrod, replaced it in the thimbles, and sprang up the rocks just as the head of the cavalry appeared around the bend of the road a few rods away.

Overtaking Harry shortly, he heard about the same time the Rebels on the road below strike into a trot.

"They know hit all now," he said, "an' hev started in chase. Let's jog on lively, an' get ter whar we kin head 'em off."

Night had fallen in the meantime, but the full moon had risen immediately, making it almost as light as day.

After half an hour's fast walking, the two Unionists had cut across the long horseshoe around which the Rebels were traveling, and had come down much ahead of them on the other side of the mountain, and just where the road led up the steep ascent of another mountain.

There was a loneliness about the spot that was terrible. Over it hung the "thought and deadly feel of solitude." The only break for miles in the primeval forest was that made for the narrow road. House or cabin there was none in all the gloomy reaches of rocks and gnarled trees. It was too inhospitable a region to tempt even the wildest squatter.

The flood of moonlight made the desolation more oppresive than ever, by making palpable and suggestive the inky abysses under the trees and in the thickets.

Fortner looked up the road to his right and listened intently.

A waterfall mumbled somewhere in the neighborhood. The pines and hemlocks near the summit sighed drearily. A gray fox, which had probably just supped off a pheasant, sat on a log and barked out his gluttonous satisfaction. A wildcat, as yet superless, screamed its envy from a cliff a half a mile away.

"I can't heah anything of Aunt Debby an' the others," said Fortner, at length; "so I reckon they're clean over the mounting, an' bout safe by this time. Them beasts are purty good travelers, I imagine, an' they hain't let no grass grow in under the'r hufs."

"But the Rebels are coming, hand over hand," said Harry, who had been watching to the left and listening. "I hear them quite plainly. Yes, there they are," he continued, as two or three galloped around a turn in the road, followed at a little interval by others.

The metallic clang of the rapid hoof-beats on the rocks rang through the somber aisles of the forest. Noisy fox and aniphonal wildcat stopped to listen to this invasion of sound.

"Quick! let's get in cover," said Fortner.

"Ye make fur thet rock up thar," said Fortner to Harry, pointing to a spot several hundred yards above them, "and stay thar tell I come. Keep close in the shadder, so's they won't see ye."

"It seems to me that I ought to stay with you,' said Harry, indecisively.

"No; go. Ye can't do no good heah. One's better nor two. I'll be up thar soon. Go, quick."

There was no time for debate, and Harry did as bidden.

Fortner stepped into the inky shadow of a large rock, against which he leaned. The great broad face of the rock, gray from its covering of minute ash-colored lichens, was toward the pursuers, and shone white as marble in the flood of moonlight. The darkness seemed banked up around him, but within his arm's length it was as light as day. The long rifle barrel reached from the darkness into the light, past the corner of the rock against which it rested. The bright rays made the little "bead" near the muzzle gleam like a diamond, and lighted up the slit as fine as a hair in the hind-sight. Three little clicks, as if of twigs breaking under a rabbit's foot, told that the triggers had been set and the hammer raised.

The horsemen, much scattered by the pursuit, clattered onward. In ones and twos, with wide intervals between, they reached along a half-mile of the road. Two--the best mounted--rode together at the head. Two hundred yards below the great white rock, which shone as innocent and kindly as a fleecy Summer cloud, a broad rivulet wound its way toward the neighboring creek. The blown horses scented the grateful water, and checked down to drink of it. The right-hand rider loosened his bridle that his steed might gratify himself. The other tightened his rein and struck with his spurs. His horse "gathered," and leaped across the stream. As the armed hoofs struck sparks from the smooth stones on the opposite side, the rider of the drinking horse saw burst out of the white rock above them a gray cloud, with a central tongue of flame, and his comrade fell to the ground.

His immediate reply with both barrels of his shotgun showed that he did not mistake this for any natural phenomenon. The sound of the shots brought the rest up at a gallop, and a rapid fire was opened on the end of the rock.

But the instant Fortner fired he sprang back behind the rock, and then ran under its cover a little distance up the mountain side to a dense laurel thicket, in which he laid down behind a log and reloaded his rifle. He listened. The firing had ceased, and a half-dozen dismounted men were carefully approaching the spot whence he had sent the fatal shot. He heard the Captain order a man to ride back and bring up the wagon, that the body of the dead man might be put in it. As the wagon was heard rumbling up, the dismounted men reported to the Captain that the bushwhacker had made good his escape and was no longer behind the rock.

"Well, he hasn't gone very far," said the Captain with a savage oath. "He can't have got any distance away, and I'll have him, dead or alive, before I leave this spot. The whole gang of Lincolnite hellhounds are treed right up there, and not one of them shall get away alive." He put a bone whistle to his lips, and sounded a shrill signal. A horseman trotted up from the rear in response to the call, leading a hound with a leash. "Take the dog up to that rock, there, Bill," said the Captain, "and set him on that devil's trail. Five more of you dismount, and deploy there on the other side of the road. All of you move forward cautiously, watching the dog, and make sure you 'save' teh whelp when he is run out."

The men left their saddles and moved forward with manifest reluctance. They had the highly emotional nature usual in the poor white of the South, and this was deeply depressed by the weird loneliness that brooded over everything, and the bloodshed they had witnessed. Their thirst for vengeance was being tempered rapidly by a growing superstitious fear. There was something supernatural in these mysterious killings. Each man, therefore, only moved forward as he felt the Captain's eye on him, or his comrades advanced.

The dog, after some false starts, got the scent, and started to follow Fortner's footsteps.

"He's done tuck the trail, Cap'n," called back one of the men.

"All right," answered the officer, "don't take your eyes off of him for a second till he trees the game."

But the logs and rocks and the impenetrable darkness in the shadows made it impossible to follow the movements of the hound every moment. Only Fortner was able to do this. He could see the great greenish-yellow eyes burn in the pitchy-depths and steadily draw nearer him. They entered the laurel thicket, and the beast growled as he felt the nearness of his prey.

"Wolf must be gitten close ter him," said one of the men.

Fortner laid his rifle across the log, and drew from his belt a long keen knife. He stirred slightly in doing this, and in turning to confront the dog. The hound sprang forward with a growl that was abruptly ended, for Fortner's left hand shot out like an arrow, and caught the loose folds of skin on the brute's neck, and the next instant his right, armed with the knife, descended and laid the animal's shoulder and neck open with a deep cut. But the darkness made Fortner mistake his distance. He neither caught the dog securely, nor sent the knife to his heart, as he intended, and the hound tearing away, ran out into the moonlight, bleeding and yelping. Before he reached his human allies Fortner had silently sped back a hundred yards, to a more secure shelter, so that the volley which was poured into he thicket only endangered the lives of the chipmunks denizened there. The mounted men rode forward and joined those on foot, in raking the copse with charges of buckshot.

Away above Fortner and Harry rose yells and the clatter of galloping horses. Before they could imagine what this meant a little cavalcade swept by at a mad gallop, yelling at the tops of their voices, and charging directly at the Rebels below. In front were Aunt Debby, Bolton and Edwards, riding abreast, and behind them three men in homespun.

The Rebels seemed totally unnerved by this startling apparition. The dismounted ones flung themselves on their horses and all fled away at a gallop, without attempting to make a stand and without taking thought of their wagon. As they scurried along the opposite mountain-side Fortner and Harry fired at them, but without being able to tell whether their shots took effect.

The pursuit was carried but a little distance. The wagon was secured and taken up the mountain. A little after midnight the summit was passed, and Fortner led the way into an opening to the right, which eventually brought up at a little level spot in front of a large cave. The horses where unhitched and unsaddled, a fire built, cedar boughs gathered to make a bed on the rocky floor of the cave, and they threw themselves down upon this to sleep the sleep of utter weariness.

In the meantime Harry had learned taht the new comers were cousins of Fortner's, who, being out on a private scouting expedition, had been encountered by Aunt Debby and the others, near the summit of the mountain, and had started back with them to the assistance of Fortner. The sound of firing had so excited them that the suggestion of a charge by Kent Edwards was eagerly acceded to.

"It must be near three o'clock," said Kent, looking up at the stars, as he came back stealthily from laying the saddle blanket, which was the only covering he and Abe had, upon the sleeping form of Aunt Debby, "and my downy couch still waits for me. My life-long habits of staid respectability have been greatly shaken recently."

Abe groaned derisively.

An inspection, the next morning of the wagon's load, showed it to be mainly made up of hams, shoulders and sides, plundered from the smokehouses visited. With these were a number of guns, including several fine rifles, and all the ammunition that could be found along the route.

A breakfast was made of slices of ham broiled on the ends of sticks, and then a consultation was held as to the plans for the day's operations.

The result of this was a decision that Aunt Debby and one of the newcomers should go back and inform the neighborhood of what had taken place, gather a party to remove the dead from the creek and bury them, to keep the water from being poisoned, and recover what property might be found with the first wagon. Kent Edwards, Abe Bolton, and two of the new comers would scout down toward London, to ascertain the truth of the rumor that Zollicoffer had evacuated the place, and retired to Laurel Bridge, nine miles south of it. Fortner and Harry Glen would take the wagon to Wildcat Gap, report what had been done, and explain to their commander the absence of the enlisted men.

"Shade of King Solomon," said Kent to Abe, after their party had ridden for two or three hours through the mountains toward London. "I wonder if there is any other kind of worldly knowledge that I know as little about as I did of scouting when we started out? My eyes have been opened to my own ignorance. I used to have the conceit that we two could play a fair hand at any game of war they could get up for our entertainment. But these Kentuckians give me points every hundred yards that I never so much as dreamed of. Theirs is the wisdom of serpents when compared with our dove-like innocence."

"I like dove-like innocence," interrupted Abe.

"But did you ever see anybody that could go through the country as these fellows can? It's just marvelous. They know every short cut to every point, and they know just where to go every time to see way ahead without being seen themselves. It would puzzle the sharpest Rebel bushwhacker to get the drop on them."

"I don't know as I want to learn their way of doing," said Abe crustily. "It looks like sneaking, on a big scale, that's all. And I'm ashamed of this laying round behind a log or a rock to pop a man over. It ain't my style at all. I believe in open and above-board fighting, give and take, and may the best man win."

"So do I, though I suppose all's fair in war. But when we scout we give them the same chance to knock us over that they give us when they scout. I'll admit it looks very much like murder to shoot men down that way, for it does not help either side along a particle. But these Kentuckians have a great many private injuries to avenge, and they can't do it any other way."

All the people of the region were intensely Union, so it was not difficult to get exact information of the movements of the Rebels, and as the scouts drew near London they became assured that not only all of Zollicoffer's infantry, but his small parties of cavalry had retreated beyond the town. Our scouts therefore, putting Edwards and Bolton to the front, that their blue uniforms might tell the character of the party, spurred into a gallop, and dashed into London, to be received with boundless enthusiasm.

"Somebody ought to ride back to Wildcat immediately," said Kent, after they had enjoyed their reception a little while, "and report this to the General."

All assented to this position.

"It is really the duty of myself and comrade here to do it," said Kent, shifting uneasily in his chair, to find a comfortable place to sit upon; "but as we have been for two days riding the hardest-backed horses over roads that were simply awful, and as previous to that time we had not taken any equestrian exercise for several years, there are some fundamental reasons--that is, reasons lying at the very base of things, (he shifted again)--why we should not be called upon to do another mile of horseback riding until Time has had an opportunity to exercise his soothing and healing influence, so to speak. Abe, I believe I have stated the case with my usual happy combination of grace and delicacy?"

"You have, as usual, flushed a tail-race of big words."

"In short," Kent went on ("Ah, thank you. That is delicious. The best I ever drank. Your mountain stills make the finest apple jack in the world. There must be something in the water--that you don't put in. It's as smooth as new-made butter. Well, here's to the anner of Beauty and Glory.) In short, as I was saying when you hospitably interrupted me, we are willing to do anything for the cause, but unless there is some other way of riding, the most painful effort I could make for our beloved country would be to mount that horse again, and ride another hundred yards.

To be messenger of this good news would be bliss; what prevents it is a blister."

The crowd laughed boisterously.

"Mister," said one of the Kentuckians who accompanied them, with that peculiar drawling inflection of the word that it were hopeless to attempt to represent in print, "ef ye want ter send some one in yer places me an' Si heah will be powerful glad ter go. Jes' git a note ter the Jineral at Wildcat ready while we saddle fresh beasts, an' we'll hev hit in his hands afore midnight."

The proposition was immediately accepted, and in a little while the Kentuckians were speeding their way back to Gen. Schoepf, with a letter giving the news, and signed: "Kent Edwards, Chief of Scouts."

That evening a party of young men who had followed the Rebel retreat some distance, brought in a wagon which had been concealed in an out-of-the-way place, and left there. It was loaded mainly with things taken from the houses, and was evidently the private collection of some freebooting subordinate, who did not intend that the Southern Confederacy should be enriched by the property. Hence, probably, the hesitation about taking it along with the main train. It was handed over to Kent as the representative of the United States, who was alone authorized to take charge of it. Assisted by Abe he started to make an inventory of the contents. A portly jug of apple jack was kept at hand, that there might not be any suffering from undue thirst during the course of the operation, which, as Kent providently remarked, was liable to make a man as dry as an Arizona plain.

The danger of such aridity seemed to grow more imminent continually, judged by the frequency of their application to the jug. It soon became more urgent than the completion of the inventory. Frequent visits of loyal Kentuckians with other jugs and botles, to drink to the renewed supremacy of the Banner of Beauty and Glory, did not diminish Kent's and Abe's apprehensions of ultimate thirst. Their clay seemed like some other kinds, which have their absorptive powers strengthened by the more they take up. They belonged to a not-unusual class of men whom it takes about as long to get thoroughly drunk as it does to heat up an iron-furnace, but the condition that they achieve then makes the intoxication of other and ordinary men seem a very mild and tame exhilaration.

By noon the next day this process was nearing its completion. A messenger galloped into town with the information that the Union forces were coming, and would arrive in the course of an hour or two.

"Shash so?" said Kent, straightening himself up with a crushing dignity that always formed a sure guage of the extent to which inebriation had progressed. "Shash so? Troops 'she United States 'bout to enter shis lovely metropolis wish all pomp and shircumshtance 'reassherted 'thority. 'Shtonishin' event; wonderful 'casion. Never happened 'fore; probably never'll happen again. Ought to be 'propriately celebrated, Abe!"

That gentleman made a strong effort to control joints which seemed unmanageable, and succeeded in assuming a tolerable erectness, while he blinked at his companion with stolid gravity.

"Abe, shis ish great 'casion. Greatest in she annalsh of she country. We're only representatives Government in she town. Burden whole shing fallsh on us. Understand? We musht do everyshing. Understand? Country 'spects every man to do his duty. Undershtand?"

Abe sank down on a bench, leaned his head against the wall, and looked at his companion with one eye closed wearily.

"Yesshir," Kent resumed, summoning up a new supply of oratorical energy, and an official gravity beneath which his legs trembeled. "Name shis town's London. Shame name's big town 'cross ocean. Lots history c'nected wish name. Shtacks an' cords of it. Old times when King went out t'meet him, wish shtyle pile on bigger'n a haystack. Fact. Clothes finer'n a peacock. Tendered him keys, freed'm city. All shat short shing. Ver' impreshive shpectacle. Everybody felt better'n for improvin' sight. Undershtand? We'll be Lord Mayor and train for shis London. We can rig out right here. Our trouseau's here in shis hair trunk."

"Shall we get anyshing t' drink?" inquired Abe making a temporary collection of his wits with a violent effort.

"Abe!" the freezing severity of Kent's tone and manner would have been hopelessly fatal to early vegetables. "Abe you've many good qualities--more of 'em shan any man I know. but a degrading passion fur shtrong drink is ruinin' you. I'm your besht fren, an' shay it wish tearsh in m' eyes. Lemme beg o' you t' reform ere it ish too late. Beware of it, my fren, beware of it. It shtingeth like a serpent, an' biteth like a multiplier--I mean an adder. You haven't got my shuperb self-control, an' so yer only shafety lies in total abstinence. Cheese it, my fren, cheese it on she sheductive but fatal lush."

"Are we goin' out t' meet she boysh?" inquired Abe.

"Shertainly we are. Yesshir. An' we're goin' out ash I proposed. Yer a shplen-did feller, Abe," continued Kent, with lofty patronage. "A shplendid feller, an' do great credit t' yer 'portunities. But y' haven't had my 'dvantages of mingling constantly in p'lite s'ciety, y'know. Rough diamond, I know, 'nall that short o' shing, but lack polish an' easy grace. So I'll be th' Lord Mayor, an' y'll be th' train. Undershtand?"

He lurched forward, and came near falling over the chair, but recovering he stiffened up and gazed on that useful article of furniture with a sternness that implied his belief that it was a rascally blackleg trying to insinuate itself into the circle of refinement and chaste elegance of which he was the particular ornament.

"Come," he resumed, "le's bedizen ourselves; le's assume th' shplendor 'propriate t' th' 'casion."

When the troops marched in in the afternoon, the encountered at the head of the crowd that met them at the crossing of the creek just ouside of town, a man who seemed filled with deep emotion, and clothed with strange fancies. He wore a tall silk hat of antique patter, carefully brushed, which he protected from the rays of the sun with a huge blue cotton umbrella. A blue broadcloth coat, with gilt buttons, sat jauntily over a black satin vest, and nankeen trousers. A pair of gold spectacles reposed in magisterial dignity about half way down his nose, and a large silver-headed cane in the left hand balanced the umbrella in the right. By the side of the man with rare vestments stood another figure of even more limpness of general bearing, whose garb consisted of a soldier's uniform pantaloons and woolen shirt--none too clean--set off by a black dress-coat, and white linen vest.

As the head of the column came up he in the blue broadcloth pulled off his hat and spectacles, and addressed himself to speech:

"Allow me, shir, to welcome you with hoshpitable hands to a bloody--no, let me tender you, shir, the liberties of our city, and reshoice shat she old banner which has braved she battle, hash---"

The column had stopped, and the Captain commanding the advance was listening patiently to what he supposed was the address of an enthusiastic, but eccentric old Kentuckian, when one of the sharp-eyed ones in the company shouted out:

"I declare, it's Kent Edwards and Abe Bolton."

The yell of laughter and applause at the ludicrous masquerade shook the hills. The Colonel rode up to see what occasioned it. He recognized his two men, and his face darkened with anger.

"You infernal rascals," he shouted, "you have been off plundering houses, have you, in place of being with your company. I'll stop this sort of thing mighty sudden. This regiment shall not degrade itself by plundering and robbing, if I have to shoot every man in it. Captain, arrest those men, and keep thim in close confinement until I can have them tried and properly punished."

Chapter XVII. Alspaugh on a Bed of Pain.

This is the very ecstacy of love,
Whose violent property foredoes itself.
And leads the will to desperate undertakings
As often as any passion under Heaven
That does afflict our natures.

--Hamlet

Endurance is made possible by reason of the element of divisibility. Metaphysical mathematicians imagine that there is possibly a "fourth dimension," by the existence of which many hitherto inexplicable phenomena may be explained. They think that probably this fourth dimension is SUCCESSION OF TIME.

So endurance of unendurable things is explainable on the ground that but a small portion of them has to be endured in any given space of time.

It is the old fable of the clock, whose pendulum and wheels stopped one day, appalled by the discovery that they would have to move and tick over three million times a year for many wearisome years, but resumed work again when reminded that they would only have to tick ONCE each second.

So it was with Rachel Bond.

The unendurable whole of a month's or a week's experience was endurable when divided in detail and spread over the hours and days.

She was a woman--young and high-natured.

Being a woman she had a martyr-joy in affliction that comes in the guise of duty. Young, she enjoyed the usefulness and importance attached to her work in the hospital. High-natured, she felt a keen satisfaction in triumphing over daily difficulties and obstacles, even though these were mainly her own feelings.

Though months had gone by it seemed as if no amount of habituation could dull the edge of the sickening disgust which continually assailed her sense and womanly instincts. The smells were as nauseating, the sights as repulsive, the sounds of misery as saddening as the day when she first set foot inside the hospital.

From throbbing heart to dainty finger-tip, every fiber in her maidenly body was in active rebellion while she ministered to the rough and coarse men who formed the bulk of the patients, and whose afflictions she could not help knowing were too frequently the direct result of their own sins and willful disobedience of Nature's laws.

One day, when flushed and wearied with the peevish exactions of a hulking fellow whose indisposition was trifling, she said to Dr. Denslow:

"It is distressing to find out how much unmanliness there is in apparently manly men."

"Yes," answered the doctor, with his customary calm philosophy; "and it is equally gratifying to find out how much real manliness there is in some apparently unmanly men. You have been having an experience with some brawny subject?"

"Yes. If the fellow's spirit were equal to his bone and brawn, he would o'ertop, Julius Caesar. Instead, he whimpers like a school-girl."

"That's about the way it usually goes. It may be that my views are colored by my lacking three or four inches of six feet, but I am sometimes strongly inclined to believe that every man--big or little--is given about the same amount of will or vital power, and the bigger and more lumbering the body he has to move with it, the less he accomplishes, and the sooner it is exhausted. You have found, I have no doubt, that as a rule the broad-chested, muscular six-footers, whose lives have ever passed at hard work in the open air, groan and sigh incessantly under the burden of minor afflictions, worry every one with their querulousness, moan for their wives, mothers, or sweethearts, and the comforts of the homes they have left, and finally fret and grieve themselves into the grave, while slender, soft-muscled boys bear real distress without a murmur, and survive sickness and wounds that by all rules ought to prove fatal."

"There is certainly a good deal in that; but what irritates me now is a display of querulous tyranny."

"Well, you know what Dr. Johnson says: 'That a sick man is a scoundrel.' There is a basis of truth in that apparent cruelty. It is true that 'scoundrel' is rather a harsh term to apply to a man whose moral obliquities have not received the official stamp in open court by a jury of his peers. The man whose imprudences and self-indulgences have made his liver slothful, his stomach rebellious, and wrecked his constitution in other ways, may--probably does--become an exasperating little tyrant, full of all manner of petty selfishness, which saps the comfort of others, as acid vapors corrode metals, but does that make him a 'scoundrel?' Opinions vary. His much enduring feminine relatives would probably resent such a query with tearful indignation, while unprejudiced outsiders would probably reply calmly in the affirmative."

"What is the medical man's view?" asked Rachel, much amused by this cool scrutiny of what people are too often inclined to regard as among the "inscrutable providences."

"I don't speak in anything for the profession at large, but my own private judgement is that any man is a scoundrel who robs others of anything that is of value to them, and he is none the less so when he makes his aches and pains, mostly incurred by his gluttony, passions or laziness, the means of plundering others of the comforts and pleasures which are their due."

Going into the wards one morning, Rachel found that Lieutenant Jacob Alspaugh had been brought in, suffering from what the Surgeon pronounced to be "febrile symptoms of a mild type, from which he will no doubt recover in a few days, with rest, quiet and proper food.

It is possibly worth while to note the coincidence that these symptoms developed with unexpected suddenness in the midst of earnest preparations by the Army of the Cumberland, for a terrible grapple at Perryville with the Rebel Army of the Tennessee.

Alspaugh recognized Rachel at once, much to her embarrassment, for her pride winced at playing the role of nurse before an acquaintance, especially when that acquaintance was her father's hired-man, whom she knew too well to esteem highly.

"O, Miss Rachel," he groaned, as she came to his cot in response to his earnest call, "I'm so glad to see you, for I'm the sickest man that ever came into this hospital.

Nothin' but the best o' care 'll carry me through, and I know you'll give it to me for the sake of old times," and Jacob's face expressed to his comrades the idea that there had been a time when his relations with her had been exceedingly tender.

Rachel's face flushed at the impudent assumption, but she overcame the temptation to make a snubbing answer, and replied quietly:

"No, Jacob, you are not so sick as you think you are." ("She calls him 'Jacob,'" audibly commented some of those near, as if this was a confirmation of Jakes insinuation.) "The Surgeons say," she continued, "that your symptoms are not at all bad, and that you'll be up again in a few days."

"O, them Doctors always talk that way. They're the flintiest-hearted set I ever see in all my born days. They're always pretending that they don't believe there is nothin' the matter with a feller. I really believe they'd a little liefer a man'd die than not. They don't seem to take no sort of interest in savin' the soldiers that the country needs so badly."

Rachel felt as if it would sweeten much hard service if she could tell Alspaugh outright her opinion that he was acting very calfishly; but other counsels prevailed, and she said encouragingly:

"You are only discouraged, Jacob--that's all. A few days rest here will restore both your health and your spirits."

"No, I'm not discouraged. I'm not the kind to git down in the mouth--you know me well enough for that. I'm sick, sick I tell you--sicker'n any other man in this hospital, an' nothin' but the best o' nursin' 'll save my life for the country. O, how I wish I was at home with my mother; she'd take care o' me."

Rachel could not repress a smile at the rememberance of Jake's termagant mother nad her dirty, comfortless cottage, an how her intemperance in administering such castisement as conveyed most grief to a boy's nature first drove Jake to seek refuge with her father.

"No doubt it would be very comfortable," she answered, "if you could get home to your mother; but there's no need of it, because you'll be well before you could possibly reach there."

"No, I'll never be well," persisted Jake, "unless I have the best o' care; but I feel much better now, since I find you here, for I'm sure you'll take as much interest in me as a sister would."

She shuddered a little at the prospect of even temporary sisterly relations to the fellow, but replied guardedly:

"Of course I'll do what I can for you, Jacob," and started to move away, but he caught her dress and whimpered:

"O, don't go, Miss Rachel; do go and leave me all alone. Stay any way till I'm fixed somehow comfortable."

"I half believe the booby will have hysterics," thought Rachel, with curling lip. "Is this the man they praised so for his heroism? Does all his manhood depend upon his health? Now he hasn't the spirit of a sick kitten." Dreading a scene, however, she took her seat at the head of the cot, and gave some directions for its arrangement.

Jake's symptoms grew worse rapidly, for he bent all his crafty energies to that end. Refuge in the hospital from the unpleasant contingencies attending duty in the field was a good thing, and it became superexcellent when his condition made him the object of the care and sympathy of so fine a young lady as Miss Rachel Bond. This he felt was something like compensation for all that he had endured for the country, and he would get as much of it as possible. His mind busied itself in recalling and imitating the signs of suffering he had seen in others.

He breathed stretorously, groaned and sighed immoderately, and even had little fits of well-feigned delirium, in which he babbled of home and friends and the war, and such other things as had come within the limited scope of his mental horizon.

"Don't leave me, Miss Rachel--don't leave me," he said, in one of these simulated paroxysms, clutching at the same time, with a movement singularly well directed for a delirious man, one of her delicate hands in his great, coarse, and not-over-clean fingers. Had it been the hand of a dying man, or of one in a raging fever, that imprisoned hers, Rachel would not have felt the repulsion that she did at a touch which betrayed to her only too well that the toucher's illness was counterfeited. She could hardly restrain the impulse to dash away the loathsome hand, as she would a toad that had fallen upon her, but she swiftly remembered, as she had in hundreds of other instances since she had been in the hospital, that she was no longer in her own parlor, but in a public place, with scores of eyes noting every movement, and that such an act of just disdain would probably be misunderstood, and possibly be ruinous to a belief in her genuine sympathy with the misfortunes of the sick which she had labored so heroically to build up.

She strove to release her fingers quietly, but at this Alspaugh's paroxysm became intense. He clung the tighter to her, and kneaded her fingers in a way that was almost maddening. Never in all her life had a man presumed to take such a familiarity with her. But her woman's wit did not desert her. With her disengaged hand she felt for and took out a large pin that fastened a bit of lace to her throat, with the desperate intent to give her tormentor a sly stab that would change the current of his thoughts.

But at the moment of carrying this into effect something caused her to look up, and she saw Dr. Denslow standing before her, with an amused look in his kindly, hazel eyes.

She desisted from her purpose and restored the pin to its place in obedience to a sign from him, which told her that he thoroughly understood the case, and had a more effective way of dealing with it than the thrust of a pin point.

"I'm very much afraid that this is a dangerous case we have here, Miss Bond," he said in a stage whisper, as if very anxious that the patient should not overhear. "Yes, a very dangerous case."

Jake grew pale, released Rachel's hand, turned over on his side and groaned.

"Do you really think so, Doctor?" said Rachel in the same tone.

"Yes, really. It's as clear a case of de gustibus non disputandum as I ever saw in my life."

"O, Lordie, hev I got all of that?" asked Jake, as he sat bolt upright, with eyes starting.

"It is my unpleasant duty to tell you that you certainly have," said the Doctor, gravely. "As plainly indicated as I ever saw it. Furthermore, it is seriously complicated with fiat justitia ruat caelum, with strong hints of the presence of in media tutissimus ibis."

"Great Scott! can I ever get well?" groaned poor Jake. Rachel's strain was on her risibles, and to make her face express only sympathy and concern.

"And," continued the remorseless Surgeon, in a tone of the kindliest commiseration, "in the absence of the least espirt de corps, and dulce et decorum est pro patria mori feeling in you it is apparent that none of your mental processes are going on properly, which deranges everything."

"Can't I be sent home to die?" whimpered the wretched Jake.

"Not in your present condition. I notice, in addition to what I have told you, that your heart is not right--its action is depraved, so to speak." This with a glance at Rachel, which brought the crimson to that damsel's cheek.

"O, Doctor, please try to do something for me right off, before I get any worse," pleaded Jake, with the tears starting in his eyes.

Rachel took this opportunity to slip away to where she could laugh unobserved. The Surgeon's facial muscles were too well trained to feel any strain. he continued in the same tone of gentle consideration:

"I have already ordered the preparation of some remedies. The Steward will be here in a few minues with the barber, who will shave your head, that we may apply a couple of fly-bisters behind your ears. They are also spreading a big mustard-plaster in th dispensary for you, which will cover your whole breast and stomach. These, with a strong dose of castor-oil, may bring you around so that you will be able to go back to duty in a short time."

Jake did not notice the unsheathed sarcasm in the Surgeon's allusion to returning to duty. He was too delighted with the chance of escaping all the horrors enumerated to think of aught else, and he even forgot to beg for Rachel to come and sit beside his bedside, as he had intended doing, until the blisters began to remind him that they stuck closer than a brother. After that he devoted his entire attention to them, as a man is apt to.

A good-sized blister, made according to the United States Pharmacopoeia, has few equals as a means of concentrating the attention. When it takes a fair hold of its work it leaves the gentleman whom it patronizes little opportunity to think of anything else than it and what it is doing. Everything else is forgotten, taht it may receive full consideration. Then comes in an opportunity for a vigorous imagination. No one ever underestimates the work done by an active blister, if it is upon himself. No one ever grumbles that he is not getting his money's worth. It is the one monumental exception, where men are willing to accept and be satisfied with a fractional part of that which they have bought and paid for.

So when the layer of fresh mustard that covered the whole anterior surface of Mr. Alspaugh's torso began to take a fair hold of its appointed work that gentlemen's thoughts became strangely focused upon it, and they succeeded each other as the minutes went by something in this fashion:

FIRST TEN MINUTES.--"I 'spect that this may become rather unpleasant and bothersome, but it will not be for long, and it'll really do me much good."

SECOND TEN MINUTES.--"I had no idead that blisters felt just this way, but they never really hurt anybody but women and children--MEN laugh at them."

THIRD TEN MINUTES.--"The thing seems to be hunting 'round for my tender spots, and pokin' pins into 'em. I begin to wish that it was all over with."

FOURTH TEN MINUTES.--"It begins to hurt real bad. I wonder if it ain't a'most time to take it off?"

FIFTH TEN MINUTES.--"The very devil seems to be in that thing. It burns like as if a sheet of red-hot iron was layin' there."

SIXTH TEN MINUTES.--"I surely believe that they've made a terrible mistake about that blister, and put in some awful thing that'll kill me if it ain't stopped. I'll swear it's not only eat all the skin off, but it's gone through my ribs, an' is gnawin' at my insides. Why don't the Doctor come 'round an' see to it? Here, nurse, call the Doctor, an' have this think taken off."

NURSE.--"No, it's all right. The Doctor left orders that it was not to be disturbed for some time yet. I'll see to it when the proper time comes. I'm watching the clock."

SEVENTH TEN MINUTES.--"Great Jehosefat! this's jest awful. That blasted stuff's cooked my innards to rags, an' I kin feel my backbone a-sizzlin'. Say, Steward, do, for the Lord's sake, come here, an' take this thing off, while there's a little life left in me."

STEWARD.--"Can't do anything yet. You must grin and bear it a little while longer."

EIGTH TEN MINUTES.--"Holy smoke! I couldn't suffer more if I was in the lake of burnin' brimstone. Every ounce of me's jest fryin'. Say, Steward! Steward!"

STEWARD (ANGRILY).--"I have told you several times that I couldn't do anything for you yet awhile. Now keep quiet."

"But Steward, can't you at least bring me a fork?"

"Why, what do you want a fork for?"

"Jest to see for myself if I ain't cooked done--that's all."

A roar of laughter went up in which even Dr. Denslow, who had just entered the ward, joined. He orderd the blister to be taken off, and the inflamed surfaces properly dressed, which was done to the accompaniment of Jake's agonizing groans.

"I think Lieutenant Alspaugh will be content to go back to the field in a few days, if we continue this vigorous treatment," Dr. Denslow said, a little later, as he came into the reading-room of the hospital where he found Rachel sitting alone.

"O, Doctor, how could you be so cruel?" she asked in tones which were meant to be reproachful, but only poorly disguised her mirthful appreciation of the whole matter.

"I wasn't cruel; I only did my duty. The fellow's a palpable malingerer, and his being here makes it ever so much worse. He's trying to shirk duty and have a good time here in the hospital. It's my place to make the hospital so unpleasant for him that he will think the field preferable, and I'm going to do it, especially if I find him squeezing your hand again."

There was that in the tone of the last sentence which sobered her instantly. Womanly prescience told her that the Surgeon had discovered what seemed to him a fitting opportunity to say that which he had long desired. Ever since she had been in the hospital he had exerted himself to smooth her path for her, and make her stay there endurable. There was not a day in which she was not indebted to him for some unobtrusive kindness, delicately and thoughtfully rendered.

While she knew quite well that these courtesies would have been as conscientiously extended to any other woman--young or old--in her position, yet her instincts did not allow her any doubt that there was about them a flavor personal to herself and redolent of something much warmer than mere kindliness. A knowledge of this had at times tainted the pleasure she felt in accepting welcome little attentions from him. She dreaded what she knew was coming. He took her hand and started to speak with tremulous lips. But almost at the same instant the door was flung open, and a nurse entered in breathless haste.

"O, Doctor," he gasped, "I've been looking for you everywhere. That Lieutenant in the First Ward thinks he's a-dyin'. He's groanin' an' cryin', and a-takin' on at a terrible rate, an' nobody can't do nothin' with him. The Steward wants you to come there right off."

"It's only the castor oil," muttered the Doctor savagely, as he rose to follow the nurse.

This was the letter that the Orderly handed Rachel some days later:

Dear Ratie: Your letter came at last, for which I was SO thankful, because I had waited SO long for it that I was SO tired and SO anxious that I was almost at my wits' end. I am SO glad that you are well, that you have got your room at last fixed up real nice and comfortable, as a young lady should have, and that you find your duties more agreeable. It is SO nice in that Dr. Denslow to help you along as he does. But then that is what every real gentleman should do for a young lady--or old one for that matter. Still, I would like to thank him SO much.

I am not at all well: my heart gives me SO much trouble--more than ever before--and as you say nothing about coming home I have about concluded to try what a change of climate and scene will do for me, and so have concluded to accept your Aunt Tabitha's invitation to spend a few months with her. Unless you hear from me to the contrary--which you will probably not, as the mails are so uncertain in Kentucky, you had better address your next letter to me at Eau Claire.

But I am so sorry to see by your letter that you show no signs of weariness with your quixotic idea of serving the country in the hospital. I had hoped so much that you would by this time have decided that you had done enough, and come home and content yourself with doing what you could for the Sanitary Fair, and the lint-scraping bees.

YOUR AFFECTIONATE MOTHER.

P.S.--Your father is well. He will go with me to Wisconsin, and then go down to Nebraska to look after his land there.

P.S.--I am SO sorry to tell you that Harry Glen has acted badly again. The last letters from the regiment say that he did not go into the fight at Wildcat, and afterward was missing. They believe he was captured, and some say he was taken prisoner on purpose. Everybody's saying, "I told you so," and Mrs. Glen has not been on the street or to church since the news came. I am so sorry for her, but then you know that she used to put on quite as many airs as her position justified.

P.S.--Hoop-skirts are getting smaller every month, and some are confident that they will go entirely out of fashion by next year. I do so hope not. I so dread having to cme back to the old way of wearing a whole clothes-basketful of white skirts.

The new bonnets are just the awfulest things you ever did see. Write soon.

Rachel crumpled the letter in her hand, with a quick, angry gesture, as if crushing some hateful, despicable thing, and her clear hazel eyes blazed.

"He is evidently a hopeless coward," she said to herself, "when all that has passed can not spur him into an exhibition of proper spirit. If he had the love for me he professed it could not help stimulating him to some show of manliness. I will fling him out of my heart and my world as I would fling a rotten apple out of a basket."

Then a sadder and gentler light shone in her face.

"Perhaps I am myself to blame a little. I may not be a good source of inspiration to acts of heroism. Other girls may have ways of stimulating their loves to high deeds that I know not of. Possibly I applied the lash too severely, and instead of rousing him up I killed all the hope in his heart, and made him indifferent to his future. Possibly, too, this story may not be true. The feeling in Sardis against him is strong, and they are hardly willing to do him justice. No doubt they misrepresent him in this, as they are apt to do in everything."

Her face hardened again.

"But it's of no use seeking excuses for him. My lover--my husband--must be a man who can hold his own with other men, in whatever relation of life the struggle may be. The man into whose hands I entrust the happiness of my life must have his qualities so clear and distinct that there never will be any question about them. He must not need continual explanation and defense, for then outraged pride would strangle love with a ruthless hand. No, I must never have reason to believe that my choice is inferior to other men in anything."

But notwithstanding this, she smoothed out the crumpled letter tenderly upon her knee, and read it over again, in the vain hope of finding that the words had less harshness than she had at first found in them.

"No," she said after a weary study of the lines, "it's surely worse than mother states it. She is so kind and gentle that she never fails to mitigate the harshness of anything that she hears about others, and she has told me this as mildly as the case will admit. I must give him up forever."

But though she made this resolution with a firm settling of the lines around her mouth that spoke strongly of its probable fulfilment, the arrival of the decision was the signal for the assault of a thousand tender memories and dear recollections, all pleading trumpet-tongued against the summary dismissal of the unworthy lover. All the ineffably sweet incidents of their love-life stretched themselves out in a vista before her, and tempted her to reverse her decision. But she stayed her purpose with repeating to herself:

"It will save untold misery hereafter to be firm now, and end a connection at once that must be the worse for both of us every day that it is allowed to continue."

There was a tap at the door, and Dr. Denslow entered.

The struggle had so shattered Rachel's self-control that she nervously grasped the letter and thrust it into her pocket, as if the mere sight of it would reveal to him the perturbation that was shaking her.

His quick eyes--quicker yet in whatever related to her--noticed her embarrassment.

"Excuse me," he said with that graceful tact which seemed the very fiber of his nature. "You are not in the mood to receive callers. I will go now, and look in again."

"No, no; stay. I am really glad to see you. It is nothing, I assure you."

She really wished very much to be alone with her grief, but she felt somehow that to shrink from a meeting would be an evasion of the path of duty she had marked out for her feet to tread. If she were going to eliminate all thoughts of her love and her lover from her life, there was no better time to begin than now, while her resolution was fresh. She insisted upon the Doctor remaining, and he did so. Conscious that her embarrassment had been noticed, her self-possession did not return quickly enough to prevent her falling into the error of failing to ignore this, and she confusedly stumbled into an explanation:

"I have received a letter from home which contains news that disturbs me." This was as far as she had expected to go.

Dr. Denslow's face expressed a lively sympathy. "No one dead or seriously ill, I trust."

"No, not as bad as that," she answered hastily, in the first impulse of fear that she had unwarrantably excited his sympathy. "Nor is it anything connected with property," she hastily added, as she saw the Doctor looked inquiringly, but as though fearing that further questioning might be an indelicate intrusion.

She picked nervously at the engagement ring which Harry had placed upon her finger. It fitted closely, and resisted her efforts at removal. she felt, when it was too late, that neither this nor its significance had escaped Dr. Denslow's eyes.

"A f-riend--an--acquaintance of mine has disgraced himself," she said, with a very apparent effort.

An ordinary woman would have broken down in a tearful tempest, but as has been said before she was denied that sweet relief which most women find in a readily responsive gush of tears. Her eyes became very dry and exceedingly hot. Her misery was evident.

The Doctor took her hand with a movement of involuntary sympathy. "I am deeply hurt to see you grieve," he said, "and I wish that I might say something to alleviate your troubles. Is it anything that you can tell me about?"

"No, it is nothing of which I can say a word to any one," she answered. "It is a trouble that I can share with no one, and least of all with a stranger."

"am I not more than a stranger to you?" he asked.

"O yes, indeed," she said, and hastening to correct her former coldness, added:

"You are a very dear, good friend, whom I value much more highly than I have given you reason to think."

His face brightened wonderfully, but he adventured his way slowly. "I am very glad that you esteem me what I have tried to show myself during our acquaintance."

"You have indeed shown yourself a very true friend. I could not ask for a better one."

"Then will you not trust me with a share of your sorrows, that I may help you bear them?"

"No, no; you can not. Nobody can do anything in this case but myself."

"You do not know. You do not know what love can accomplish when it sets itself to work with the ardor belonging to it."

"Love! O, do not speak to me of that," she said, suddenly awaking to the drift of his words, and striving to withdraw her hand.

"No, but I must speak of it," he said with vehemence entirely foreign to his usual half-mocking philosophy. "I must speak of it," he repeated with deepening tones.

"You surely can not be blind to the fact that I love you devotedly--absorbingly. Every day's intercourse must have shown you something of this, which you could not have mistaken. You must have seen this growing upon me continually, until now I have but few thoughts into which your image does not appear, to brighten and enhance them. Tell me now that hopes, dearer--infinitely dearer--than any I have ever before cherished, are to have the crown of fruition."

"I can not--I can not," she sighed.

"What can you not? Can't you care for me at least a little?"

"I do; I care for you ever so much. I am not only grateful for all that you have been to me and done for me, but I have a feeling that goes beyond mere gratitude. But to say that I return the love you profess for me--that I even entertain any feeling resembling it--I can not, and certainly not at this time."

"But you certainly do not love any one else?"

"O, I beg of you not to question me."

"I know I have no right to ask you such a question. I have no right to pry into any matter which you do not choose to reveal to me of your own free will and accord. But as all the mail of the hospital goes through my hands, I could not help noticing that in all the months that you have been here you have written to no man, nor received a letter from one. Upon this I have built my hopes that you were heartfree."

"I can not talk of this, nor of anything now. I am so wrought up by many things that have happened--by my letter from home; by your unexpected declaration--that my poor brain is in a whirl, and I can not think clearly and connectedly on any subject. Please do not press me any more now."

The torrent of his passion was stayed by this appeal to his forbearance. He essayed to calm down his impetuous eagerness for a decision of his fate, and said penitently:

"I beg your pardon. I really forgot. I have so long sought an opportunity to speak to you upon this matter, and I have been so often balked at the last moment, that when a seeming chance came I was carried away with it, and in my selfish eagerness for my own happiness, I forgot your distress. Forgive me--do."

"I have nothing to forgive," she said frankly, most touched by his tender consideration. "You never allow me an occasion for forgiveness, or to do anything in any way to offset the favors you continually heap upon me."

"Pay them all a thousand times over by giving me the least reason to hope."

"I only wish I could--I only wish I dared. But I fear to say anything now. I can not trust myself."

"But you will at least say something that will give me the basis of a hope," he persisted.

"Not now--not now," she said, giving him her hand, which he seized and kissed fervently, and withdrew from the room.

She bolted the door and gave herself up to the most intense thought.

Assignment to duty with an expedition took Dr. Denslow away the next morning, without his being able to see her. When he returned a week later, he found this letter lying on his desk:

MY VERY DEAR FRIEND: The declaration you honored me with making has been the subject of many hours of the most earnest consideration possible. I am certain that it si due to you and to the confession that you have made of your feelings, that I should in turn confess that I am deeply--what shall I say--INTERESTED in you? No; that is too prim and prudish a term. There is in you for me more than a mere attraction; I feel for you something deeper than even warm friendship. That you would make such a husband as I should cherish and honor, of whom I should be proud, and whose strong, kindly arms would be my secure support and protection until death claimed us, I have not the slightest doubt. But when I ask myself whether this is really love--the sacred, all-pervading passion which a woman should feel for the man to whom she gives herself, body and soul, I encounter the strongest doubts. These doubts have no reference to you--only to myself. I feel that it would be a degradation--a deep profanation--for me to give myself to you, without feeling in its entirety such a love as I have attempted to define. I have gone away from you because I want to consider this question and decide it with more calmness and impartiality than I can where I meet you daily, and daily receive some kindness from your hands. These and the magnetism of your presence are temptations which I fear might swerve me from my ideal, and possibly lead to a mistake which we both might ever afterward have reason to regret.

I have, as you will be informed, accepted a detail to one of the hospitals at Nashville. Do not write me, except to tell me of a change in your postoffice address.

I will not write you, unless I have something of special moment to tell you. Believe me, whatever may betide, at least your very sincere friend,

Rachel Bond.

Chapter XVIII. Secret Service.

The flags of war like storm-birds fly,
  The charging trumpets blow,
Yet rolls no thunder in the sky,
  No earthquake strives below.

And calm and patient Nature keeps
  Her ancient promise well,
Though o'er her bloom and greenness sweeps
  The battle's breath of hell.

Ah! eyes may well be full of tears,
  And hearts with hate are hot,
But even-paced come round the years,
  And Nature changes not.

She meets with smiles out bitter grief,
  With songs our groans of pain;
She mocks with tint of flower and leaf
  The war-field's crimson stain.

--Whittier's "Battle Autumn of 1862"

The Summer and Fall of the "Battle Year" of 1862 had passed without the Army of the Cumberland--then called the Army of the Ohio--being able to bring its Rebel antagonist to a decisive struggle. In September the two had raced entirely across the States of Tennessee and Kentucky, for the prize of Louisville, which the Union army won. In October the latter chased its enemy back through Kentucky, without being able to inflict upon it more than the abortive blow at Perryville, and November found the two opponents facing each other in Middle Tennessee--the Army of the Cumberland at Nashville, and the Rebel Army of the Tennessee at Murfeesboro, twenty-eight miles distant. There the two equally matched giants lay confronting each other, and sullenly making ready for the mighty struggle which was to decide the possession of a territory equaling a kingdom in extent.

In the year which had elapsed since the affair at Wildcat Harry Glen's regiment had not participated in a single general engagement. It had scouted and raided; it had reconnoitered and guarded; it had chased guerrillas through the Winter's rain and mud for days and nights together; it had followed John Morgan's dashing troopers along limestone turnpikes that glowed like brick-kilns under the July sun until three-fourths of the regiment had dropped by the roadside in sheer exhaustion; it had marched over the mountains to Cumberland Gap, and back over the mountains to Lexington; across Kentucky and Tennessee to Huntsville, Ala., back across those States to the Ohio River, and again back across Kentucky to Nashville, beside side marches as numerous as the branches on a tree; 50 per cent. of its number had fallen vicitms to sickness and hardship, and 10 per cent. more had been shot, here and there, a man or two at a time, on the picket or skirmish line, at fords or stockades guarding railroad bridges. But while other regiments which had suffered nothing like it had painted on their banners "Mill Springs," "Shiloh," and "Perryville," its colors had yet to receive their maiden inscription. This was the hard luck of many of the regiments in the left wing of Buell's army in 1862.

Kent Edwards, whose promotion to the rank of Sergeant, and reduction for some escapade had been a usual monthly occurence during the year, was fond of saying that the regiment was not sent to the field to gain martial glory, but to train as book agents to sell histories of the struggle, "When This Cruel War is Over." Whereupon Abe Bolton would improve the occasion to invoke a heated future for every person in authority, from the President down to the Fifth Corporal.

But for all this the 400 hardy boys who still remained to answer roll-call, out of the 1,100 that had crossed the Ohio River in September, 1861, were as fine a body of fighting men as ever followed a flag, and there was no better soldier among them than Harry Glen. Every day had been a growth to him, and every trial had knit his spirit into firmer texture. For awhile he had made it a matter of conscience to take an active part in everything that his comrades were called upon to do. Soon this became a matter of pleasure, for the satisfaction of successfully leading them through difficulties and dangers more than compensated for the effort. But while he had vindicated himself in their estimation, he yet lacked that which the ordeal of a battle would give him at home, and more than all, in Rachel's eyes. He heard nothing from or of her, but he consoled himself with the hope that the same means by which she had been so promptly informed of his misstep, would convey to her an intimation of how well he was deserving her. When he gained his laurels he would himself lay them at her feet. Until then he could only hope and strive, cherishing all the while the love for her that daily grew stronger in his heart.

A patient in her ward, recovering from a fever, attracted Rachel's attention soon after her entrance upon duty at Nashville.

Womanly intuition showed her that no ordinary spirit slumbered underneath the usual mountaineer characteristics. The long, lank, black hair, the angular outlines, and the uncouth gestures were common enough among those around her, but she saw a latent fire in the usually dull and languid eyes, which transformed the man into one in whose brain and hand slept many possibilities that were liable to awaken at any moment. Still womanly, she could not help betraying this fact by singling him out as the recipient of many little attentions somewhat more special than those she bestowed on others.

On the other hand, often as she moved about the ward she would in turning discover his eyes fixed upon her movements with an expression of earnest study. After awhile the study seemed to show that it had been satisfactory, and one day, when the Surgeon had informed him that he was now in a condition to return to duty whenever he saw fit to do so, he asked Rachel:

"Kin I speak ter ye a moment in private, Miss?"

"Certainly," she replied. "Come right in here."

Entering the room he closed the door behind them, and made a minute survey of the windows, and other points of vantage for eavesdroppers. This done, he returned to where Rachel was watching his operations with much curiosity, and said:

"Let's set down. I guess no one'll overhear us, ef we're keerful.

"Hev ye enny idee who I am?" he asked abruptly, as they sat down on one of the rude benches with which the room was furnished.

"Not the slightest," she answered, "except that you appear on the roll as 'James Brown, No. 23,' no company or regiment given."

"Very good. D'ye reckon thet enny o' them in thar hev?"--pointing over his shoulder with his thumb to the ward.

"Of course I can not tell as to that. I never hear them say anything about you. They seem to think that you are one of the loyal East Tennesseans that are plentiful about here."

"I've been afeered fur the last few days that some uv 'em were Rebels in disguise, an' thet they sort o' suspicioned me. I hev seed two on 'em eyein' me mouty hard. One has a red head, an' 'tother a long black beard."

"I can perhaps set your anxiety at rest on that score. They ARE Southerners, but loyal ones. They were forced into the Rebel army, but made their escape at the first opportunity. They naturally watch every Southern-looking man with great interest, fearing that he may be an unpleasant acquaintance."

"Desarters from the Rebel army, be they? Thet makes me so'. I thot I'd seen 'em afore, an' this makes me sartin. They're mouty bad pills, an' they hain't heah fur no good. but whar did I see 'em? In some Rebel camp somewhar? No; now I remember. Ef I hain't powerfully fooled them's the two laddie-bucks thet Harry Glen an' me gobbled up one fine mornin' an' tuck inter Wildcat. They're bad aigs, ef ther ever war bad aigs."

"Harry Glen, did you say? What do you know of Harry Glen?" Her heart was in her mouth.

"What do I know of harry Glen? Why, jest heaps an' more yit. He's one o' the best men thet ever wore blue clotes. But thet's nuther heah nor thar. Thet hain't what I brung ye out heah ter talk on."

"Go on," said Rachel, resisting her eagerness to overwhelm him with questions concerning the one man of all the world she most desired to learn about. "I can spare you but little time."

"All right, Miss. Ter begin with, my name's not Brown. Nary a time. Hit's Fortner--Jim Fortner--the 'noted Scout,' ez I heered ye readin' 'bout 'tother day, when ye war givin' the boys the war news in the papers. I'm well-known ez a secret-sarvice man--tu well-known, I'm afeered. I could git 'long 'ithout quite ez menny 'quaintances ez I hev gethered up lately. More 'specially o' the kind, fur menny on 'em ar' only waitin' a good opportunity ter gin me a gran' interduction to 'tarnity. I'd ruther know fewer folks an' better ones, ez I wunst heered Harry Glen say."

"What do you know of---" Rachel started to say, but before she could finish the sentence Fortner resumed:

"I'm now 'bout ter start on the most 'portant work I ever done fur the Gover'mint. Things ar' ripenin' fast fur the orfulest battle ever fit in this ere co'ntry. Afore the Chrismuss snow flies this ere army'll fall on them thar Rebels 'round Murfressboro like an oak tree on a den o' rattlesnakes. Blood'll run like water in a Spring thaw, an' them fellers'll hev so menny fun'rals ter tend thet they won't hev no time for Chrismuss frolics. They've raced back an' forrard, an' dodged up an' down fur a year now, but they're at the eend uv ther rope, an' hit'll be a deth-nooze fur 'em. May the pit o' hell open fur 'em."

He watched Rachel's face closely as he spoke. She neither blanched nor recoiled, but her eyes lighted up as if with anticipation of the coming conflict, and she asked eagerly:

"O, are you only quite sure that our army will be victorious?"

His eyes shown with gratification.

"I knowed thet's the way ye'd take the news. I knowed the minit I sot eyes on ye thet ye war good grit. I never git fooled much in my guess o' people's backbone. Thar wuz Harry Glen--all his own comrades thot he wuz white 'bout the liver, but I seed the minit I laid my eyes onter him thet he hed ez good, stan'-up stuff in him ez ennybody, w'en he got over his fust flightiness."

Had this man some scheme that would bring her lover and her together? "But what do you want of me?" Rachel asked, with all the composure she could summon.

"Suthing a cussed sight more hon'rable an' more useful ter ther Gover'mint then stayin' 'round heah nussin' these loafers," he answered roughly. "Hist! thar's a shadder nigh yon winder." He crossed the room with the quick, silent tread of a panther, and his face darkened as he saw the objectionable red-headed and black-bearded men walking away toward the parade-ground, with their backs to the window. "Yer orful cute," he said talking to himself, and alluding to the retiring figures, "but ef I don't gin ye a trip afore long thet'll make yer heels break yer pizen necks I hope I may never see Rockassel Mountings agin. I'd do hit now, but I'm a-trailin' bigger game. When hit's my day fur killin' skunks look out--thet's all."

Returning to the expectant Rachel he continued:

"I leave ter-night fur the Rebel army at Murfreesboro. Ole Rosy hisself sends me, but I'm ter pick out the messengers ter send my news back ter him by. I must hev sev'ral so's ter make dead sho' thet ev'rything reaches 'im. I want ye fur the main one, becase ye've got brains an' san', and then ye kin git thru the lines whar a man can't. thar'll be nothin' bad 'bout hit. Ye'll ride ter Murfreesboro an' back on yer own hoss, ez a young lady should, an' if ye accomplish ennything hit'll be a greater sarvice tew the country then most men kin do in ther lives. Hit'll be sum'thing ter be proud of ez long's ye live. Will ye try hit?"

"Why don't you bring back the information yourself? Can't you come back through the lines as easily as you go?"

"I mout, an' then ag'in I moutn't. Every time I go inter the Rebel camps the chances get stronger thet I'll never come back ag'in. Ez Harry Glen sez, the circle o' my onpleasant acquaintances--the fellers thet's reachin' fur my top-knot--widens. Thar's so many more on 'em layin' fur me all the time, thet the prospects keeps gittin' brighter every day thet by-an'-by they'll fetch me. the arrant I'm a-gwine on now is too important ter take any resks 'bout. I'm sartin to git the information thet Ginteral Rosy wants, but whether I kin git hit back ter him is ruther dubersome. I must hev 'some help. Will ye jine in with me?"

"But how am I to know that all this is as you say?"

"By readin' these 'ere passes, all signed by Ginteral Rosencrans's own hand, or by takin' a walk with me up ter headquarters, whar they'll tell ye thet I'm all right, an' ez straight ez a string."

"But how can I do what you want? I know nothing of the country, nor the people, and still less of this kind of service. I would probably make a blunder that would spoil all."

"I'll resk the blunders. ye kin ride critter-back can't ye?"

Rachel owned that she was a pretty fair horse-woman.

"Then all ye hev ter do is ter git yerself up ez ye see the young women who are ridin' 'round heah, an' airly on the day arter to-morrow mornin', mount a blooded mar that ye'll find standin' afore the door thar, all rigged out ez fine ez silk, an' go down the Lavergne turnpike, at a sharp canter, jes ez though ye war gwine somewhar. Nobody on our lines 'll be likely ter say anything ter ye, but ef they do, ye'll show 'em a pass from Gineral Rosy, which, howsoever, ye 'll tar up afore ye reach Lavergne, fur ye 'll likely find some o' t' other folks thar. Ef any o' them at Lavergne axes ye imperent questions, ye must hev a story ready 'bout yer being the Nashville niece o' Aunt Debby Brill, who lives on the left hand o' the Nashville pike, jest north o' the public squar in Murfreesboro, an' ye 're on yer way ter pay yer ole Aunty a long-promised visit."

"there is such a woman in Murfreesboro?"

"Yes, an' she's talked a great deal 'bout her niece in Nashville, who's comin' ter see her. I thought"--the earnestness of the eyes relaxed to a suspicion of a twinkle--"thet sometime I mout come across sich a niece fur the ole lady, an' hit wuz well ter be prepared fur her."

"But suppose they ask me about things in Nashville?"

"W'll, ye must fix up a story 'bout thet too. Ye needn't be ver partickelar what hit is, so long's hit's awful savage on the Yankees. Be keerful ter say frequently thet the yankees is awful sick o' their job o' holdin' Nashville; that their new Dutch Gineral is a mean brute, an' a coward beside, thet he's skeered 'bout out'n his wits half the time, an' he's buildin' the biggest kind o' forts to hide behind, an' thet he won't dar show his nose outside o' them--leastways not this 'ere Winter. Talk ez much ez ye kin 'bout the sojers gwine inter Winter quarters; 'bout them being mortally sartin not ter do anything tell next Spring, an' 'bout them desartin' by rijimints an' brigades, an' gwine home, bekase they're sick an' tired o' the war."

"My," said Rachel, with a gasp, "what awful things to tell!"

"Yes," returned the scout complacently, "I s'posed hit'd strike you thet-a-way. But my experience with war is thet hit's jest plum full o' awful things. In fact hit don't seem ter hev much else in hit. All ye hev ter ax yerself is whether this is nigh on ter ez awful ez the the things they 'uns do to we 'uns. Besides, we 'uns are likely ter give they 'uns in a few days a heap more interestin' things ter think about then the remarkable stories told by young ladies out fur a mornin' ride."

"I'll take some hours to think this matter over," said Rachel, "and give you your answer this afternoon. That'll be time enough, will it not?"

"Heaps an' plenty, ma'am," he answered, as he rose to go. "She'll go," he added to himself. "I'm not fooled a mite on thet 'ere stock. I'll jest go to headquarters an' git things ready for her."

He was right. The prospect of doing an important service on a grand occasion was stimulous enough for Rachel's daring spirit, to make her undertake anything, and when Fortner returned in the afternoon he found her eager to set out upon the enterprise.

But as the evening came on with its depressing shadows and silence, she felt the natural reaction that follows taking an irrevocable step. The loneliness of her unlighted room was peopled with ghostly memories of the horrors inflicted upon spies, and of tales she had heard of the merciless cruelty of the Rebels among whom she was going. She had to hold her breath to keep from shrieking aloud at the terrors conjured up before her vision. Then the spasm passed, and braver thoughts reasserted themselves. Fortner's inadvertent words of praise of Harry Glen were recalled, and began glowing like pots of incense to sweeten and purify the choking vapors in her imagination.

Could it be that Harry had really retrieved himself? He had certainly gained the not-easily-won admiration of this brave man, and it had all been to render himself worthy of her! There was rapture in the thought. Then her own heroic aspirations welled up again, bringing intoxication at the prospect of ending the distasteful routine of nursing, by taking an active part in what would be a grand event of history. Fears and misgivings vanished like the mists of the morning. She thought only of how to accomplish her mission.

She lighted a candle and wrote four letters--one to her mother, one to Dr. Denslow, one to Harry Glen in care of his mother, and one to the Hospital Steward, asking him to mail the letters in case he did not receive any contrary request from her before the 10th of January.

She was too excited to sleep in the early part of the night, and busied her waking hours in packing her clothing and books, and maturing her plans.

She had much concern about her wardrobe. Never in all the days of her village belleship had she been so anxious to be well-dressed as now, when about to embark upon the greatest act of her life. She planned and schemed as women will in such times, and rising early the next morning she visited the stores in the city, and procured the material for a superb riding habit. A cutter form a fashionable establishment in Cincinnati was found in an Orderly Sergeant in one of the convalescent wards, and enough tailors responded to the call for such artisans, to give him all the help required. By evening she was provided with a habit that, in material and that sovereign but indescribable quality called "style," was superior to those worn by the young ladies who cantered about the streets of Nashville on clean-limbed throroughbreds.

As she stood surveying the exquisite "set" of the garment in such mirrors as she could procure, she said to herself quizzically:

"I feel now that the expedition is going to be a grand success. No woman could fail being a heroine in such an inspiration of dress. There is a moral support and encouragement about a perfectly made garment that is hardly equaled by a clear conscience and righteousness of motive."

The next morning she came forth from her room attired for the journey. A jaunty hat and feather sat gracefully above her face, to which excitement had given a striking animation. One trimly-gauntleted hand carried a dainty whip; the other supported the long skirts of her riding habit as she moved through the ward with such a newly-added grace and beauty that the patients, to whom her appearance had become familiar, raised in their beds to follow the lovely spectacle with their eyes, and then turned to each other to comment upon her beauty.

At the door she found an orderly, holding a spirited young mare, handsome enough for a Queen's palfrey, and richly caparisoned.

She sprang into the saddle and adjusted her seat with the easy grace of an accomplished horsewoman.

A squad of "Convalescents" standing outside, and a group of citizes watched her with an admiration too palpable for her to be unconscious of it.

She smiled pleasantly upon the soldiers, and gave them a farewell bow as she turned the mare's head away, to which they responded with cheers.

A few hundred yards further, where an angle in the street would take her from their view, she turned around again and waved her handkerchief to them. The boys gave her another ringing cheer, with waving hats and handkerchiefs; her steed broke into a canter and she disappeared from view.

"Where is she going?" asked one of the soldiers.

"I don't know," responded another gallantly; "but wherever it is, it will be better than here, just because she's there."

The sight of an orderly, coming with the morning mail, ended the discussion by scattering the squad in a hurry.

Rachel cantered on, her spirits rising continually.

It was a bright, crisp morning--a Tennessee Winter morning--when the air is as wine to the blood, and sets every pulse to leaping. Delicate balsamic scents floated down from groves of shapely cedars. Gratefully-astringent odors were wafted from the red oaks, ranked upon the hillsides and still covered with their leaves, now turned bright-brown, making them appear like serried phalanges of giant knights, clad in rusted scale armor. The spicy smell of burning cedar rose on the lazily-curling smoke from a thousand camp-fires. The red-berried holly looked as fresh and bright as rose-bushes in June, and the magnolias still wore their liveries of Spring. The sun shone down with a tender fervor, as if wooing the sleeping buds and flowers to wake from a slumber of which he had grown weary, and start with him again through primrose paths on the pilgrimage of blossoming and fruitage.

Rachel's nostrils expanded, and she drank deeply of the exhilarating draughts of mountain air, with its delicious woodsy fragrance. Her steed did the same, and the hearts of both swelled with the inspiration.

Away she sped over the firm, smooth Murfreesboro Pike, winding around hillsides and through valleys filled with infantry, cavalry and artillery, through interminable masses of wagons, hers of braying mules, and crowds of unarmed soldiers trudging back to Nashville, on leave of absence, to spend the day seeing the sights of the historic Tennessee capital. In the camps the soldiers were busy with evergreen and bunting, and the contents of boxes received from the North, preparing for the celebration of Christmas in something like the manner of the old days of home and peace.

Like the sweet perfume of rose-attar from a bundle of letters unwittingly stirred in a drawer, rose the fragrant memory of the last of those Christmases in Sardis before the war, when winged on he scent of evergreens, and the merry laughter of the church decorators, came to her the knowledge that she had found a lodgment in the heart of Harry Glen.

Was memory juggling with her senses, or was that really his voice she heard in command, in a field to her left? She turned a swift, startled look in that direction, and saw a Sergeant marching a large squad at quick time to join a heavy "detail." His back was toward her, but his figure and bodily carriage were certainly those of Harry Glen. But before she could make certain the squad was merged with the "detail," to the obliteration of all individuality, and the whole mass disappeared around the hill.

She rode on to the top of the rim of hills which encircle that most picturesque of Southern cities, and stopped for a moment for a farewell to the stronghold of her friends, whose friendly cover she was abandoning to venture, weak and weaponless, into the camp of her enemies.

Above her the great black guns of a heavy fort pointed their sinister muzzles down the Murfreesboro road, with fearful suggestiveness of the dangers to be encountered there.

She remembered Lot's wife, but could not resist the temptation to take a one backward look. She saw as grand a landscape picture as the world affords.

Serenely throned upon the hill that dominated the whole of the lovely valley of the Cumberland, stood the beautiful Capitol of Tennessee.

Ionic porticos and graceful Corinthian columns of dazzling white limestone rose hundreds of feet above the fountains and magnolia-shaded terraces that crowned the hill--still more hundreds of feet above the densely packed roofs and spires of the city crowded upon the hill's rocky sides. It was like some fine and pure old Greek temple, standing on a romantic headland, far above the murk and toil of sordid striving. But over the symmetrical pile floated a banner that meant to the world all that was signified even by the banners which Greece folded and laid away in eternal rest thousands of years ago.

At the foot of the hill the Cumberland, clear as when it descended from its mountains five hundred miles away, flowed between its high, straight walls of limestone, spanned by cobweb-like bridges, and bore on its untroubled breast a great fleet of high-chimneyed, white-sided transports, and black, sullen gunboats. Miles away to her left she saw the trains rushing into Nashville, unrolling as they came along black and white ribbons against the sky.

"They're coming from the North," she said, with an involuntary sigh; "they're coming from home."

She touched her mare's flank with the whip and sped on.

She soon reached the outer line of guards, by whom she was halted, with a demand for her pass.

She produced the one furnished her, which was signed by Gen. Rosencrans. While the Sergeant was inspecting it it occured to her that now was the time to begin the role of a young woman with rebellious proclivities.

"Is this the last guard-line I will have to pass?" she asked.

"Yes'm," answered the Sergeant.

"You're quite sure?"

"Yes'm."

"Then I won't have any further use for this--thing?" indicating the pass, which she received back with fine loathing, as if it were something infectious.

"No'm."

"Quite sure?"

"Yes'm, quite sure."

She rode over to the fire around which part of the guard were sitting, held the pass over it by the extremest tips of her dainty thumb and forefinger, and then dropped it upon the coals, as if it were a rag from a small-pox hospital. Glancing at her finger-tips an instant, as if they had been permanently contaminated by the scrawl of the Yankee General, she touched her nag, and was off like an arrow without so much as good day to the guards.

"She-cesh--clean to her blessed little toe-nails," said the Sergeant, gazing after her meditatively, as he fished around in his pouch for a handful of Kinnikinnick, to replenish his pipe, "and she's purtier'n a picture, too."

"Them's the kind that's always the wust Rebels," said the oracle of the squad, from his seat by the fire. "I'll bet she's just loaded down with information or oui-nine. Mebbe both."

She was now fairly in the enemy's country, and her heart beat faster in momentary expectation of encountering some form of the perils abounding there. But she became calm, almost joyous, as she passed through mile after mile of tranquil landscape. The war might as well have been on the other side of the Atlantic for any hint she now saw of it in the peaceful, sun-lit fields and woods, and streams of crystal spring-water. She saw women busily engaged in their morning work about all the cabins and houses. With bare and sinewy arms they beat up and down in tiresomely monotonous stroke the long-handled dashers of cedar churns standing in the wide, open "entries" of the "double-houses;" they arrayed their well-scalded milk crocks and jars where the sun's rays would still further sweeten them; they plied swift shuttles in the weaving sheds; they toiled over great, hemispherical kettles of dye-stuffs or soap, swinging from poles over open fires in the yard; they spread out long webs of jeans and linen on the grass to dry or bleach, and all the while they sang--sang the measured rhythm of familiar hymns in the high soprano of white women--sang wild, plaintive lyrics in the liquid contralto of negresses. Men were repairing fences, and doing other Winter work in the fields, and from the woods came the ringing staccato of choppers. She met on the road leisurely-traveling negro women, who louted low to her, and then as she passed, turn to gaze after her with feminine analysis and admiration for every detail of her attire. Then came "Uncle Tom" looking men, driving wagons loaded with newly-riven rails, breathing the virile pungency of freshly-cut oak. Occasionally an old white man or woman rode by, greeting her with a courteous "Howdy?"

The serenity everywhere intoxicated her with a half-belief that the terrible Rebel army at Murfreesboro was only a nightmare of fear-oppressed brains, and in her relief she was ready to burst out in echo of a triumphant hymn ringing from a weaving-shed at her right.

Her impulse was checked by seeing approach a figure harshly dissonant to Arcadian surroundings.

It was a young man riding a powerful roan horse at an easy gallop, and carrying in his hand, ready for instant use, a 16-shooting Henry rifle. He was evidently a scout, but, as was usual with that class, his uniform was so equally made up of blue and gray that it was impossible to tell to which side he belonged. He reined up as he saw Rachel, and looked at her for a moment in a way that chilled her. They were now on a lonely bit of road, out of sight and hearing of any person or house. All a woman's fears rose up in her heart, but she shut her lips firmly, and rode directly toward the scout. Another thought seemed to enter his mind, he touched his horse up with his heel, and rode by her, saying courteously:

"Good morning, Miss," but eyeing her intently as they passed. She returned the salutation with a firm voice, and rode onward, but at a little distance could not resist the temptation to turn and look backward. To her horror the scout had stopped, half-turned his horse, and was watching her as if debating whether or not to come back after her. She yielded to the impulse of fear, struck her mare a stinging blow, and the animal flew away.

Her fright subsided as she heard no hoof-beats following her, and when she raised her eyes, she saw that she was approaching the village of Lavergne, half-way to Murfreesboro, and that a party of Rebel cavalry were moving toward her. She felt less tremor at this first sight of the armed enemy than she had expected, after her panic over the scout, and rode toward the horsemen with perfect outward, and no little inward composure.

The Lieutenant in command raised his hat with the greatest gallantry.

"Good morning, Miss. From the city, I suppose?" he inquired.

"Yes," she answered in tones as even as if speaking in a parlor; "fortunately, I am at last from the city. I have been trying to get away ever since it seemed hopeless that our people would not redeem it soon."

The conversation thus opened was carried on by Rachel giving copious and disparaging information concerning the "Yankees," and the Lieutenant listening in admiration to the musical accents, interrupting but rarely to interject a question or a favorable comment. He was as little critical as ardent young men are apt to be of the statements of captivating young women, and Rachel's spirits rose as she saw that the worst she had to fear from this enemy was an excess of devotioni. The story of her aunt at Murfreesboro received unhesitating acceptance, and nothing but imperative scouting orders prevented his escorting her to the town. He would, however, send a non-commissioned officer with her, who would see that she was not molested by any one. He requested permission to call upon her at her aunt's, which Rachel was compelled to grant, for lack of any ready excuse for such a contingency. With this, and many smiles and bows, they parted.

All the afternoon she rode through camps of men in gray and butternut, as she had ridden through those of men in blue in the morning. In these, as in the others, she heard gay songs, dance music and laughter, and saw thousands of merry boys rollicking in the sunshine at games of ball and other sports, with the joyous earnestness of a school-house playground. She tried, but in vain, to realize that in a few days these thoughtless youths would be the demons of the battle-field.

Just before dusk she came to the top of a low limestone ridge, and saw, three miles away, the lights of Murfreesboro. At that moment Fortner appeared, jogging leisurely toward her, mounted on a splendid horse.

"O there's my Cousin Jim!" she exclaimed gleefully, "coming to meet me. Sergeant, I am deeply obliged to you and to your Lieutenant, for your company, and I will try to show my appreciation of it in the future in some way more substantial than words. You need not go any farther with me. I know that you and your horse are very tired. Good by."

The Sergeant was only too gald of this release, which gave him an opportunity to get back to camp, to enjoy some good cheer that he knew was there, and bidding a hasty good-night, he left at a trot. Fortner and Rachel rode on slowly up the pike, traversing the ground that was soon to run red with the blood of thousands.

They talked of the fearful probabilities of the next few days, and halted for some minutes on the bridge across Stone River, to study the wonderfully picturesque scene spread out before them. The dusk was just closing down. The scowling darkness seemed to catch around woods and trees and houses, and grow into monsters of vast and somber bulk, swelling and spreding like the "gin" which escaped from the copper can, in the "Arabian Nights," until they touched each other, coalesced and covered the whole land. Far away, at the edge of the valley, the tops of the hills rose, distinctly lighted by the last rays of the dying day, as if some strip of country resisting to the last the invasion of the dark monsters.

A half-mile in front of the bridge was the town of Murfreesboro. Bright lights streamed from thousands of windows and from bonfires in the streets. Church bells rang out the glad acclaim of Christmas from a score of steeples. The happy voices of childhood singing Christmas carols; the laughter of youths and maidens strolling arm in arm through the streets; the cheery songs of merry-making negroes; silver-throated bands, with throbbing drums and gently-complaining flutes, playing martial airs; long lines of gleaming camp-fires, stretching over the undulating valley and rising hills like necklaces of burning jewels on the breast of night,--this was what held them silent and motionless.

Rachel at last spoke:

"It is like a scene of enchantment. It is more wonderful than anything I ever read of."

"Yes'm, hit's mouty strikin' now, an' when ye think how hit'll all be changed in a little while ter more misery then thar is this side o' hell, hit becomes all the more strikin'. Hit seems ter me somethin' like what I've heered 'em read 'bout in the Bible, whar they went on feastin' an' singin', an' dancin' an' frolickin', an' the like, an' at midnight the inimy broke through the walls of ther city, an' put 'em all ter the sword, even while they wuz settin' round thar tables, with ther drinkin' cups in ther hands."

"To think what a storm is about to break upon this scene of happiness and mirth-making!" said Rachel, with a shudder.

"Yes, an' they seem ter want ter do the very things thet'll show ther contempt o' righteousness, an' provoke the wrath o' the Lord. Thar, where ye see thet house, all lit up from the basement ter the look-out on the ruf, is whar one o' the most 'ristocratic families in all Tennessee lives. There datter is bein' married to-night, an' Major-Gineral Polk, the biggest gun in all these 'ere parts, next ter ole Bragg, an' who is also 'Piscopalian Bishop o' Tennessee, does the splicin'. They've got ther parlors, whar they'll dance, carpeted with 'Merican flags, so thet the young bucks an' gals kin show ther despisery of the banner thet wuz good enough for ther fathers, by trampin' over hit all night. But we'll show hit ter 'em in a day or two whar they won't feel like cuttin' pigeon-wings over hit. Ye jes stand still an' see the salvation o' the Lord."

"I hope we will," said Rachel, her horror of the storm that was about to break giving away to indignation at the treatment of her country's flag. "Shan't we go on? My long ride has made me very tired and very hungry, and I know my horse is the same."

Shortly after crossing the river they passed a large tent, with a number of others clustered around it. All were festooned with Rebel flags, and brilliantly lighted. A band came up in front of the principal one and played the "Bonnie Blue Flag."

"Thet's ole Gineral Bragg's headquarters," explained Fortner. "He's the king bee of all the Rebels in these heah parts, an' they think he kin 'bout make the sun stand still ef he wants ter."

They cantered on into the town, and going more slowly through the great public square and the more crowded streets, came at last to a modest house, standing on a corner, and nearly hidden by vines and shrubbery.

A peculiar knock caused the door to open quickly, and before Rachel was hardly aware of it, she was standing inside a comfortable room, so well lighted that her eyes took some little time to get used to such a change.

When they did so she saw that she was in the presence of a slender, elderly woman, whose face charmed her.

"This is yer Aunt Debby Brill," said Fortner, dryly, "who ye came so fur ter see, an' who's bin 'spectin' ye quite anxiously."

"Ye're very welcome, my dear," said Aunt Debby, after a moment's inspection which seemed to be entirely satisfactory. "Jest lay off yer things thar on the bed, an' come out ter supper. I know ye're sharp-set. A ride from Nashville sech a day ez this is mouty good for the appetite, an' we've hed supper waitin' ye."

Hastily throwing off her hat and gloves, she sat down with the rest, to a homely but excellent supper, which they all ate in silence. During the meal a muscular, well knit man of thirty entered.

"All clar, outside, Bill?" asked Fortenr.

"All clar," replied the man. "Everybody's off on a high o' some kind."

Bill sat down and ate with the rest, until he satisfied his hunger, and then rising he felt along the hewed logs which formed the walls, until he found a splinter to serve as a tooth-pick. Using this for a minute industriously, he threw it into the fire and asked:

"Well?"

"Well," answered Fortner. "I reckon hit's ez sartin ez anything kin well be thet Wheeler's and Morgan's cavalry hez been sent off inter Kentucky, and ez thet's what Ole rosy's been waitin' fur, now's the time fur him ter put in his best licks. Ye'd better start afore midnight fur Nashville. Ye'll hev this news, an' alos thet thar's been no change in the location o' the Rebels, 'cept thet Polk's an' Kirby Smith's corps are both heah at Murfreesboro, with a strong brigade at Stewart's creek, an' another at Lavergne. Ye'd better fallin with Boscall's rijiment, which'll go out ter Lavergne to-night, ter relieve one o' the rijiments thar. Ye'd better not try to git back heah ag'in tell arter the battle. Good by. God bless ye. Miss, ye'd better git ter bed now, ez soon ez possible, an' rest yerself fur what's comin'. We'll need every mite an' grain of our strength."

Chapter XIX. The Battle of Stone River.

O, wherefore come ye forth, in triumph from the North,
  With your hands and your feet, and your raiment all red?
And wherefore doth your rout, send forth a joyous shout?
  And whence be the grapes of the wine-press that ye tread?

O, evil was the root, and bitter was the fruit,
  And crimson was the juice of the vintage that we tred;
For we trampled on the throng, of the haughty and the strong,
  Who sat in the high places and slew the saints of God.

* * * * * * * * * * * * * *

They are here--they rush on--we are broken--we are gone-- Our left
is borne before them like stubble in the blast. O, Lord, put forth
thy might! O, Lord, defend the right!   Stand back to back, in
God's name! and fight it to the last.

--"Battle of Naseby."*/

The celebration of Christmas in the camps around Nashville was abruptly terminated by the reception of orders to march in the morning, with full haversacks and cartridge-boxes. The next day all the roads leading southward became as rivers flowing armed men. Endless streams of blue, thickly glinted everywhere with bright and ominous steel, wound around the hills, poured over the plains, and spread out into angry lakes wherever a Rebel outpost checked the flow for a few minutes.

Four thousand troopers under the heroic Stanley--the foam-crest on the war-billow--dashed on in advance. Twelve thousand steadily-moving infantry under the luckless McCook, poured down the Franklin turnpike, miles away to the right; twelve thousand more streamed down the Murfreesboro pike on the left, with the banner of the over-weighted Crittenden, while grand old Thomas, he whose trumpets never sounded forth retreat, but always called to victory, moved steadfast as a glacier in the center, with as many more, a sure support and help to those on either hand.

The mighty war-wave rolling up the broad plateau of the Cumberland was fifteen miles wide now. It would be less than a third of that when it gathered itself together for its mortal dash upon the rocks of rebellion at Murfreesboro.

It was Friday morning that the wave began rolling southward. All day Friday, and Saturday, and Sunday, and Monday it rolled steadily onward, sweeping before it the enemy's pickets and outposts as dry sand by an incoming tide. Monday evening the leading divisions stood upon the ridge where Rachel and Fortner had stood, and looked as they did upon the lights of Murfreesboro, two miles away.

"Two days from to-morrow is New Year's," said Kent Edwards. "Dear Festival of Egg-Nogg! how sweet are thy memories. I hope the Tennessee hens are doing their duty this Winter, so that we'll have no trouble finding eggs when we get into Murfreesboro to-morrow."

"We are likely to be so busy tendering the compliments of the season to Mr. Bragg," said Harry, lightly, "that we will probably have but little time to make calls upon the lady-hens who keep open nests."

"We all may be where we'll need lots o' cold water more than anything else," said Abe grimly.

"Well," said Kent blithely, "if I'm to be made a sweet little angel I don't know any day that I would rather have for my promotion to date from. It would have a very proper look to put in the full year here on earth, and start in with the new one in a world of superior attractions."

"Well, I declare, if here isn't Dr. Denslow," said Harry, delightedly, as he recognized a horsemna, who rode up to them. "How did you come here? We thought you were permanently stationed at the grand hospital."

"So I was," replied the Doctor. "So I was, at least so far as general orders could do it. But I felt that I could not be away from my boys at this supreme moment, an

I am here, though the irregular way in which I detached myself from my post may require explanation at a court-martial. Anyhow, it is a grateful relief to be away from the smell of chloride of lime, and get a breath of fresh air that is not mingled with the groans of a ward-full of sick men. It looks," he continued, with a comprehensive glance at the firmament of Rebel camp-fires that made Murfreesboro seem the center of a ruddy Milky-way, "as if the climax is at last at hand. Bragg, like the worm, will at last turn, and after a year of footraces we'll have a fight which will settle who is the superfluous cat in this alley. There is certainly one too many."

"The sooner it comes the better," said Harry firmly. "It has to be sometime, and I'm getting very anxious for an end to this eternal marching and countermarching."

"My winsome little feet," Kent Edwards put in plaintively, "are knobby as a burglar-proof safe, with corns and bunions, all of them more tender than a maiden's heart, and painful as a mistake in a poker hand. They're the ripe fruit of the thousands of miles of side hills I've had to tramp over because of Mr. Bragg's retiring disposition. Now, if he's got the spirit of a man he'll come out from under the bed and fight me."

"O, he'll come out--he'll come out--never you fear," said Abe, sardonic as usual. "He's got a day or two's leisure now to attend to this business. A hundred thousand of him will come out. They'll swarm out o' them cedar thickets there like grasshoppers out of a timothy field."

"Boys," said Harry, returning after a few minutes' basence, "the Colonel says we'll go into camp right here, just as we stand. Kent, I'll take the canteens and hunt up water, if you and Abe will break some cedar boughs for the bed, and get the wood to cook supper with."

"All right," responded Kent, "I'll go after the boughs."

"That puts me in for the wood," grumbled Abe. "And, I don't suppose there's a fence inside of a mile, and if there is there's not a popular rail in it."

"And, Doctor," continued Harry, flinging the canteens over his shoulder, "you'll stay and take a cup of coffee and sleep with us to-night, won't you? The trains are all far behind, and the hospital wagon must be miles away."

"Seems to me that I've heard something of the impropriety of visiting your friends just about mealtime," said the Doctor quizzically, "but a cup of coffee just now has more charms for me than rigid etiquette, so I'll thankfully accept your kind invitation. Some day I'll reciprocate with liberality in doses of quinine."

In less time than that taken by well-appointed kitchens to furnish "Hot Meals to Order" the four were sitting on their blankets around a comfortable fire of rails and cedar logs, eating hard bread and broiled fat pork, and drinking strong black coffee, which the magic of the open air had transmuted into delightfully delicate and relishable viands.

"You are indebted to me," said Dr. Denslow, as he finished the last crumb and drop of his portion of the food, "for the accession to your company at this needful time, of a tower of strength in the person of Lieutenant Jacob Alspaugh."

Abe groaned; the Doctor looked at him with well-feigned astonishment, and continued:

"That gore-hungry patriot, as you know, has been home several months on recruiting duty, by virtue of a certificate which he wheedled out of old Moxon. At last, when he couldn't keep away any longer, he started back, but he carefully restrained his natural impetuosity in rushing to the tented field, and his journey from Sardis to Nashville was a fine specimen of easy deliberation. There was not a sign of ungentlemanly hurry in any part of it. He came into my ward at Nashville with violent symptoms of a half-dozen speedily fatal diseases. I was cruel enough to see a coincidence in this attack and the general marching orders, and I prescribed for his ailments a thorough course of open air exercise. To be sure that my prescription would be taken I had the Provost-Marshal interest himself in my patient's case, and the result was that Alspaugh joined the regiment, and so far has found it difficult to get away from it. It's the unexpected that happens, the French say, and there is a bare possibility that he may do the country some service by the accidental discharge of his duty."

"The possibility is too remote to waste time considering," said Harry.

They lay down together upon a bed made by spreading their overcoats and blankets upon the springy cedar boughts, and all but Harry were soon fast asleep. Though fully as weary as they he could not sleep for hours. He was dominated by a feeling that a crisis in his fate was at hand, and as he lay and looked at the stars every possible shape that that fate could take drifted across his mind, even as the endlessly-varying cloud-shapes swept--now languidly, now hurriedly--across the domed sky above him. And as the moon and the stars shone through or around each of the clouds, making the lighter ones masses of translucent glory, and gilding the edges of even the blackest with silvery promise, so the thoughts of Rachel Bond suffused with some brightness every possible happening to him. If he achieved anything the achievement would have for its chief value that it won her commendation; if he fell, the blackness of death would be gilded by her knowledge that he died a brave man's death for her sweet sake.

He listened awhile to the mournful whinny of the mules; to the sound of artillery rolling up the resonant pike; to the crashing of newly-arrived regiments through the cedars as they made their camps in line-of-battle; to little spurts of firing between the nervous pickets, and at last fell asleep to dream that he was returning to Sardis, maimed but honor-crowned, to claim Rachel as his exultant bride.

The Christmas forenoon was quite well-advanced before the fatigue of Rachel Bond's long ride was sufficiently abated to allow her to awaken. Then a soft hum of voices impressed itself upon her drowsy senses, and she opened her eyes with the idea that there were several persons in the room engaged in conversation. But she saw that there was only Aunt Debby, seated in a low rocking-chair by the lazily burning fire, and reading aloud from a large Bible that lay open upon her knees. The reading was slow and difficult, as of one but little used to it, and many of the longer words were patiently spelled out. But this labored picking the way along the rugged path of knowledge, stumbling and halting at the nouns, and verbs, and surmounting the polysyllables a letter at a time, seemed to give the reader a deeper feeling of the value and meaning of each word, than is usually gained by the more facile scholar. As Rachel listened she became aware that Aunt Debby was reading that wonderful twelfth chapter of St. Luke, richest of all chapters in hopes and promises and loving counsel for the lowly and oppressed. She had reached the thirty-fifth verse, and read onward with a passionate earnestness and understanding that made every word have a new revelation to Rachel:

"Let your loins be girded up, and your lights burning;

"And ye yourselves like unto men that wait for their Lord when he will return from the wedding; that when he cometh and knocketh they may open unto him immediately.

"Blessed are those servants whom the Lord when he cometh shall find watching; verily I say unto you that he shall gird himself and make them to sit down to meat, and will come forth and serve them.

"And if ye shall come in the second watch, or come in the third watch, and shall find them so, blessed are those servants.

"And this now that if the good man of the house had known what the hour the thief would come he would have watched, and not suffered his house to be broken through.

"Be ye therefore ready also, for the Son of Man cometh at an hour when ye think not."

Rachel stirred a little, and Aunt Debby looked up and closed the book.

"I'm afeared I've roused ye up too soon," she said, coming toward the bed with a look of real concern upon her sad, sweet face. "I raylly didn't intend ter. I jest opened the book ter read teh promise 'bout our Father heedin' even a sparrer's fall, an' forgot 'bout our Father heedin' even a sparrer's fall, an' forgot, an' read on; an' when I read, I must read out loud, ter git the good of hit. Some folks pretend they kin understand jest ez well when they read ter themselves. Mebbe they kin."

"O, no," replied Rachel cheerfully, "you didn't disturb me in the least. It was time that I got up, and I was glad to hear you read. I'm only troubled with the fear that I've overslept myself, and missed the duty that I was intended for."

"Make yourself easy on that 'ere score. Ye'll not be needed to-day, nor likely to-morrow. Some things hev come up ter change Jim's plans."

"I am very sorry," said Rachel, sitting up in the bed and tossing back her long, silken mane with a single quick, masterful motion. "I wished to go immediately about what I am expected to do. I can do anything better than wait."

Aunt Debby came impulsively to the bedside, threw an arm around Rachel's neck, and kissed her on the forehead. "I love ye, honey," she said with admiring tenderness. "Ye' 're sich ez all women orter be. Ye 'll make heroes of yer husband and sons. Ye 've yit ter l'arn though, thet the most of a woman's life, an' the hardest part of hit, is ter wait."

In her fervid state of mind Rachel responded electrically to this loving advance, made at the moment of all others when she felt most in need of sympathy and love. She put her strong arms around Aunt Debby, and held her for a moment close to her heart. From that moment the two women became of one accord. Womanlike, they sought relief from their high tension in light, irrelevant talk and care for the trifling details of their surroundings. Aunt Debby brought water and towels for Rachel's toilet, and fluttered around her, solicitous, helpful and motherly, and Rachel, weary of long companionship with men, delighted in the restfulness of association once more with a gentle, sweet-minded woman.

The heavy riding-habit was entirely too cumbersome for indoor wear, and Rachel put on instead one of Aunt Debby's "linsey" gowns, that hung from a peg, and laughed at the prim, demure mountain girl she saw in the glass. After a good breakfast had still farther raised her spirits she ventured upon a little pleasantry about the dramatic possibilities of a young lady who couls assume different characters with such facility.

The day passed quietly, with Rachel studying such of the Christmas festivities as were visible from the window, and from time to time exchanging personal history with Aunt Debby. She learned that the latter had left her home in Rockcastle Mountains with the Union Army in the previous Spring, and gone on to Chattanooga, to assist her nephew, Fortner, in obtaining the required information when Mitchell's army advanced against that place in the Summer. When the army retreated to the Ohio, in September, she had come as far back as Murfreesboro, and there stopped to await the army's return, which she was confident would not be long delayed.

"How brave and devoted you have been," said Rachel warmly, as Aunt Debby concluded her modestly-told story. "No man could have done better."

"No, honey," replied the elder woman, with her wan face coloring faintly, "I've done nothin' but my plain duty, ez I seed hit. I've done nothin' ter what THEY would've done had n't they been taken from me afore they had a chance. Like one who speaks ter us in the Book, I've been in journeyin's often, in peril of robbers, in perils of mine own countrymen, in perils in the city, in perils in the wilderness, in weariness an' painfulness, in watchings often, in hunger an' thirst, in fastings often, in cold an' nakedness, but he warns us not ter glory in these things, but in those which consarn our infirmities."

"How great should be your reward!"

"Don't speak of reward. I only want my freedom when I've 'arned hit--the freedom ter leave an 'arth on which I've been left behind, an' go whar my husband an' son are waitin' fur me."

She rose and paced the floor, with her face and eyes shining.

"Have you no fear of death whatever?" asked Rachel in amazement.

"Fear of death! Child, why should I fear death? Why should I fear death, more than the unborn child fears birth? Both are the same. Hit can't be fur ter thet other world whar THEY wait fur me. Hit is not even ez a journey ter the next town--hit's only one little step though the curtain o' green grass an' violets on a sunny hillside--only one little step."

She turned abruptly, and going back to her chair by the fireside, seated herself in it, and clasping her knees with her hands, rocked back and forth, and sang in a low, sweet croon:

"Oh, the rapturous, transporting scene,   That rises ter my sight; Sweet fields arrayed in livin' green,   An' rivers of delight.

"All o'er those wide, extended plains   Shines one eternal day; Thar God, the Son, forever reigns,   An scatters night away.

"No chillin' winds or poisonous breath   Kin reach thet healthful shore; Sickness an' sorrow, pain an' death,   Are felt an' feared no more."

After dark Fortner came in. Both women studied his face eagerly as he walked up to the fire.

"Nothin' yet, honey," he said to Aunt Debby, and "Nothin' yet, Miss," to Rachel, and after a little stay went out.

When Rachel awoke the next morning the sky was lowering darkly. On going to the window she found a most depressing change from the scene of bright merriment she had studied the night before. A chill Winter rain was falling with dreary persistence, pattering on the dead leaves that covered the ground, and soaking into the sodden earth. A few forlorn little birds hopped wearily about, searching in vain in the dry husks and empty insect shells for the food that had once been so plentiful there. Up and down the streets, as far as she could see, men in squads or singly, under officers or without organization, plodded along dejectedly, taking the cold drench from above, and the clinging mud around their feet, with the dumb, stolid discontent characteristic of seasoned veterans. When mules and horses went by they seemed poor and shrunken. They drew their limbs and bodies together, as if to present the least surface to the inclement showers, and their labored, toilsome motion contrasted painfully with their strong, free movement on brighter days. Everything and everybody in sight added something to increase the dismalness of the view, and as Rachel continued to gaze upon it the "horrors" took possession of her. She began to brood wretchedly over her position as a spy inside the enemy's lines, and upon all the consequences of that position.

It was late that night when Fortner came in. As he entered the two expectant women saw, by the ruddy light of the fire, that his face was set and his eyes flashing. He hung his dripping hat on a peg in the chimney, and kicked the blazing logs with his wet boots until a flood of meteor sparks flew up the throat of the fireplace. Turning, he said, without waiting to be questioned:

"Well, the hunt's begun at last. Our folks came out'n Nashville this morning in three big armies, marchin' on different roads, an they begun slashin' at the Rebels wherever they could find 'em. Thar's been fouten at Triune an' Lavergne, an' all along the line. They histed the Rebels out'n ther holes everywhar, an' druv' em back on the jump. Wagon load arter wagon load o' wounded's comin' back. I come in ahead of a long train agwine ter the hospital. Hark! ye kin heah 'em now."

The women listened.

They heard the ceaseless patter and swish of the gloomy rain--the gusty sighs of the wind through the shade-trees' naked branches--louder still the rolling of heavy wheels over the rough streets; and all these were torn and rent by the shrieks of men in agony.

"Poor fellows," said Rachel, "how they are suffering!"

"Think ruther," said Aunt Debby calmly, "of how they've made others suffer. Hit's God's judgement on 'em."

Rachel turned to Fortner. "What will come next? Will this end it? Will the Rebels fall back and leave this place?"

"Hardly. This's on'y like the fust slap in the face in a fight atween two big savage men, who've locked horns ter see which is the best man. Hit's on'y a sorter limberin' the jints fur the death rassel."

"Yes; and what next?"

"Well, Rosy's started fur this 'ere place, an' he's bound ter come heah. Bragg's bound he sha'n't come heah, an' is gittin' his men back to defend the town."

"What am I--what are we to do in the meanwhile?"

"Ye're ter do nothin', on'y stay in the house ez close ez ye kin, an' wait tell the chance comes ter use ye. Hit may be ter-morrer, an' hit mayn't be fur some days. These army moves are mouty unsartin. Aunt Debby 'll take keer on ye, an' ye 'll not be in a mite o' danger."

"But we'll see you frequently?"

"Ez offen ez I kin arrange hit. I'm actin' ez orderly an' messenger 'bout head-quarters, but I'll come ter ye whenever I kin git a chance, an' keep ye posted."

This was Friday night. All day Saturday, as long as the light lasted, Rachel stood at the window and watched with sinking heart the steady inflow of the Rebels from the north. That night she and Aunt Debby waited till midnight for Fortner, but he did not come. All day Sunday she stood at her post, and watched the unabated pouring-in on the Nashville pike. Fortner did not come that night. She was downcast, but no shade disturbed the serenity of Aunt Debby's sweet hymning. So it was again on Monday and Tuesday. The continually-swarming multitudes weighed down her spirits like a millstone. She seemed to be encompassed by millions of armed enemies. They appeared more plentiful than the trees, or the rocks, or the leaves even. They filled the streets of the little town until it seemed impossible for another one to find standing room. Their cavalry blackened the faces of the long ranges of hills. Their artillery and wagons streamed along the roads in a never-ending train. Their camp-fires lighted up the country at night for miles, in all directions.

Just at dusk Tuesday night Fortner came in, and was warmly welcomed.

"There are such countless hosts of the Rebels," Rachel said to him after the first greetings were over, "that I quite despair of our men being able to do anything with them. It seems impossible that there can be gathered together anywhere else in the world as many men as they have."

"I don't wonder ye think so, but ef ye'd been whar I wuz to-day ye'd think thet all the world wuz marchin' round in blue uniforms. Over heah hit seems ez ef all the cedars on the hills hed suddintly turned inter Rebel soldiers. Three miles from heah the blue-coats are swarmin' thicker'n bees in a field o' buckwheat."

"Three miles from here! Is our army within three miles of here?"

"Hit sartinly is, an' the Lord-awfullest crowd o' men an' guns an' hosses thet ever tromped down the grass o' this ere airth. Why, hit jest dazed my eyes ter look at 'em. Come ter this other winder. D' ye see thet furtherest line o' campfires, 'way on yander hill? Well, them's Union. Ef ye could see far enuf ye'd see they're 'bout five miles long, an' they look purtier'n the stars in heaven."

"But if they are so close the battle will begin immediately, will it not?"

"Hit ain't likely ter be put off very long, but thar's no tellin' what'll happen in war, or when."

"When is my time to come?"

"Thet's what I've come furt ter tell ye. Ef we're agwine ter be of sarvice ter the Guv'MENT, we must do hit to-night, fur most likely the battle'll begin in the mornin'. Hit's not jest the way I intended ter make use of ye, but hit can't be helped now. I hev information thet must reach Gineral Rosencrans afore daybreak. The vict'ry may depend on hit. Ter make sure all on us must start with hit, fur gittin' through the lines is now mouty dangersome, an' somebody--mebbe several--is bound to git cotcht, mebbe wuss. The men I expected ter help me are all gone. I hain't nobody now but ye an Aunt Debby. D'ye dar try an' make yer way through the lines to-night?"

Rachel thought a minute upon the dreadful possibilities of the venture, and then replied firmly:

"Yes I dare. I will try anything that the rest of you will attempt."

"Good. I knowed ye'd talk thet-a-way. Now we must waste no time in gittin' started, fur God on'y knows what diffikilties we'll meet on the way, an' Rosencrans can't hev the information enny too soon. Ev'ry minute hit's kep' away from him'll cost many vallerable lives--mebbe help defeat the army."

"Tell me quickly, then, what I must do, that I may lose no time in undertaking it."

"Well, heah's a plan of the position at sundown of the Rebels. Hit's drawed out moughty roughly but hit'll show jest whar they all are, an' about the number there is at each place. Hit begins on the right, which is south of Stone River, with Breckenridge's men; then across the river is Withers, an' Cheatham, an' Cleburne, with McCown's division on the left, an' Wharton's cavalry on the flank. But the thing o' most importance is thet all day long they've been movin' men round ter ther left, ter fall on our right an' crush hit. They're hid in the cedar thickets over thar, an' they'll come out to-morrow mornin' like a million yellin' devils, an' try ter sweep our right wing offen the face o' the arth. D'ye understand what I've tole ye?"

"Yes. Breckenridge's division is on their right, and south of Stone River. Withers, Cheatham, and Cleburne come next, on the north of the river, with McCown's division and Wharton's cavalry on the left, as shown in the sketch, and they are moving heavy forces around to their left, with the evident intention of falling overwhelmingly on our right early in the morning."

"Thet's hit. Thet's hit. But lay all the stres ye kin on the movin' around ter ther left. Thar's mo' mischief in thet than all the rest. Say thet thar's 20,000 men gwine round thar this arternoon an' evening'. Say thet thar's the biggest thunder-cloud o' danger thet enny one ever seed. Say hit over an' over, tell everybody understands hit an' gits ready ter meet hit. Tell hit till ye've made ev'ry one on 'em understand thet thar can't be no mistake about hit, an' they must look out fur heeps o' trouble on ther right. Tell hit ez ye never tole anything afore in yer life. Tell hit ez ye'd pray God Almighty fur the life o' the one thet ye love better then all the world beside. An' GIT THAR ter tell hit--git thru the Rebel lines--ef ye love yer God an' yer country, an' ye want ter see the brave men who are ter die tomorrer make their deaths count somethin' to'ard savin' this Union. Hit may be thet yore information'll save the army from defeat. Hit may be--hit's most likely--thet hit'll save the lives o' thousands o' brave men who love ther lives even ez yo an' me loves ourn."

"Trust me to do all that a devoted woman can. I will get through before daybreak or die in the attempt. But how am I to go?"

"Hide this paper somewhar. Aunt Debby'll fix ye up ez a country gal, while I'm gittin' yer mar saddled an' bridled with some common harness, instid o' the fancy fixin's ye hed when ye rode out heah. Ef ye're stopt, ez ye likely will be, say that ye've been ter town fur the doctor, an' some medicine fur yer sick mammy, an' are tryin' ter git back ter yer home on the south fork o' Overall's Creek. Now, go an' git ready ez quick ez the Lord'll let ye."

As she heard the mare's hoofs in front of the door, Rachel came out with a "slat-sun-bonnet" on her head, and a long, black calico riding-skirt over her linsey dress. Fortner gave her attire an approving nod. Aunt Debby followed her with a bottle. "This is the medicine ye've bin ter git from Dr. Thacker heah in town," she said, handing the vial. "Remember the name, fur fear ye mout meet some one who knows the town. Dr. Thacker, who lives a little piece offen the square, an' gives big doses of epecac fur everything, from brakebone fever ter the itch."

"Dr. Thacker, who lives just off the square," said Rachel. "I'll be certain to remember."

"Take this, too," said Fortner, handing her a finely-finished revolver, of rather large caliber. "Don't pull hit onless ye can't git along without hit, an' then make sho o' yer man. Salt him."

"Good-by--God bless ye," said Aunt Debby, taking Rachel to her heart in a passionate embrace, and kissing her repeatedly. "God bless ye agin. No one ever hed more need o' His blessin' then we'uns will fur the next few hours. Ef He does bless us an' our work we'll all be safe an' sound in Gineral Rosencrans' tent afore noon. But ef His will's different we'll be by thet time whar the Rebels cease from troublin', and the weary are at rest. I'm sure thet ef I thot the Rebels war gwine ter whip our men I'd never want ter see the sun rise ter-morrer. Good-by; we're all in the hands o' Him who seeth even the sparrer's fall."

Fortner led the mare a little ways, to where he could get a good view, and then said:

"Thet second line o' fires which ye see over thar is our lines--them fires I mean which run up inter the woods. The fust line is the Rebels. Ye'll go right out this road heah tell ye git outside the town, an' then turn ter yer right an' make fur the Stone River. Ford hit or swim your mar' acrost, an' make yer way thru or round the Rebel line. Ef ye find a good road, an' everything favorable ye mout try ter make yer way strait thru ef ye kin fool the gyards with yer story. Ef ye're fearful ye can't then ride beyond the lines, an' come inter ours thet-a-way Aunt Deby'll go ter the other flank, an' try ter git a-past Breckinridge's pickets, an' I'll 'tempt ter make my way thru the center. We may all or none o' us git thru. I can't gin ye much advice, ez ye'll hev ter trust mainly ter yerself. But remember all the time what hangs upon yer gittin' the news ter Rosy afore daybreak. Think all the time thet mebbe ye kin save the hull army, mebbe win the vict'ry, sartinly save heeps o' Union lives an' fool the pizen Rebels. This is the greatest chance ye'll ever hev ter do good in all yer life, or a hundred more, ef ye could live 'em. Good-by. Ef God Almighty smiles on us we'll meet ter-morrer on yon side o' Stone River. Ef He frowns we'll meet on yon side o' the Shinin' River. Good-by."

He released her hand and her horse, and she rode forward into the darkness.

Her course took her first up a main street, which was crowded with wagons, ambulances and artillery. Groups of men mingled with these, and crowded upon the sidewalks. When she passed the light of a window the men stared at her, and some few presumed upon her homely garb so far as to venture upon facetious and complimentary remarks, aimed at securing a better acquaintance.

She made no reply, but hurried her mare onward, as fast as she could pick her way. She soon passed out of the limits of the town and was in the country, though she was yet in the midst of camps, and still had to thread her way through masses of men, horses and wagons moving along the road.

The first flutter of perturbation at going out into the darkness and the midst of armed men had given way to a more composed feeling. No one had stopped her, or offered to, no one had shown any symptom of surprise at her presence there at that hour. She began to hope that this immunity would continue until she had made her way to the Union lines. she had left the thick of the crowd behind some distance, and was going along at a fair pace, over a clear road, studying all the while the line of fires far to her right, in an attempt to discover a promising dark gap in their extent.

She was startled by a hand laid upon her bridle, and a voice saying:

"Say, Sis, who mout ye be, an' whar mout ye be a-mosyin' ter this time o' night?"

She saw a squad of brigandish-looking stragglers at her mare's head.

"My name's Polly Briggs. I live on the South Fork o' Overall's Creek. I've done been ter Dr. Thacker's in Murfreesboro, fur some medicine fur my sick mammy, an' I'm on my way back home, an' I'd be much obleeged ter ye, gentlemen, ef ye'd 'low me ter go on, kase mammy's powerful sick, an' she's in great hurry fur her medicine."

She said this with a coolness and a perfect imitation of the speech and manner of the section that surprised herself. As she ended she looked directly at the squad, and inspected them. She saw she had reason to be alarmed. They were those prowling wolves found about all armies, to whom war meant only wider opportunities for all manner of villainy and outrage. An unprotected girl was a welcome prize to them. It was not death as a spy she had to fear, but worse. Now, if ever, she must act decisively. The leader took his hand from her bridle, as if to place it on her.

"Yer a powerful peart sort of a gal, an' ez purty ez a fawn. yer mammy kin git 'long without the medicine a little while, an'---"

He did not finish the sentence, for before his hand could touch her Rachel's whip cut a deep wale across his face, and then it fell so savagely upon the mare's flank that the high-spirited animal sprung forward as if shot from a catapult, and was a hundred yards away before the rascals really comprehended what had happened.

Onward sped the mettled brute, so maddened by the first cruel blow she had ever received that she refused to obey the rein, but made her own way by and through such objects as she encountered. When she at last calmed down the road was clear and lonely, and Rachel began searching for indications of a favorable point of approach to the river, that hinted at a bridge or a ford. While engaged in this she heard voices approaching. A moment's listening to teh mingling of tones convinced her that it was another crowd of stragglers, and she obeyed her first impulse, which was to leap her horse over a low stone wall to her right. Taking her head again, the mare did not stop until she galloped down to the water's edge.

"I'll accept this as lucky," said Rachel to herself. "The ancients trusted more to their horses' instincts than their own perceptions in times of danger, and I'll do the same. I'll cross here."

She urged the mare into the water. The beast picked her way among the boulders on the bottom successfully for a few minutes. The water rose to Rachel's feet, but that seemed its greatest depth, and in a few more yards she would gain the opposite bank, when suddenly the mare stepped upon a slippery steep, her feet went from under her instantly, and steed and rider rolled in the sweeping flood of ice-cold water. Rachel's first thought was that she should surely drown, but hope came back as she caught a limb swinging from a tree on the bank. With this she held her head above water until she could collect herself a little, and then with great difficulty pulled herself up the muddy, slippery bank. The weight of her soaked clothes added greatly to the difficulty and the fatigue, and she lay for some little time prone upon her face across the furrows of a cotton field, before she could stand erect. At last she was able to stand up, and she relieved herself somewhat by taking off her calico riding skirt and wringing the water from it. Her mare had also gained the bank near the same point she had, and stood looking at her with a world of wonder at the whole night's experience in her great brown eyes.

"Poor thing," said Rachel sympathetically. "This is only the beginning. Heaven knows what we won't have to go through with before the sun rises."

She tried to mount, but her watery garments were too much for her agility, and with the wet skirts fettering her limbs she began toiling painfully over the spongy, plowed ground, in search of a stump or a rock. She thought she saw many around her, but on approaching one after another found they were only large cotton plants, with a boll or two of ungathered cotton on them, which aided the darkness in giving them their deceptive appearance. She prevented herself from traveling in a circle, by remembering this aptitude of benighted travelers, and keeping her eye steadily fixed on a distant camp-fire. When she at last came to the edge of the field she had to lean against the fence for some minutes before she could recover from her fatigue sufficiently to climb upon it. While she sat for a minute there she heard some cocks, at a neighboring farm-house, crow the turn of night.

"It is midnight," she said feverishly, "and I have only begun the journey. Now let every nerve and muscle do its utmost."

She rode along the fence until she came to an opening which led into what appeared in the darkness to be another cotton field, but proved to be a worn-out one, long ago abandoned to the rank-growing briars, which clung to and tore her skirts, and seamed the mare's delicate skin with bleeding furrows. The flinching brute pressed onward, in response to her mistress's encouragement, but the progress was grievously slow.

Presently Rachel began to see moving figures a little way ahead of her, and hear voices in command. She eralized that she was approaching the forces moving to the attack on the Union right. There was something grotesque, weird, even frightful in the sounds and the aspect of the moving masses and figures, but she at last made out that they were batteries, regiments and mounted men. She decided that her best course was to mingle with and move along with them, until she could get a chance to ride away in advance. For hours that seemed weeks she remained entangled in the slow-moving mass, whose bewildering vagaries of motion were as trying to the endurance of her steed as they were exasperating to her own impatience. Occasionally she caught glimpses of the Union camp-fires in the distance, that, low and smoldering, told of the waning night, and she would look anxiously over her left shoulder for a hint of the coming of the dreaded dawn. Her mare terrified her with symptoms of giving out.

At last she saw an unmistakable silvery break in the eastern clouds. Half-frantic she broke suddenly out of the throng by an abrupt turn to the right, and lashing her mare savagely, galloped where a graying in the dense darkness showed an opening between two cedar thickets, that led to the picket-fires, half a mile away. The mare's hoofs beat sonorously on the level limestone floor, which there frequently rises through the shallow soil and starves out the cedar.

"Halt! Go back," commanded a hoarse voice in front of her, which was accompanied with the clicking of a gunlock. "Ye can't pass heah."

"Lemme pass, Mister," she pleaded. "I'm on'y a gal, with medicine fur my mammy, an' I'm powerful anxious ter git home."

"No, ye can't git out heah. Orders are strict; besides, ef ye did the Yankees 'd cotch ye. They're jest out thar."

She became aware that there were heavy lines of men lying near, and fearing to say another word, she turned and rode away to the left. She became entagled with a cavalry company moving toward the extreme Union right, and riding with it several hundred yards, turned off into a convenient grove just as the light began to be sufficient to distinguish her from a trooper. She was now, she was sure, outside of the Rebel lines, but she had gone far to the south, where the two lines were wide apart. The Union fifes and drums, now sounding what seemed an unsuspicous and cheerful reveille, were apparently at least a mile away. It was growing lighter rapidly, and every passing moment was fraught with the weightiest urgency. She concentrated all her energies for a supreme effort, and lashed her mare forward over the muddy cotton-field. The beast's hoofs sank in the loose red loam, as if it were quicksand, and her pace was maddeningly slow. At last Rachel came in sight of a Union camp at the edge of a cedar thicket. The arms were stacked, the men were cooking breakfast, and a battery of cannon standing near had no horses attached.

Rachel beat the poor mare's flanks furiously, and shouted.

"Turn out! The Rebels are coming! The Rebels are coming!"

Her warning came too late. Too late, also, came that of the pickets, who were firing their guns and rushing back to camp before an awful wave of men that had rolled out of the cedars on the other side of the cotton field.

A hundred boisterous drums were now making the thickets ring with the "long roll." Rachel saw the men in front of her leave their coffee-making, rush to the musket stacks and take their places in line. In another minute they were ordered forward to the fence in front of them, upon which they rested their muskets. Rachel rode through their line and turned around to look. The broad cotton field was covered with solid masses of Rebels, rushing forward with their peculiar fierce yell.

"Fire!" shouted the Colonel in front of her. The six field-pieces to her right split her ears with their crash. A thousand muskets blazed out a fire that withered the first line of the advancing foe. Another crash, and the Rebels had answered with musketry and artillery, that tore the cedars around her, sent the fencerails flying into the air, and covered the ground with blue-coats. Her faithful mare shied, caught her hoof in a crack in the limestone, and fell with a broken leg.

So began that terrible Wednesday, December 31, 1862.

Bragg's plan of battle was very simple. Rosencrans had stretched out a long thin wing through the cedars to the right of the pike. At the pike it was very strong, but two miles away it degenerated into scattered regiments, unskilfully disposed. Bragg threw against these three or four to one, with all the fury of the Southern soldier in the onset. The line was crumbled, and before noon crushed back to the pike.

Rachel disengaged herself from her fallen steed, and leaning against a sapling, watched the awful collision. She forgot the great danger in the fascination of the terrible spectacle. She thought she had seen men scale the whole gamut of passion, but their wildest excesses were tame and frothy beside this ecstacy of rage in the fury of battle. The rustic Southerners whom she had seen at ball-play, the simple-hearted Northerners whom she had alarmed at their coffee-making, were now transformed into furies mad with the delirium of slaughter, and heedless of their own lives in the frenzy of taking those of others.

"You had better run back, young woman," said some one touching her elbow. "The whole line's going to fall back. We're flanked."

A disorderly stream of men, fragments of the shattered right, caught her in its rush, and she was borne back to the open fields lying along the pike. There, as when a turbulent river empties into a bay, the force of the current subsided, and she was dropped like silt. The cowardly ones, hatless and weaponless, ran off toward the pike, but the greater portion halted, formed in line, called for their comrades to join them, and sent for more cartridges.

Almost dropping with fatigue, Rachel made her way to a pile of cracker-boxes by an Osage-orange hedge, on a knoll, and sat down. Some fragments of hard-bread, dropped on the trampled sod while rations were being issued, lay around. She was so hungry that she picked up one or two that were hardly soiled, and nibbled them.

The dreadful clamor of battle grew louder continually. The musketry had swollen into a sullen roar, with the artillery pulsating high above it. Crashing vollies of hundreds of muskets fired at once, told of new regiments joining in the struggle. Rebel brigades raised piercing treble yells as they charged across the open fields against the Union positions. The latter responded with deep-lunged cheers, as they hurled their assailants back. Clouds of slowly curling smoke rose above thickets filled with maddened men, firing into one another's breasts. Swarms of rabbits and flocks of birds dashed out in terror from the dark coverts in which they had hitherto found security.

No gallantry could avail against such overwhelming numbers as assailed the Union right. The stream of disorganized men flowing back from the thickets became wider and swifter every minute; every minute, too, the din of the conflict came closer; every minute the tide of battle rolled on to regiments lying nearer the pike.

A Surgeon with a squad of stretcher-bearers came up to where Rachel was sitting.

"Pull down some of those boxes, and fix a place to lay the Colonel till we can make other arrangements," said a familiar voice. Rachel looked up, and with some difficulty reconciled a grimy-faced man in torn clothes with the trim Hospital Surgeon she had known.

"Can that be you, Dr. Denslow?" she said.

He had equal difficulty in recognizing her.

"Is it possible that it is you, Miss Bond?" he said in amazement, after she had spoken to him again. "Yes, this is I, or as much as is left of me. And here," and his voice trembled, "is about all that is left of the regiment. The rest are lying about the roots of those accursed cedars, a full mile from here."

"And Harry Glen--where is he?" she said, rising hurriedly from the boxes and passing along the line of stretchers, scanning each face.

A new pain appeared in the Doctor's face, as he watched her.

"You'll not find him there," he said. "The last I saw of him he was forming a handful of the regiment that were still on their feet, to retake cannon which the Rebels had captured. I was starting off with the Colonel here, when they dashed away."

"Come," he said, after making some temporary provisions for the comfort of his wounded. "You must get away from here as quickly as possible. I fear the army is badly defeated, and it may be a rout soon. You must get away before the rush begins, for then it will be terrible."

He took her over the pike, and across it to where some wagons were standing. As he was about to put Rachel in one of these their attention was arrested by an officer, apparently acting as Provost Marshal, dragging from behind a huge rock a Lieutenant who was skulking there. They were too far away to hear what was said, but not so far that they could not recognize the skulker as Lieutenant Jacob Alspaugh. The Provost Marshal apparently demanded the skulker's name, and wrote it in a book. Alspaugh seemed to give the information, and accompanied it with a lugubrious pointint to a bandage around his knee. The Provost Marshal stooped and took the handkerchief off, to find that not even the cloth of the pantaloons had been injured. He contemptuously tore the straps from Alspaugh's shoulders, and left him.

"The rascal's cowardice is like the mercy of God," said Denslow, "for it endureth forever."

He put Rachel in the wagon, and ordered the driver to start at once for Nashville with her. She pressed his hand, as they separated with fatigue and grief.

How had it been faring all this time with Harry Glen and those with him?

The fierce wave had dashed against the regiment early in the morning, and although the first fire received from the Rebels made gaps in the ranks where fifty men fell, it did not recoil a step, but drove its assailants back with such slaughter that their dead, lying in the open ground over which they crossed, were grimly compared by Abe Bolton to "punkins layin' in a field where the corn's been cut off."

Then the fight settled into a murderous musketry duel across the field, in which the ranks on both sides melted away like frost in the sun. In a few minutes all the field officers were down, and the only Captain that remained untouched took command of the regiment, shouting to Harry Glen at the same moment to take command of the two companies on the right, whose Captains, and Lietenants had fallen. Two guns escaping from the crush at the extreme right, had galloped down, and opened gallantly to assist the regiment. Almost instantly horses and men went down under the storm of bullets. An Aide broke through the cedars behind.

"Fall back--fall back, for God's sake!" he shouted. "The Rebels have got around the right, and will cut you off."

"Fall back, boys," shouted the Captain in command, "but keep together, listen to orders, and load as you go." The same instant he fell with a ball through his chest.

"Sergeant Glen, you're in command of the regiment, now," shouted a dozen voices.

The Lieutenant of the battery--a mere boy--ran up to Harry. A stream of blood on his jacket matched its crimson trimmings.

"Don't go off and leave my guns, after I've helped you. Do not, for the love of Heaven! I've saved them so far. Bring them off with you."

Harry looked inquiringly around upon the less than one hundred survivors, who gathered about him, and had heard the passionate appeal. Every face was set with mortal desperation. An Irish boy on the left was kissing a cross which he had drawn from his bosom.

The tears which strong men shed in wild fits of rage were rolling down the cheeks of Edwards, Bolton, and others.

"I don't want to live always!" shouted Kent with an oath; "let's take the ----- guns!"

"I don't want no better place to die than right here!" echoed Abe, still more savagely profane. "Le's have the guns, or sink into hell getting 'em!"

The remnant of the Rebel regiment had broken cover and rushed for the guns.

"Attention!" shouted Harry. "Fix bayonets!"

The sharp steel clashed on the muzzles.

"FORWARD, CHARGE!"

For one wild minute shining steel at arm's length did its awful work. Then three-score Rebels fled back to their leafy lair, and as many blue-coats with drew into the cedars, pulling the guns after them.

"Pick up the Lieutenant, there, some of you who can do a little lifting," said Kent, as they came to where the boy-artillerist lay dead. "This prod in my shoulder's spoilt my lifting for some time. Lay him on the gun and we'll take himj back with us. He deserves it, for he was game clear through. Harry, that fellow that gave you that beauty-mark on the temple with his saber got his discharge from the Rebel army just afterwards, on the point of Abe's bayonet."

"Is that so? Did Abe get struck at all?"

"Only a whack over the nose with the butt of a gun, which will doubtless improve his looks. Any change would."

"Guess we can go back now with some peace and comfort," said Abe, coming up, and alluding to the cessation of the firing in their front. "That last round took all the fight out of them hell-hounds across the field."

"Some of you had better go over to the camp there and get our axes. We'll have to cut a road through the cedars if we take these guns off," said Harry, tieing a handkershief around the gaping saber wound in his temple. "The rest of you get around to the right, and keep a sharp look out for the flank."

So they worked their way back, and a little after noon came to the open fields by the pike.

As the wagon rolled slowly down the pike toward Nashville Rachel, in spite of anxiety, fell asleep. Some hours later she was awakened by the driver shaking her rudely.

"Wake up!" he shouted, "ef ye value yer life!"

"Where are we?" she asked, rubbing her eyes.

"At Stewart's Creek," answered the driver, "an' all o' Wheeler's cavalry are out thar' in them woods."

She looked out. She could see some miles ahead of her, and as far as she could see the road was filled with wagons moving toward Nashville. A sharp spurt of firing on the left attracted her attention, and she saw a long wave of horsemen ride out of the woods, and charge the wagon-guards, who made a sharp resistence, but at length fled before overwhelming numbers. The teamsters, at the first sight of the formidable line, began cutting their wheel-mules loose, and escaping upon them. Rachel's teamster followed their example.

"The off-mule's unhitcht; jump on him, an' skip," he shouted to her as he vanished up the pike.

The Rebels were shooting down the mules and such teamsters as remained. Some dismounted, and with the axes each wagon carried, chopped the spokes until the wagon fell, while others ran along and started fires in each. In a little while five hundred wagons loaded with rations, clothing, amunition and stores were blazing furiously. Their work done, the cavalry rode off toward Nashville in search of other trains.

Rachel leaped from the wagon, before the Rebels approached, and took refuge behind a large tree, whence she saw her wagon share the fate of the rest. When the cavalry disappeared, she came out again into the road and walked slowly up it, debating what she could do. She was rejoiced to meet her teamster returning. He had viewed the occurence from a prudent distance, and being kindly-natured had decided to return to her help, as soon as it could be done without risk.

He told her that there was a wagon up the pike a little ways with a woman in it, to which he would conduct her, and they would go back to the army in front of Murfreesboro.

"It seems a case of 'twixt the devil and the deep sea," he said, despairingly. "At any rate we can't stay out here, and my experience is that it is always safest where there is the biggest crowd."

They found the wagon with the woman in it. Its driver had bolted irrevocably, so Rachel's friend assumed the reins. It was slow work making their way back through the confused mass, but Rachel was lucky enough to sleep through most of it. When she awoke the next morning the wagon was still on the pike, but in the center of the army, which filled all the open space round-about.

Everywhere were evidences of the terrible work of the day before, and of preparations for renewing it. The soldiers, utterly exhausted by the previous days' frightful strain, lay around on the naked ground, sleeping, or in a half-waking torpor.

An officer rode up to the wagon. "There seems to be some flour on this wagon," said the voice of Dr. Denslow. "Well, that may stay the boys' stomachs until we can get something better. Go on a little ways, driver."

"O, Doctor Denslow," called out Rachel, as the wagon stopped again, "what is the news?"

"You here again?" said the Doctor, recognizing the voice: "well that is good news. When I heard about Wheeler's raid on our trains I was terribly alarmed as to your fate. This relieves me much."

"But how about the army?"

"Well it seems to have been a case of hammer and anvil yesterday, in which both suffered pretty badly, but the hammer go much the worst of it. We are in good shape now to give them some more, if they want it, which so far they have not indicated very strongly. Here, Sergeant Glen, is a couple barrels of flour, which you can take to issue to your regiment."

Had not the name been called Rachel could never have recognized her former elegant lover in the salwart man with tattered uniform, swollen face, and head wrapped in a bloody bandage, who came to the wagon with a squad to receive the flour.

A tumult of emotions swept over her, but superior to them all was the feminine feeling that she could not endure to have Harry see her in her present unprepossessing plight.

"Don't mention my name before those men," she said to Dr. Denslow, when he came near again.

"Very good," he answered. "Sit still in the wagon, and nobody will see you. I will have the wagon driver over to the hospital presently, with the remainder of the flour, and you can go along."

All the old love seemed to have been out at compound interest, from the increment that came back to her at the sound of Harry Glen's voice, now so much deeper, fuller and more masterful than in the fastidious days of yore. She lifted the smallest corner of the wagon-cover and looked out. The barrel heads had been beaten in with stones, and a large cupful of flour issued to each of the hungry men. They had mixed it up into dough with water from the ditch, and were baking it before the fire on large flat stones, which abounded in the vicinity.

"I'll mix up enough for all three of us on this board," she heard Harry say to Abe and Kent. "With your game arm, Kent, and Abe's battered eyes, your cooking skill's about gone. You ought to both of you go to the hospital. You can't do any good, and why expose yourself for nothing? I've a mind to use my authority and send you to the hospital under guard."

"You try it if you dare, after my saving your life yesterday," said Abe. "I can see well enough yet to shoot toward the Rebels, and that's all that's necessary."

"I enlisted for the war," said Kent, "and I'm going to stay till peace is declared. I went into this fight to see it through, and I'm going to stay until we whhip them if there's a piece of me left that can wiggle. Bragg's got to acknowledge that I'm the best man before I'll ever let up on him."

Rachel longed to leap out of the wagon, and do the bread-making for these clumsy fellows, but pride would not consent.

The dough was browning slowly on the hot stones, but not yet nearly done, when the spiteful spirits of firing out in front suddenly burst into a roar, with a crash of artillery. A bugle sounded near.

"Fall in, boys," shouted Harry, springing to his feet, and tearing off the flakes of dough, which he hastily divided with his comrades. "Right dress. Right face, forward, file right--march!"

"If there is anything that I despise, it's disturbing a gentleman at his meals," said Kent, giving the fire a spiteful kick, as he tucked the bread under his lame arm, took his musket in his other hand, and started off in the rear of the regiment, accompanied by the purblind Abe.

Rachel's heart sank, as she saw them move off, but it rose again when the firing died down as suddenly as it had flamed up.

Soon Dr. Denslow took the wagon off to a cabin on a high bank of Stone River, which he was using as a hospital.

She called some question to him, as he turned away to direct the preparation of the flour into food for his patients, when some one cried out from the interior of the cabin:

"Rachel Bond! Is that you? Come in heah, honey."

She entered, and found Aunt Debby lying on the rude bed of the former inhabitants of the cabin.

"O my love--my darling--my honey, is that you?" said the elderly woman, with streaming eyes, reaching out her thin arms to take Rachel to her heart. "I never expected ter see ye ag'in! But God is good."

"Aunt Debby, is it possible? Are you hurt, dear?"

"No, not hurt child; on'y killed," she answered with a sweet radiance on her face.

"Killed? It is not possible."

"Yes, honey, it is possible. It is true. The gates open for me at last."

"How did it happen?"

"I got through Breckenridge's lines all right, an' reached the river, but thar was a picket thar, hid behind a tree, and ez he heered my hoss's feet splash in the ford, he shot me through the back. An' I didn't get through in time," she added, with the first shade of melancholy that had yet appeared in her face. "Did YOU?"

"No, I was too late, too."

"An' Jim must've been, too. Hev ye seed him any whar?"

"No," said Rachel, unable to restrain her tears.

"Now, honey, don't cry for me--don't," said Aunt Debby, pulling the young face down to where she could kiss it. "Hit's jest ez I want hit. On'y let me know thet Bragg is whipt, an' I die happy."

All day Thursday the two bruised armies lay and confronted each other, as two bulldogs, which have torn and mangled one another, will stop for a few minutes, to lick their hurts and glare their hatred, while they regain breath to carry on the fight.

Friday morning it was the same, but there was a showing of teeth and a rising fierceness as the day grew older, which was very portentous.

While standing at the door of the cabin Rachel had seen Harry Glen march down the bank at the head of the regiment, and cross the ford to the heights in front of Breckenridge. She picked up a field-glass that lay on a shelf near, and followed the movements of the force the regiment had joined.

"What d' ye see, honey?" called out Aunt Debby. She was becoming very fearful that she would die before the victory was won.

"Our people," answered Rachel, "seem to be concentrating in front of Breckenridge. There must be a division over there. Breckenridge sees it, and his cannon are firing at our men. He is bringing men up at the double quick." She stopped, for a spasm of fear in regard to Harry choked her.

"Go on, honey. What are they doing now?"

"Our men have formed a long line, reaching from the river up to the woods. They begin to march forward. Breckenridge opens more guns. They cut lanes through them. Now the infantry begins firing. A cloud of smoke settles down and hides both sides. I can see no more. O my God, our men are running. The whole line comes back out of the smoke, with men dropping at every step. If Harry were only safely out of there, I'd give my life."

Aunt Debby groaned. "Look again, honey," she said after a moment's pause.

"It's worse than ever. Breckenridge's men are swarming out of their works. There seems to be a myriad of them. They cover the whole hillside until I can not see the ground. They yell like demons, and drive our men down into the river. They follow them to the water's edge and shoot them down in the stream. Ah, there goes a battery on the gallop to the hill in front of us. It has opened on the Rebels, and its shells dig great holes in the black masses, but the Rebels still come on. There goes another battery on the gallop. It has opened. There is another. Still another. They are galloping over here from every direction."

"Glory!" shouted Aunt Debby.

"There's a fringe of trees near the water's edge, whose tops reach nearly tot he top of the hill. The cannon shots tear the branches off and dash down the great ranks of Rebels with them."

"The arth rocks as when He lays his finger upon hit," said Aunt Debby.

The ground was trembling under the explosion of the fifty-eight pieces of artillery which Rosencrans hastily massed at four o'clock Friday, for the relief of his overpowered left. "What's them that go 'boo-woo-woo,' like great big dogs barkin'?"

"Those are John Mendenhall's big Napoleons," said a wounded artillery officer. "Go on, Miss. What now?"

"The Rebels have stopped coming on. They are apparently firing back. The shells and the limbs of the trees still break their lines and tear them to pieces. Now our men dash across the river again, and begin a musketry fire that mows them down. They start to run, and our men charge after them, cheering as they run. Our men have taken their cannon away from them. The Rebels are running for life to get inside their works. The hillside is dotted with those who have fallen, and there are rows of them lying near the water. Now everything is quieting down again."

"Glory ter God! for He has at last given the enemy inter our hands. Come and kiss me, honey, an' say good-by."

From the throats of twenty-five thousand excited spectators of the destruction of Breckenridge's division rose cheers of triumph that echoed to the clouds.

"What sweet music that is!" said Aunt Debby, half unclosing her eyes. "God bless ye, honey. Good-by."

The gentle eyes closed forever.

Late in the evening Dr. Denslow's stretcher corps brough in Harry Glen, who had fallen in the last charge with a flesh wound in the leg. Until he woke the next morning to find her sitting by his bedside, Harry thought he had been dreaming all the time that Rachel Bond had come to him, dressed in quaint country garb, and loosed with gentle, painless fingers the stiff, blood-encrusted bandage about his head, and replaced it with something that soothed and eased his fevered temples.

"I have very good news for you," she said, later in the day. "Kent Edwards says that you are promoted to Captain, by special orders, for 'Conspicuous gallantry on the battle-field of Stone River.'"

"And when are we to be married?" he asked.

"Just as soon as you are able to travel back to Sardis."

They looked up and saw Dr. Denslow standing beside them. A stunned look on his face indicated that he had heard and understood all. This speedily gave away to his accustomed expression of serene philosophy.

"Forget me, except as a friend," he said. "It is better as it is for you, Harry, and certainly better for her. Possibly it is better for"--with a little gasp--"me. The sweets of love are not for me. They are irrational, and irrational things are carefully eliminated from my scheme of life."

Towards evening Fortner came in with the news "Thet ole Bragg picked up his traps and skipped out fur Tullahoma, ter nuss his hurts, leavin' his wounded and lots o' stores in our hands."

So was gained the great victory of Stone River.

The Codes Of Hammurabi And Moses
W. W. Davies

QTY

The discovery of the Hammurabi Code is one of the greatest achievements of archaeology, and is of paramount interest, not only to the student of the Bible, but also to all those interested in ancient history...

Religion   **ISBN:** *1-59462-338-4*   **Pages:132**
MSRP $12.95

The Theory of Moral Sentiments
Adam Smith

QTY

This work from 1749. contains original theories of conscience amd moral judgment and it is the foundation for systemof morals.

Philosophy   **ISBN:** *1-59462-777-0*   **Pages:536**
MSRP $19.95

Jessica's First Prayer
Hesba Stretton

QTY

In a screened and secluded corner of one of the many railway-bridges which span the streets of London there could be seen a few years ago, from five o'clock every morning until half past eight, a tidily set-out coffee-stall, consisting of a trestle and board, upon which stood two large tin cans, with a small fire of charcoal burning under each so as to keep the coffee boiling during the early hours of the morning when the work-people were thronging into the city on their way to their daily toil...

Pages:84

Childrens   **ISBN:** *1-59462-373-2*   *MSRP $9.95*

My Life and Work
Henry Ford

QTY

Henry Ford revolutionized the world with his implementation of mass production for the Model T automobile. Gain valuable business insight into his life and work with his own auto-biography... "We have only started on our development of our country we have not as yet, with all our talk of wonderful progress, done more than scratch the surface. The progress has been wonderful enough but..."

Pages:300

Biographies/   **ISBN:** *1-59462-198-5*   *MSRP $21.95*

The Art of Cross-Examination
Francis Wellman

QTY

I presume it is the experience of every author, after his first book is published upon an important subject, to be almost overwhelmed with a wealth of ideas and illustrations which could readily have been included in his book, and which to his own mind, at least, seem to make a second edition inevitable. Such certainly was the case with me; and when the first edition had reached its sixth impression in five months, I rejoiced to learn that it seemed to my publishers that the book had met with a sufficiently favorable reception to justify a second and considerably enlarged edition. ..

Reference   **ISBN:** *1-59462-647-2*   **Pages:412**
MSRP $19.95

On the Duty of Civil Disobedience
Henry David Thoreau

QTY

Thoreau wrote his famous essay, On the Duty of Civil Disobedience, as a protest against an unjust but popular war and the immoral but popular institution of slave-owning. He did more than write—he declined to pay his taxes, and was hauled off to gaol in consequence. Who can say how much this refusal of his hastened the end of the war and of slavery ?

Law   **ISBN:** *1-59462-747-9*   **Pages:48**
MSRP $7.45

Dream Psychology Psychoanalysis for Beginners
Sigmund Freud

QTY

Sigmund Freud, born Sigismund Schlomo Freud (May 6, 1856 - September 23, 1939), was a Jewish-Austrian neurologist and psychiatrist who co-founded the psychoanalytic school of psychology. Freud is best known for his theories of the unconscious mind, especially involving the mechanism of repression; his redefinition of sexual desire as mobile and directed towards a wide variety of objects; and his therapeutic techniques, especially his understanding of transference in the therapeutic relationship and the presumed value of dreams as sources of insight into unconscious desires.

Psychology   **ISBN:** *1-59462-905-6*   **Pages:196**
MSRP $15.45

The Miracle of Right Thought
Orison Swett Marden

QTY

Believe with all of your heart that you will do what you were made to do. When the mind has once formed the habit of holding cheerful, happy, prosperous pictures, it will not be easy to form the opposite habit. It does not matter how improbable or how far away this realization may see, or how dark the prospects may be, if we visualize them as best we can, as vividly as possible, hold tenaciously to them and vigorously struggle to attain them, they will gradually become actualized, realized in the life. But a desire, a longing without endeavor, a yearning abandoned or held indifferently will vanish without realization.

Self Help   **ISBN:** *1-59462-644-8*   **Pages:360**
MSRP $25.45

The Rosicrucian Cosmo-Conception Mystic Christianity by *Max Heindel*   ISBN: *1-59462-188-8*   **$38.95**
The Rosicrucian Cosmo-conception is not dogmatic, neither does it appeal to any other authority than the reason of the student. It is: not controversial, but is: sent forth in the, hope that it may help to clear...   New Age/Religion Pages 646

Abandonment To Divine Providence by *Jean-Pierre de Caussade*   ISBN: *1-59462-228-0*   **$25.95**
"The Rev. Jean Pierre de Caussade was one of the most remarkable spiritual writers of the Society of Jesus in France in the 18th Century. His death took place at Toulouse in 1751. His works have gone through many editions and have been republished...   Inspirational/Religion Pages 400

Mental Chemistry by *Charles Haanel*   ISBN: *1-59462-192-6*   **$23.95**
Mental Chemistry allows the change of material conditions by combining and appropriately utilizing the power of the mind. Much like applied chemistry creates something new and unique out of careful combinations of chemicals the mastery of mental chemistry...   New Age Pages 354

The Letters of Robert Browning and Elizabeth Barret Barrett 1845-1846 vol II   ISBN: *1-59462-193-4*   **$35.95**
by *Robert Browning* and *Elizabeth Barrett*   Biographies Pages 596

Gleanings In Genesis (volume I) by *Arthur W. Pink*   ISBN: *1-59462-130-6*   **$27.45**
Appropriately has Genesis been termed "the seed plot of the Bible" for in it we have, in germ form, almost all of the great doctrines which are afterwards fully developed in the books of Scripture which follow...   Religion/Inspirational Pages 420

The Master Key by *L. W. de Laurence*   ISBN: *1-59462-001-6*   **$30.95**
In no branch of human knowledge has there been a more lively increase of the spirit of research during the past few years than in the study of Psychology, Concentration and Mental Discipline. The requests for authentic lessons in Thought Control, Mental Discipline and...   New Age/Business Pages 422

The Lesser Key Of Solomon Goetia by *L. W. de Laurence*   ISBN: *1-59462-092-X*   **$9.95**
This translation of the first book of the "Lernegton" which is now for the first time made accessible to students of Talismanic Magic was done, after careful collation and edition, from numerous Ancient Manuscripts in Hebrew, Latin, and French...   New Age/Occult Pages 92

Rubaiyat Of Omar Khayyam by *Edward Fitzgerald*   ISBN:*1-59462-332-5*   **$13.95**
Edward Fitzgerald, whom the world has already learned, in spite of his own efforts to remain within the shadow of anonymity, to look upon as one of the rarest poets of the century, was born at Bredfield, in Suffolk, on the 31st of March, 1809. He was the third son of John Purcell...   Music Pages 172

Ancient Law by *Henry Maine*   ISBN: *1-59462-128-4*   **$29.95**
The chief object of the following pages is to indicate some of the earliest ideas of mankind, as they are reflected in Ancient Law, and to point out the relation of those ideas to modern thought.   Religion/History Pages 452

Far-Away Stories by *William J. Locke*   ISBN: *1-59462-129-2*   **$19.45**
"Good wine needs no bush," but a collection of mixed vintages does. And this book is just such a collection. Some of the stories I do not want to remain buried for ever in the museum files of dead magazine-numbers an author's not unpardonable vanity..."   Fiction Pages 272

Life of David Crockett by *David Crockett*   ISBN: *1-59462-250-7*   **$27.45**
"Colonel David Crockett was one of the most remarkable men of the times in which he lived. Born in humble life, but gifted with a strong will, an indomitable courage, and unremitting perseverance...   Biographies/New Age Pages 424

Lip-Reading by *Edward Nitchie*   ISBN: *1-59462-206-X*   **$25.95**
Edward B. Nitchie, founder of the New York School for the Hard of Hearing, now the Nitchie School of Lip-Reading, Inc, wrote "LIP-READING Principles and Practice". The development and perfecting of this meritorious work on lip-reading was an undertaking...   How-to Pages 400

A Handbook of Suggestive Therapeutics, Applied Hypnotism, Psychic Science   ISBN: *1-59462-214-0*   **$24.95**
by *Henry Munro*   Health/New Age/Health/Self-help Pages 376

A Doll's House: and Two Other Plays by *Henrik Ibsen*   ISBN: *1-59462-112-8*   **$19.95**
Henrik Ibsen created this classic when in revolutionary 1848 Rome. Introducing some striking concepts in playwriting for the realist genre, this play has been studied the world over.   Fiction/Classics/Plays 308

The Light of Asia by *sir Edwin Arnold*   ISBN: *1-59462-204-3*   **$13.95**
In this poetic masterpiece, Edwin Arnold describes the life and teachings of Buddha. The man who was to become known as Buddha to the world was born as Prince Gautama of India but he rejected the worldly riches and abandoned the reigns of power when...   Religion/History/Biographies Pages 170

The Complete Works of Guy de Maupassant by *Guy de Maupassant*   ISBN: *1-59462-157-8*   **$16.95**
"For days and days, nights and nights, I had dreamed of that first kiss which was to consecrate our engagement, and I knew not on what spot I should put my lips..."   Fiction/Classics Pages 240

The Art of Cross-Examination by *Francis L. Wellman*   ISBN: *1-59462-309-0*   **$26.95**
Written by a renowned trial lawyer, Wellman imparts his experience and uses case studies to explain how to use psychology to extract desired information through questioning.   How-to/Science/Reference Pages 408

Answered or Unanswered? by *Louisa Vaughan*   ISBN: *1-59462-248-5*   **$10.95**
Miracles of Faith in China   Religion Pages 112

The Edinburgh Lectures on Mental Science (1909) by *Thomas*   ISBN: *1-59462-008-3*   **$11.95**
This book contains the substance of a course of lectures recently given by the writer in the Queen Street Hail, Edinburgh. Its purpose is to indicate the Natural Principles governing the relation between Mental Action and Material Conditions...   New Age/Psychology Pages 148

Ayesha by *H. Rider Haggard*   ISBN: *1-59462-301-5*   **$24.95**
Verily and indeed it is the unexpected that happens! Probably if there was one person upon the earth from whom the Editor of this, and of a certain previous history, did not expect to hear again...   Classics Pages 380

Ayala's Angel by *Anthony Trollope*   ISBN: *1-59462-352-X*   **$29.05**
The two girls were both pretty, but Lucy who was twenty-one who supposed to be simple and comparatively unattractive, whereas Ayala was credited, as her Bombwhat romantic name might show, with poetic charm and a taste for romance. Ayala when her father died was nineteen...   Fiction Pages 484

The American Commonwealth by *James Bryce*   ISBN: *1-59462-286-8*   **$34.45**
An interpretation of American democratic political theory. It examines political mechanics and society from the perspective of Scotsman James Bryce   Politics Pages 572

Stories of the Pilgrims by *Margaret P. Pumphrey*   ISBN: *1-59462-116-0*   **$17.95**
This book explores pilgrims religious oppression in England as well as their escape to Holland and eventual crossing to America on the Mayflower, and their early days in New England...   History Pages 268

QTY

The Fasting Cure *by Sinclair Upton*
ISBN: *1-59462-222-1* **$13.95**
In the Cosmopolitan Magazine for May, 1910, and in the Contemporary Review (London) for April, 1910, I published an article dealing with my experiences in fasting. I have written a great many magazine articles, but never one which attracted so much attention... New Age/Self Help/Health Pages 164

Hebrew Astrology *by Sepharial*
ISBN: *1-59462-308-2* **$13.45**
In these days of advanced thinking it is a matter of common observation that we have left many of the old landmarks behind and that we are now pressing forward to greater heights and to a wider horizon than that which represented the mind-content of our progenitors... Astrology Pages 144

Thought Vibration or The Law of Attraction in the Thought World
by William Walker Atkinson
ISBN: *1-59462-127-6* **$12.95**
Psychology/Religion Pages 144

Optimism *by Helen Keller*
ISBN: *1-59462-108-X* **$15.95**
Helen Keller was blind, deaf, and mute since 19 months old, yet famously learned how to overcome these handicaps, communicate with the world, and spread her lectures promoting optimism. An inspiring read for everyone... Biographies/Inspirational Pages 84

Sara Crewe *by Frances Burnett*
ISBN: *1-59462-360-0* **$9.45**
In the first place, Miss Minchin lived in London. Her home was a large, dull, tall one, in a large, dull square, where all the houses were alike, and all the sparrows were alike, and where all the door-knockers made the same heavy sound... Childrens/Classic Pages 88

The Autobiography of Benjamin Franklin *by Benjamin Franklin*
ISBN: *1-59462-135-7* **$24.95**
The Autobiography of Benjamin Franklin has probably been more extensively read than any other American historical work, and no other book of its kind has had such ups and downs of fortune. Franklin lived for many years in England, where he was agent... Biographies/History Pages 332

Name	
Email	
Telephone	
Address	
City, State ZIP	

☐ **Credit Card**   ☐ **Check / Money Order**

Credit Card Number	
Expiration Date	
Signature	

Please Mail to: Book Jungle
PO Box 2226
Champaign, IL 61825
or Fax to: 630-214-0564

ORDERING INFORMATION
web: *www.bookjungle.com*
email: *sales@bookjungle.com*
fax: *630-214-0564*
mail: *Book Jungle PO Box 2226 Champaign, IL 61825*
or PayPal *to sales@bookjungle.com*

Please contact us for bulk discounts

DIRECT-ORDER TERMS

20% Discount if You Order Two or More Books
Free Domestic Shipping!
Accepted: Master Card, Visa, Discover, American Express